THIS IS THE CIRCLE

The Psionics, Book Four

Tash McAdam

A NineStar Press Publication

Published by NineStar Press
P.O. Box 91792,
Albuquerque, New Mexico, 87199 USA.
www.ninestarpress.com

This is the Circle

Printed in the USA
First Edition
December, 2019

Print ISBN: 978-1-951880-11-8

Also available in eBook, ISBN: 978-1-951880-01-9

Warning: This book contains scenes of graphic violence and cannibalism, depictions of PTSD and disassociation, death of secondary characters.

In the middle of two wars, including one that they didn't want and didn't ask for, the Psionics of ARC struggle to turn back the Eaters. The Institute is still waiting for an opportunity to regain control of the city, but right now there are more pressing concerns. Outside the Wall, chaos reigns, and the slums are overrun. Citizens and dwells alike are panicked and rioting. Cassandra hides in Epsilon 17's body, convincing those closest to her that everything is normal as she pieces together plans to escape in the confusion.

But when the Eaters take her, Thea manages to regain control. The tables have turned. Now she has to pretend to be Cassandra to survive—but fortunately her time in the Institute prepared her well. If she tries to flee, she'll be killed, but if she stays with the cannibal hordes she's bound to be discovered. Escape seems impossible, but help—and friendship—comes from an unlikely source.

Toby and Serena have their hands full fighting the invading Eaters and trying to track down leads on where Thea could be. Cut off from his twin, Toby's relationships with ARC deepen and grow, but he's consumed by his guilt and his need to find Thea.

The cannibal threat looms ever closer, and with one of their best weapons either lost or disabled, ARC has to decide what their priorities are. Should they try to kill her, or save her?

For all the lonely queer kids, whether you're young or grown. Don't stop looking until you find your circle.

Chapter One

TOBY

They're coming over the wall, Serena pushes the thought to me as we duck into a doorway, looking for our next targets. People are running and screaming, I see a toddler dashed out of his mother's arms, grabbed by an invisible hand, and send a puff of telekinesis out to catch him, whisking him out of danger and back safe onto her shoulder. A scream of frustration rings in the empty air.

The woman doesn't know what happened, but she takes her child and keeps running. The streets are clearing now, the gates shut to keep the attackers out, cutting off the flood of dwells. I can't help but think they'd be safer if they'd all stayed outside. The Eaters are here; they're in the City, but we can't see them.

I desperately try to comm base, but everything's down, my datapad blinking uselessly as it tries to connect.

Serena marks two falling shapes that are invisible to me as they tumble down the huge white edifice. They're using their power like parachutes, skidding their feet down the surface of the wall and wafting their telekinesis above themselves, slowing their descent; it's unbelievable. Via our hand-to-hand connection I get a faint impression of Serena skidding down a wall by herself, long ago, young and scared, with devastation woven into the heart of the memory. She digs her nails into my hand, jogging me out of the private moments she didn't mean to share, and points our joined hands at the first descending Eater.

I send out a burst of power, flatten the body-snatcher against the massive white blocks of steel-hard stone, feel his bones break, and his scream of pain reverberates through the air. Serena yanks the other attacker down, but he...no, *she*, flips in the air and lands on her feet, dodging into the panicked shapes before Serena can keep track of her.

A massive figure shunts refugee bodies aside like a battering ram—Tudor: he can see them, just like Leaf could in the desert—and heaves upward. The woman Serena lost sight of flickers into view for a moment, and Tudor hammers a huge fist into her chest. Everything is so sharp and clear in my vision. I see her rib bones bow inward, snap. *Battlesight,* Serena crows, adrenaline pounding through her, making her forget the deaths around us and focus only on the joy of war.

Together we race toward the fading trail of another invisible attacker as they sprint down a street after the fleeing crowds. *They want the children,* Serena sends to me, her inner voice shocked and disbelieving. *I caught it on her before Tudor took her down; they're here for the kids.* The powered kids, she means. I feel it.

Why? My feet smash into the pavement. I wish these boots were older, broken in, the tight synth-leather making my strides just a touch uncertain on the slippery solar panels.

You should try doing this in the rain, Serena jokes, not knowing the answer to my question. Then we're on the escaping Eater and have to focus. She reads and finds his feet for me, bare, soles like hide but used to hot sands not smooth glassy surfaces. I thread a noose of power around his ankle, ready to trip him. But I forgot what they can do with an open line, and I gasp as he yanks on the tendril I sent toward him. He pulls a gob of power right out of my chest, absorbing it with a shuddery cry I can hear with my mundane ears, not needing Serena to read it and pass it to me.

I stagger, almost falling with the shock of it, but Serena catches me with a strong hand around my belt, saving me from a nosedive onto the ground. *Toby.* It's a cry, thick with fear, but I'm okay. I let go of the power and let him take it rather than try to keep the connection open and fight him for it. I don't know how to do that, and the memory of my twin taking everything out of me is still too fresh in my mind to want to try.

I'm good, I spit it, finding my balance and yanking Serena along, urging her to look for our prey, but he's disappeared, and she can't find him. *If they want the kids, they'll be at ARC,* I realize and share at the same time, and Serena blanches.

Damon.

She's washed with fear. *Lost him once; can't lose him again* swirls in her so thickly I can hardly breathe past the crushing weight of responsibility and loneliness and hopelessness and loss that makes her feet slow and her spine bow with the pressure.

I slap her, because I'm drowning in the emotions she's accidentally forcing on me, and the impact of my hand turns her cheek, stings scarlet blood into the skin, and she shakes her head vigorously, working her jaw but refocused. She gives me a pulse of gratitude and looks around for a path to the city center.

The roads are packed, abandoned belongings being picked over by some of the hardier souls in the crowd, vehicles tipped over and deserted, desperate families searching for loved ones. Kids. There are kids missing here too. The absence of them is washing over Serena, open as she is now to our surroundings. Gifted kids the Institute and ARC missed? Slum kids strong enough that the Eaters want them.

Oh, Google. Serena stumbles, drops to one knee, and vomits on the shiny, blood-smeared solar panel right next to my foot.

What? But in reply, she just reaches up to take my hand again.

Our fingers wind together. We're both sweaty, sticky; there's a fingerprint of red smudged down the back of my hand. And then she shows me, and I stop thinking about my hand.

There's an Eater near, very near, and now I know how they got their names. He's smashed open the head of an infant, no more than six months, and he's digging his hand into the bowl of the child's skull, scooping out brains and shoveling them into his mouth. He's so intent on what he's doing, he hasn't realized Serena's clocked him, but she's too shaken by the secondhand emotions and the firsthand horror of witnessing such vileness, she can't do anything more than bring up her meager dinner.

I'm not much better, to be honest, but the extra layer between myself and the carnage, the filter of Serena and her disgust, her fear, is enough to keep me on my feet.

He's crouched, this monster, in the corner of two buildings, safe out the way of the madding crowd. There's another child with him, a girl, still breathing, but unconscious, shrouded by the Eater's invisible cover.

I don't have a Zap. We were unarmed—in as far as we ever can be—to help keep the atmosphere friendly and minimize the chance of aggression. I'll have to be quick, have to try to haul the limp body of the living child away from the Eater. Pin the man back at the same time, crush his skull, maybe. He doesn't get to live; not after I've seen this. There's nothing of humanity left in this monster.

Serena pulls herself upright using me as a ladder. *I'll get the kid. You get the...Eater,* her mind voice twists around the word, rippled through with new meaning, new understanding. It sounds like a curse when she shapes it. I send a flash of understanding, and she counts for us both: *three, two, one.*

We move at the same time, like lightning, like one entity. I spare a sliding second of thought for how well we do this, how together we are, how in sync our minds can be when we fight. And then Serena's pulling the second victim free of her position, wedged behind the Eater in the corner, and I'm pinning limbs with flashing, repeated shots. I can't keep a thread open, wrap it around him like rope in case he pulls my power out of me again; I can only hit him—hit him—hit him with blasts like ball bearings, repeated impact shoving his hands up and into the steel behind him.

He drops the corpse he was feeding on, roars his disgust at us. I can only feel-see him through Serena's hand linked to mine; if we let go of each other, I'll lose him completely, and our grip is sweat slick and slippery. There's a small gang of people running toward us, trying to get away from something, someone, and I can't pin the Eater down, but Serena has the child scooped into her arm, hoisting the small figure over her narrow shoulder and turning her attention to helping me.

Together we lift him up, smash him against the wall, and he loses his control for a second, flickers into view with gore and blood smeared down his chin like a beard.

Then someone barges into us, and we stagger, jostled, our hands sliding apart, and I've lost my grip on Serena, and with it, my understanding of where the Eater is.

I stumble, spinning, my hands up and searching for Serena, for a target, but there are people everywhere, and I can't see her. *Serena,* I mind shout at her, and then realize that might have been a mistake as a heavy weight crushes me to the ground. Stupid. I may as well have sent up a flare! At least I know where the enemy is now. On top of me, with his hands around my throat, sweat and child's blood lubricating his grip as he chokes the life out of me, batting my weakening telekinesis away with less effort than I expend on swatting flies.

Stars dance in my vision, the world is fading gray at the edges, my arms are pinned under his knees, and the agony of his bones digging into my biceps—grinding my muscles into the ground—is second only to the hot fear rising in my throat, sparking panic through me. I flail and twist, flesh and power alike looking for a chink, a moment of weakness, something that will save me.

He's stronger than I am and has me at a complete disadvantage, my lungs straining for air, and I don't know how I'm going to die, if I'm going to suffocate or if my spine will snap first. His hands are so strong...

Serena saves me, again; I've lost count of how many times I would have died without her at my side. She blasts the Eater off me with a shout of rage. His ragged fingernails tear stinging lines in my throat, and I lie there uselessly, gasping for sweet, sweet air as my lungs remember how to inflate.

My throat hurts badly, inside and out; it feels swollen and hot and wet, but I manage to turn my head sideways and watch Serena smashing her fist into the Eater's face.

Her expression is masklike, unnervingly still. She's holding him down with one hand, and her other is already dripping with blood. Sunlight glances off the lurid scarlet wetness. Watching her cave his face in is almost beautiful.

"Get up." She doesn't bother mind sending it, just yells it at me, and sound rushes back into my ears, making me realize how quiet everything had gone while I was being throttled.

The kids, ARC, of course. We have to get back there. I swallow past the tightness of the imprint of his fingers on my neck.

She leaves the corpse of the Eater, bloody and almost unrecognizable as human—if these monsters even count as such—and yanks me to my feet, leaving her arm around my waist, under my shirt for skin contact and to help keep me upright.

Hauling the kid the Eater wanted up into her arms again, she basically carries both of us down the rapidly emptying street. Her strength is immutable, making my feet steady and my lungs stop juddering. I'm glad she didn't leave the kid, but I might not have thought of it. We gotta shove her somewhere safe, where the Eaters can't get her, but they're invisible and everywhere? I can hear screaming. Half of me wants to head that way, but I know Serena's right. We have to get back to base and tell them what we know, try to save the highest concentration of gifted kids.

The streets empty quickly. I think it's been less than fifteen minutes since it all started. I wonder what happened at the park. All those people in tents. Maybe the citizens let them into their houses. At least houses have doors, are sealable. The Eaters don't seem to have weaponry, really, relying on their invisibility to cover them.

We sprint down the silent roads, past a watch station that bears the black marks of Zap fire on its walls, with a caved-in front door dangling from its hinges.

The silence feels tangible; inhaling it makes me think of memories that aren't mine, swallowing gel until I drown in it. I can't feel Thea at all right now; she must be sleeping. I can sense the ambient presence of our bond though, so I'm not worried she's dead. I'd feel it if she was. I know I would.

Our harsh breathing and heavy footsteps are the only sounds close to us, save the distant bangs and yelling of unseen fights. Serena stumbles, and I send *Gimme the kid,* laced with the knowledge I am physically stronger than her when she's not pumping telekinesis into every cell. I'm also a better runner, but slow to react, and her unfettered responses might keep us alive.

She grunts agreement and hands me the child without missing a step, bracing the limp body with tendrils of power until I have the small, warm girl slung over my broad shoulder.

She doesn't weigh much, and we speed up now Serena's relieved of her burden. *But we're taking her to them?* I ask, meaning that we are headed for where we think the fight will be, where the kids are, and Serena flashes a reply back to me: *Nowhere's safe; at least we can keep the kids together,* and I see what she means.

We can take the Eaters in a fight, if we know where they are; they're under-equipped even if they are strong in ways we don't understand. If we can gather the kids in one place and surround them with fighters, we might be able to save them.

The girl in my arm stirs slightly, and I abruptly realize that "them" doesn't include the kids not at ARC, the kids who weren't at the Institute, or kids like the girl in my arms. Serena catches the thought off me and responds grimly: *There's nothing we can do; we don't know how they're finding them.*

Thea? I send back to Serena, wrapped with the reminder that my twin is the most powerful Reader we have. If anyone can find latent telepaths, assuming that's what the Eaters are after, it'd be her.

Can you reach her? She already knows I can't; it's not a real question. Serena yanks us off the main path, around a bloody heap I don't want to look too closely at, and I see the walls of ARC ahead of us, the side of the grounds. There's no gate here, but Serena throws me her plan to jump the wall, and we seamlessly release our grip on each other.

I pull ahead, gently deposit the girl on the ground, and turn... One, two, three... I cup my hands over my thigh, Serena steps up, and I hurl her skyward. The nuking show-off does a flip in the air before landing on the narrow top of the wall, crouching immediately, and throwing up a shield—I can tell by the way she moves her hands—before reaching down for me.

I pick up the girl, brace her with one arm, as well as I can, and then take a short run up. My feet pound the hard road, sending shocks through my shinbones as I increase the pressure of my weight, hurling my power out through my feet when I'm a mere three meters from the rising stone.

My feet pedal wildly in the air—I'm flying—Serena wraps her power around my torso and increases my speed, yanking me up to join her on the wall top.

She steadies me as I land and then leaps off before I have a chance to get my stomach back into my body, landing as lightly as a cat at the base of the wall, her shoes barely indenting the mud more than the flat cushion of telekinesis she sent before her did.

I carefully lower the girl down to her using telekinesis, and Serena catches the weight of her before she drops the final few meters.

Groaning, I close my eyes and step outward, wrapping my legs and bones in power to reinforce them while bursting a pad of energy out to absorb my momentum.

My landing is a lot messier than hers, dirt blasting out for a few feet, flowers torn up by the roots, and I pitch forward, getting my elbows and knees covered in mud. Serena spares a split second to make sure I didn't break anything and then hauls me to my feet, brushes me off, and hands me the girl back.

And then we run, hand in hand, Serena reading, and me, well, I'm just trying to stay on my feet.

The scars of the earlier conflict are still scraped deep in the grasses under the beat of our shoes, but there's no sign of newer battle.

Where is everyone? I ask.

On the streets? It's a bloodbath out there. But we have to find the kids. Even Serena's internal voice sounds breathless and stressed.

Dorms? It's where I'd go if I knew what was going on outside.

Emergency procedure is head for the canteen, Serena responds after a second, slowing down while we figure out where to go. The sun is bright, high in the sky, like a white eye blasting down on us without the protection of the transal shields we're used to. I have to squint just to see.

We could split up? I offer. It's dangerous, more dangerous for me 'cause I can't read, and they could take me by surprise, but I can shield myself, and once they've hit me, I can fight.

Serena looks torn for a minute, and then nods. *If you don't find anyone in the dorms, head for the canteen down B block. If it's jammed, or you can't get through, yell for me. I'll do the same; if they're not in the canteen, I'll come down B looking for you.*

All right. I give her my best attempt at a grin, and she clenches her jaw.

Gimme the kid. She's right. The girl stands a better chance with her. It's hard to keep a shield up over someone who isn't yourself. I'm not that good even though I'm stronger.

See you in ten, I send, trying to sound positive, and she hits me on the shoulder affectionately, hard enough to make me miss a step as I pass the kid over.

Later, Tobes.

We don't need to say anything else; all the emotion is wrapped up in the thoughts, and I nod at her and peel off across the abandoned grounds, heading for the dorms. I wish I knew where Thea was, or Aly, or Darcy. Leaf would be a great guy to have around right now, but as a Blank, not even Serena will find him if he doesn't want to be found.

The corridors are eerily silent; there's a thick smear of dark blood congealing on the floor, and I avoid it. So, they're here. Definitely here. My heart hammers in my chest. I can hear my footsteps echoing, and I try to mute them, pillow them with power like Serena does so naturally, her control a light touch and redirection of energy. For me, it only helps a little. I won't take anyone by surprise, but it's better.

The lights are still on, which is good, because I can see, but adds to the feeling of wrongness pervading the whole place, the *offness* of the empty: empty halls and the doors with no bustle behind them.

Someone touches me on the shoulder, and I'm swinging for them as I turn, reinforcing my forearm until it's hard as steel, arcing toward...my twin's face. I'm too committed to the movement to pull up, but she laughs lightly as she steps back, flutters her hand up, and spins my powerful blow past her head. I lose my balance and just about fall to the floor, staggering forward a step, bouncing my shoulder painfully off the wall.

"Toby, what are you doing?" She sounds light, airy, and I blink, taken aback.

"Don't you know?" I reach for her hand to fill her in, to show her the carnage outside, but she jerks backward, avoiding my touch. Oh, Google, maybe it's too much for her. I think of the wave of disastrous emotions from Serena that almost dropped me when she found the Eater earning his name.

Her face hardens into more familiar lines, and she nods, sharp and jerky. "Of course, sorry... It was just... funny. You almost..." She sounds a little strange, and I frown at her, willing her to get with the program.

"I'm heading for the dorms; Serena's in the canteen; the Eaters are here and they're after the children." I fill her in as fast as I can, already moving again. She'll come with me, of course. We're better as a team.

"Damon, Jake, and Ana are hiding in the ceiling over Ana's room. There's two Eaters looking for them." She sounds so dramatically unconcerned I flinch, whirling around.

"What's wrong with you?" I snap, glaring before breaking into a run toward the boys room, my stomach swirling with fear.

"Wait, Toby," she calls after me, but I don't have time for whatever nervous breakdown she's having. She can read better than anyone. The Eaters won't catch her by surprise, and she's better than me in hand to hand now. She can take care of herself. I'm shocked by the anger pounding in my chest. I thought she'd help if she already knew where any of the kids are. *Why isn't she helping? Maybe she's headed to a more dangerous group*, I tell myself, feet skidding as I round the corner, forgoing stealth for speed.

I can't feel them, but I sure as hell can find them.

I send a shockwave of energy out of me, the kind that earned me my nickname right at the beginning of everything, the kind that makes the pictures fall off the wall and the tiles rattle. I blast it down the corridor ahead of me, slamming it wall to ceiling to floor. No space for them to slip past this wave of power.

One of them is on the ceiling, coming toward me. The blast knocks him down like an ant being shaken off a leaf; he smashes to the floor, landing on his hands and feet. I kick him in the face as I run past him. His head snaps back with a sound audible even over the thud of the second Eater being thrown backward.

This one is female; she bares sharpened teeth at me as she shimmers into view when her back hits the wall where the corridor turns. The air puffs out past her self-made fangs, but she's gone again before I can hit her with a follow-up.

I close my eyes, reinforce my skin all over—a net of energy over every millimeter of me—and wait for the blow. It's hard to concentrate, but it's not for long.

Her knife slams into the skin over my kidney, and she yells her triumph before she realizes her blade has snapped at the hilt with the impact into rock-hard flesh. My protection's shattered, dropped away with the blow, but I have her.

My hands wrap around her wrist. I twist it upward, step through the loop of her arm, and drive my foot into her knee, folding her downward.

I follow her to the floor hard enough her arm snaps when we hit, and she squeals in pain before I use my free hand to drive her forehead into the hard tile and knock her out.

Panting, I roll off her, then get to my feet. "Jake? Damon? It's me, Toby," I call softly, fearful I could be calling more Eaters to our location.

"Toby!" A triumphant whisper sounds from halfway down the corridor, and then a ceiling tile moves. Jake pokes his head out, sees me, and then flips down to the ground before turning and holding his hands up. Damon dangles his feet over the edge and jumps. Jake catches him with steady hands. Both the boys lock hands and help Ana down. She almost knocks them over, but they steady her, and all three run to me, run into me.

Down the corridor, Thea rounds the corner and grins at me. "Nice catch, brother mine."

Chapter Two

CASSANDRA

He has the kids with him, annoyingly. They'll bring the Eaters down on us. I was hoping they'd be dead before he found them. The smile I plastered on my face at the sight of them itches. I usually practice smiling in my new bodies before trying it out in front of people, let alone when I'm trying to pretend I'm someone else. Fortunately, E17 hasn't learned much about social niceties since she escaped the Institute. An uncomfortable smile on her face shouldn't raise any eyebrows.

Toby looks delighted to see me, and in the deepest depth of my mind the twin stirs. They have a connection, always, and I can read on him that it's strange for him to not feel her. I'll have to play the trauma card—I caught him assuming that before—and keep him busy. I need to figure out a way to get him away with me, somewhere with time and space to leech his power properly.

There's eleven Eaters in the building with us. I can feel them like blips in the web that connects everything, small blurs of wrongness, greed and sickness. They bristle with tumors, pressing on nerves and neurons. I've never been confused by what they are, what they want. Not since the first time I came across a mad psi.

Watching Pollux devour his own brother's brain was a bit of an eye-opener. He thought it would save Castor, thought that was a way to keep them together. It didn't work of course, but it did, helpfully, let the madness he'd been toying with for years come out in full force.

Toby's eyeing me with confusion, and I snap out of the bloodied memories, jerking my head at him. "Kion's got a small core of resistance in the armory with the kids—those he could gather in time. There are six Eaters over there, but the soldiers are holding them off fine. Eleven in this building. Serena's fighting two in the canteen."

"Let's go." He pushes Jake's shoulder, getting the kids to jog over to me, and then looks at me with his dark, serious eyes. "You bring up the rear; let me know if they're coming. Damon, can you read for me?"

Damon nods, his small face lined with fear, and Toby takes his hand gently, care in every line of his body. Ridiculous. The urge to roll my eyes is so strong I look away, blink like I'm holding back tears.

Ana and Jake hold hands, making a smaller duo between the brother and me, and he catches my eyes one last time before turning and heading down the corridor.

We don't encounter any more Eaters on the way. I'm beginning to enjoy myself, in control for the first time in months, with Reader power beyond my prior considerable skills at my disposal. My own telekinesis was always barely there, but once I have the boy...well. Empires will tremble. I smirk at my thoughts, confident that no one can see me, as they tiptoe nervously through the empty, yawning hallways. I'm still not sure what my play is here; as soon as the chaos of the invading Eaters is dealt with, I'll be in a much more precarious position. I need to render Toby incapable of fighting me. He's too heavy to carry unconscious; he must be half his twin's weight again. Growing up with plentiful protein in the lap of luxury has allowed him to pack on muscle, and his brief stay with ARC hasn't skinnied him down any.

I think, for now, my best option is to lay low and hope we don't encounter anyone who knows about what happened with Icarus. My stomach twists in anger as I think of my fine son, pushed back by that stupid boy. Icarus didn't even want to take Cassius, at first, pleaded with me for another option even while devoured by unbearable pain. Like taking a different life would be better somehow.

He thought he loved Cassius, but love is weak and easily manipulated, twisted. In the end, the agony drove him into actions he would have sworn impossible, and I got to keep Icarus with me, albeit damaged by what he'd experienced. I always hoped eventually the memory of his burning body would leave him, that we could iron it out of him, but even four years on, he still couldn't cement the transfer process. He was too broken, Cassius too strong in him.

Should have just dipped him. It's not like he'd remember the promise I made him once he came out of the Tank. Oh well, live and learn.

The children in front of me are walking close together, as huddled as they can be while still on their feet, and they shriek in surprise when an Eater bursts out of a doorway in front, visible to me in the Read spectrum and to Toby only by the swinging of the door behind him.

Toby's reflexes are atrocious; it has to be said. I frown disapprovingly and then remember Epsilon 17 would probably not stand idly and watch, so I grab the three kids and urge them backward, stand in front of them protectively with my knife drawn, watching the brother dispatch the attacker with brute force and very little nuance.

Leaving the Eater a bloody mess on the floor, Toby whirls around, sees me "protecting" the kids and relaxes, giving me a lopsided grin riddled with his fear that he'll get us all killed. The way this boy projects, I'm surprised there weren't Eaters beating the doors down months ago. Maybe just one flame, no matter how strong, wasn't enough to draw them? Not until ARC brought all the young ones up and let them send their willfulness where they wished.

A little hand finds mine, curls small fingers around the edge of my palm. A second of hot disgust boils through me, and the girl, the small, quiet girl looks up at me with hurt painted on her elfin face. I force a soft expression, meld the aversion with the sight of the Eater on the floor, and her face clears easily.

Children. Idiots, every single one of them.

Urging Ana ahead of me, we continue toward Serena. I'm not too worried. She's a strong Reader, but she's never really spent a lot of time with Epsilon 17, and she's insensitive by nature. Kion and Darcy will be the hardest to fool. He is very attuned to Epsilon 17's psyche, and while Darcy's not overly strong, she's very intuitive. Only a few points off being an empath, I'd guess. She knows Epsilon 17 better than anyone, really, even Kion. Even her brother. Toby sees her, feels her, but can't possibly understand her. Their points of view are so disparate he tries to view her through his own lens, which warps and distorts everything he sees. Very, very useful. He's so blinded by his assumptions that I doubt he'll ever really see what's happening here, how I've stolen his twin's body like a set of new clothes.

The battle in the canteen is over by the time we arrive, not that I felt the need to inform Toby of such. Maybe he's wondering why I'm not passing him information, but Epsilon 17 hasn't slotted easily into a sharing role, failing to become part of the fabric of a team. She isolates herself, still, and that gives me an edge. Even if she *would* be helping now, if she could, she's not really worked with him before. Her desire for independence from him gives me a chance.

Serena stands, gasping, her shoulders heaving, in the middle of the canteen. Tables are scattered everywhere, and three bodies lie around the room. A quick read of the ambient energies remaining in the room lets me know that the third body isn't an Eater—one of the ARC residents then. There's a small girl on a table, hiding her head in her knees. They'll all be damaged by what's happening today, and to think, we could fix it by dipping them, and they'd never know the difference. We could take this day back out of their hearts without them missing a beat. But ARC never would. Stupidity at its most selfish.

Assuming Epsilon 17 would be concerned about the corpse, I drop Ana's hand and race over to the ARC body, a blond-haired man in his early twenties. Daine, Epsilon 17's suppressed mind provides, the name floating up laced with anguish and rage. I emulate it admirably in my own tone. "Daine!"

"I got here too late," Serena sounds hollow, exhausted. I abruptly realize there's a fourth body in the room, a young corpse. One of the Eaters found a child here. Daine found them both, was overmatched by the two of them, and was dead before Serena stumbled upon the gruesome scene.

I close his blank eyes because I assume that's the thing to do, the thing that people who cared would do, and catch Serena eyeing me with what could be gratitude on her face.

She scrubs her hand over her eyes and turns away from me, her shoulders slumped, and Toby takes a few long strides across the room, pulls her into his chest.

The sobs she lets escape are quiet, and it's easy to hear Toby over her as he catches my eyes. "Where are they?" He means the Eaters, the others who weren't here in this fight.

I close my eyes and spin my stolen hyperawareness through the building. "Four in the upper levels; they're going room to room; there's two kids up there...Sandy and Mario." Epsilon 17 helpfully identifies the two children for me. "Two in the grounds looking for stragglers, three heading for the armory to join the attack there."

Toby looks torn; he doesn't know what to do, so far from being a leader it's hard to hide my amusement. I bite my lip until the taste of iron stings my tongue. Serena pushes him back, shakes off some of the sorrow and despair, and assumes command of the room. She, at least, has some idea of how to take charge. I'd like to beat that spirit out of her, but I doubt I'll get the opportunity to break her fully. She's too strong to take chances with. I'll probably just snap her neck and be done with it. My palms itch to do it now, to neutralize the threat.

"We have to stick together. There's not enough of us to split up. Who's at the armory, Thea?" Serena turns to me.

I try to make my face intent and serious to match Serena's tone. "Your dad, Kion, Ria, Johan, Marty, Domas, Darcy, four soldiers, and I don't know, twenty-seven kids." I count through the power signatures of the people I can sense with Epsilon 17's abundant power.

Mine now. I have to resist the urge to shiver with glee. "And a Blank, I think. Could be Leaf."

Google! She's so powerful she can separate their essences from this far away; it's mind-blowing. It's hard not to let my excitement show in her face. Being solely a Reader has a huge advantage here, though. No wonder she managed to hide herself from me for so long. With almost null projection, people just have to listen to what you say and look at your face. It's like they're all deaf to my thoughts, but in reality, I'm so quiet they can't hear me.

Serena relaxes when I say her girlfriend's name. I should have said it first, as E17 would have done. A foolish mistake but no one seems to have noticed. "We go for Andy and Mario, then take out the two in the grounds on the way to back up the armory after." It is the obvious thing to do, but Toby looks impressed anyway.

Jake, Damon, and Ana are standing together in a cluster in the doorway, and even though Damon is a weak projector, I hear his thought before he speaks it.

"I'm a girl." He blurts it out, his voice shaking, and Serena moves closer to him, a quizzical look on her face. Damon gulps and stands in a weak attempt at a military stance, legs braced. "I don't want to die and have everyone not know. I'm a girl."

"She's a girl. Demi. Her name is Demi, not Damon." Jake moves closer to his smaller friend, winding their hands together in a show of solidarity, and then Serena's in front of them both. She crouches down so they're taller than her, and I watch with interest to see her response.

"Damon...Demi?" It's a question, and then she takes the kid's other hand, and her face clears as Demi connects with her. "Okay, Demi. I love you; you're my sibling, and

I'll always love and support you, okay? I'm glad you told me. It's gonna be okay," she says, like we're not at war. Like we have time for any of this. I resist the urge to make a "get on with it" gesture. Pronouns, words—they all attempt to summarize complex aspects of one's experience and identity and boil it down into a simplistic sound. Everything's reductive and inaccurate, moving on.

So Damon's a girl, Demi, now. Whatever. The Eaters don't care; they'll come for her anyway. I keep my thoughts locked down, though, make sure sympathy is on my face instead of mild irritation.

Toby, however, looks confused. "Wait, what?"

Serena snorts, straightens, pulls Demi in for a quick hug, and then offers her hand to Toby. He strides across the room to take it, and then his brow clears of confusion as she uses the efficacy of mental connection to explain to him the complexities of gender identity.

"You ready?" she asks Demi, who's still holding her other hand, and the girl nods.

"Yeah, I just wanted... I just wanted to make sure." Serena squeezes Demi's hand and lets go of Toby.

"Twins, take the lead."

We pad down the corridor, Toby and I at the front; we don't need to hold hands for me to pass him information, and there's nothing to share right now anyway. The majority of the ARC personnel were on the streets, apart from the commanders who stayed at base to oversee. I can catch bursts of telekinesis and power out in the City, where presumably they have their own battles to fight. And here, the building is empty, except for the few dead we pass.

In my head, Epsilon 17 tallies their names. Three doors down from us, Leah lies dead on the stretcher that used to trap my son. She's covered with a white sheet, stained red in uneven, flowering patches that vibrate with her last memories of pain and fear. I make sure to keep my awareness of that locked down.

I don't know where Icarus is. They must have drugged him, shut him down, but I'll find him, and then we'll escape from here. The list of things I have to do is getting longer, more complex. Ideally, I'll take this body, take Toby as well—their connection makes me believe it will be relatively easy to merge the two, the frequencies of their power identical as far as I can tell. No one has ever done anything like this; the closest I know of would be Pollux trying to absorb his brother and *keep* him present inside. A shared body with two separate minds. And of course, my Icarus, battling for dominance with Cassius day and night.

So taking Icarus *and* the boy are musts. Somewhere safe with time for me to explore the possibilities. My destination has to be Second City, the Institute there. I have the girl's recent trip to inform me of the state of transportation though. So, a helichopper is the only real solution.

I need to split us up from the rest of the group, get Toby to the helipad, knock him out, dose him and restrain him, go back for Icarus, and then get out immediately. To my delight, I realize E17 has two small, white pills pressing against her hipbone in a secret pocket hand sewn into her pants. I almost laugh as I realize they are Institute issue phenolum gel pills, ones she stole on the day her brother's powers emerged. I have phenolum ready to stuff down Toby's throat, I just have to wait for an opportunity to arise.

We make quick work of the two Eaters hunting the children on the upper levels, and once we've dealt with them, the child-to-adult ratio makes me very uncomfortable. We must look like easier targets than the armory. I'm on full alert, awareness spread everywhere, but Leaf still shocks me when he drops out of a window frame at the top of the corridor wall, which looks much too small to disgorge an adult-sized person.

"Wotcher," he greets us, sweat shining on his high forehead, the dip of his philtrum above his upper lip. I notice it more than I should and swallow the indignation Epsilon 17 throws at me. In my head, she's a kitten struggling to get out of a bag before it's drowned. So, she likes this boy. Could be useful.

Leaf fills us in on what we already know: the rest of the kids are pinned down in the armory with Kion, Johan, and more soldiers. The Eaters have surrounded them, but with us on the outside we should have a shot at trapping them between our two forces.

We approach quietly. Leaf is to stay with the kids in the shadow of the wall, to protect them as a last line of defense if Eaters get through the rest of us. His hand is clenching nervously on the baton he's carrying, but he seems to know how to hold it. He keeps looking at me, though, in a way I can't quite make sense of. Hopefully, the nascent romance between these two is what has his attention.

Outside the sun is streaming down on us all, as hot as liquid pouring over me, thrilling me at the sensation. The *sun*—it's been so long since I felt the sun on my skin!

There's another wave of Eaters heading toward ARC, but I decide to keep that close to my chest, for now. It could be the exact distraction I need. The ones we're after are trying to break down the door to the square, squat building that comprises the armory. The defenders are safe enough inside as there's no battering ram or door killer in use, yet, but with no windows to let them shoot back, they're under siege conditions.

Serena and Toby take point, wordlessly fanning out so I am the rear point of a triangle they front. I send my brother the sparks of where the Eaters are, what they're doing, and pretty much relax to watch the carnage unfold.

They're exquisite. Killing machines. It's been a while since I've seen such brutal efficiency. It warms me, my blood tingling with excitement as they destroy the Eaters without hesitation, smashing them to the ground and throwing them in the air. My breathing is fast, and I feel flushed and hot by the time the last one is supine, and Serena hammers on the wall, shouting that they can open it.

The relief on the faces of the soldiers and kids inside unsettles me, and I turn away as Serena greets her lover with an enthusiastic, blood-smeared kiss. It's desperate and romance-laced, not sexual, and I have no interest in that.

"Thea," Leaf's voice comes quietly, he's snuck up on me again, but instead of touching me, he's letting me know he's there. Epsilon 17 experiences a wave of affection that makes me grimace. I try to keep my distaste off my face. "You a'right?" he inquires as if anyone could possibly be all right in this mess.

I nod instead of replying, but he won't stop looking at me, his head cocked to one side, dark eyes narrowed in the sun's glare, assessing me. Aly and Darcy race over, leaving Serena talking to Kion at the barracks door, no doubt discussing tactics. Before I can dodge, Darcy wraps me in a hug, making me stiffen and freeze in her arms. Her hand slides across my bare neck.

No.

It's whispered, almost nonexistent, but I'm caught; I know I'm caught.

It's almost a relief.

I spin backward, away from them physically and wrap my mental grip around the connection strumming the air between Toby and me.

I yank.

He drops to his knees hard, like he's been poleaxed, his eyes finding me across the meters between us, wide and vacant and brimming with tears before he topples backward, and his power surges through me, an avalanche of strength. It feels so *good* I laugh.

The girl who caught me is an artist, so I stomp on her hand and grind it down. She'll remember me and wish she'd acted differently.

There are too many soldiers, too many Zaps, and all hope of stealth is gone now anyway. I've never had enough telekinetic power to try this before, but Toby's power is washing over me, excessive, too much, almost; it burns in my veins, and I slam it out of me in a telekinetic shockwave that throws the people turning toward me to the ground, shatters the windows above me. That's how Toby got his nickname, years ago, and now it's easy to see why. It's better than I expected. I could knock a helichopper out of the sky with this strength.

Most of the soldiers drop, unconscious. Some have the wind knocked out of them at the very least, but Leaf— of course—is still standing, his face a soft, shocked, open target. I punch him in the mouth, winding power around my fist as easily as breathing. His teeth slice into my knuckles where I haven't reinforced my skin properly, not used to having that as an option. It stings, but it's negligible for now. It'll need stitches later, but Leaf falls to the ground, dizzy and blinking, his mouth a bloody red O of fear.

There's a threat.

A short, enraged man throws power at me; it lifts me off the floor, but I laugh as I throw threads of Toby's Talent in every direction, make a web of it, and spin myself to my feet to land softly, using the strength in Epsilon 17's muscles gratefully.

Johan launches himself at me. The man who trained Toby in the art of Talent fighting, who has never been beaten in real combat, whose thoughts scream out what he's going to do to me when he drags me out of Epsilon 17's head... I react without thinking, power surging uncontrollable and wild out of my hands.

Chapter Three

E17

Cassandra uses my hands and Toby's power to *shred* Johan. I can't even make sense of what I'm seeing. He was Johan, snarling in rage, picked up by invisible chains and then he was...meat. Gone. A mist of blood in the air, sticky residue plopping to the floor. My hands, when Cassandra looks down, are pink with sprayed gore. The last lines of defense I'd been holding up flicker into nothing in my shock.

I'm expelled from my body, pushed out by the tidal wave of force that is Cassandra-using-Toby. My vision fades to brown, sepia tones scarring everything. The world whirs and spins, and I am alone. Hands that don't belong to anyone tug at my skin, and I realize, with a moan of despair, where I am. The nothing space. The lost land. The place Damon...Demi was flung by Toby's psychic explosion, and I am here with only the barest trickle of connection back to my flesh and bone. A connection Cassandra is trying to destroy. Curling up, for lack of a better way to think of the idea of shrinking myself as small as possible, hiding from the distraught cries and screams of the souls that are trapped here, I try to remember who I am in the face of nothingness.

The fierce anger in Toby's eyes when he found me when we first saw each other, and the anger for *me*. The squeeze of Kion's hand on my shoulder. The pride in his expression when I exceed his expectations. The crinkle at the corners of Leaf's eyes when he looks at me. The way Darcy will always, always know what I am feeling when I don't even understand it myself. The shouts of Jake and Demi as they try to get me to play with them, knowing I'll give in and run and dance through the soft grass, yelling with the joy of it. The camaraderie of the operatives getting ready to go out together where I am one of them, and they respect me and trust me to do my part. The smirk on Johan's lips when he tells me my next challenge. Curling up with Alyssa and Darcy and Serena and watching a movie together, safe and cozy. The people who love me. The people I love. I hold them to my mind and try not to vanish. The tenuous thread holding me to my physical self strengthens, and I painstakingly force myself back into my own flesh. I can't take it back from her, but I won't let go.

Cassandra pins the soldiers and the children to the ground indiscriminately, a web of power smashing down on their heads and dropping them flat to the floor. There are screams of pain as bones break.

Cassius yells defiance, somehow fighting his way to his knees, his face a mask of rage. I can feel the horror, the anger pouring off of him, and it's all directed at her, at Cassandra. The idea of her doing to me what was done to him seems to have brought him to his senses momentarily.

Cassandra rolls her eyes, waves a hand, and drops a wall on him. The building—damaged weeks ago, and since repaired—crumbles to one side and crushes him where he kneels. She drags him out again with Toby's power, and sighs when she sees the mess she's made of him. She practically dances over the tangles of slumped bodies, grabs one by the neck, and hauls him with her. Andrea, Toby's roommate, struggles in her grip. With less effort than I could possibly imagine to be true, Cassandra drops Andrea next to Cassius, puts a hand on both of their heads, drags Icarus clear of Cassius's mangled form, and stuffs him into Andrea.

I *feel* her do it, and it's a sick, sliding sensation of utter wrongness, emphasized by her pleasure in the sheer power she has accessible to her right now. If Toby wanted to, he could do this to any of us, his strength... She uses it like an extension of herself. Like a gun in her hand.

Cassius slumps, empty. Icarus no more. Just a damaged, mess of meat with broken legs and a shredded stomach. I can see his intestines; they're *moving*. Andrea drops to his knees, retching.

Leaf pushes himself up, wild terror painting his beautiful face, his eyes rolling wildly, taking in the carnage that surrounds him. He's the only one not crushed to the ground, the only one who could stop her. But I'm a much better fighter than him, and he only has a slight edge on me in physical strength, not enough to achieve anything against the woman wearing my body.

His eyes are dark and hard, like I've never seen him. He struggles upright, dabbing at the corner of his mouth with his hand. The impact of my fist in his face was hard, too hard. The Serena Slam, reinforced muscles and bone, doesn't care if you're a Blank or not, doesn't care if you're immune to Psionic power. I think it hurt him less than it would have if he had Talent, but he's still dizzy and unsteady on his feet as he faces off against me.

Cassandra doesn't even spare Leaf a glance, just picks up a block of concrete from the torn-up grass and hurls it at him. He barely reacts in time to avoid taking it full in the head, but it smashes into his shoulder, dashing him to the ground in a heap. He groans and rolls sideways, crying out with pain as he slowly drags himself to his knees.

He meets my eyes, and his are full of hatred, but somehow also softness, surety. "It's okay, Thea," he mouths, blood staining his crooked teeth.

He has a knife, somehow. And for a flashing, brutal moment, I see what's going to happen, the chain of light in the air as he pulls it back and throws it. The hot heat where it will slide into my flesh and sever my last connection to the world, but with me, Cassandra. We'll both die, if he aims true.

But he's not trying to throw it, not moving his hand back. Instead, he places his limp left hand on the floor, his shoulder ruined by the crashing block of concrete. There's blood streaking the inside of his wrist. It looks out of place against his pale tan skin.

He drives the knife into his palm, and for a long, strung-out second, I think she has him. Cassandra is holding him, making him hurt himself. But no, that's not right. Leaf's a Blank, and she can hit him, but she can't control him.

Leaf looks deliberately from me to Toby, where he's lying on the cold hard ground, his back arched as if he's having a seizure. His hands grip at nothing in the grass, fists clench, his truncated finger looks strange and off even though I'm used to seeing it.

And then I realize what Leaf is doing, what he's trying to do. Trauma-induced power—that's how Toby went from being a true Blank to what he is now, an overpowered, overgifted boy with so little Reading ability he's operating on a lower level than the average non-Talented human.

Hope surges in me. Maybe Leaf's plan will work. Maybe he's right. Maybe the hellish looking injury he just inflicted on himself will save us all. He closes his eyes, grits his jaw, and instead of sending out a wash of power, he collapses backward in a heap, the knife still sticking obscenely out of his pink, delicate palm. His fingers flutter and then are still.

The sight of him falling ruins me. I'm fading, Cassandra pushes me back, shoving me down inside my own mind, roaring through me. Toby's limp body lies in front of me; he's as gray as a statue made of ash, frozen-looking, making horrible choking noises instead of breathing.

She moves my hands in the air like a conductor, dragging his power out in a long string. I can almost see it, a shimmering of the air. Toby retches and jerks, shuddering like a fish on a hook. I scream impotently from the corner of my mind she's crushing me into. The nothing space drags at me, shredding my thoughts to tatters.

"No! I won't let you!" The voice shocks Cassandra and me both. She whirls my body around, hands upraised, already forming a field of power, ready to smash whoever has dared speak. I force down my awareness of the other bodies approaching, trying to hide them from her.

Jake stands in front of me, hands clenched at his side so tightly his knuckles are bone-colored. His face is set, fear and determination warring in his brown eyes. He looks so young it breaks my heart, and I redouble my attempts to break free of Cassandra's insidious hold. I didn't know I had more in me, but I find it. She swats my attempts aside, using Toby's stolen power to repress me.

It doesn't recognize me anymore, where it used to be almost mine. She smirks, twisting my face into an unfamiliar, uncomfortable shape.

"Well, little man. How do you plan to stop me?" She's unbearably smug; my Reader power combined with Toby's Projection must be off the scale. She's not concerned. She's superhuman. Unstoppable. She can, however, sense the soldiers throughout the city. Many of them are injured, but there are still a lot of them. She knows her time is finite. If enough of them band together, they might be able to contain her. She vividly remembers Toby keeping back thirty Institute agents that first day, the first time we met. *But how many soldiers are coming, Cassandra?* I make her think of that. Focus every ounce of willpower I have on keeping my memories away from Jake, hiding my knowledge of him, hoping against hope that she'll dismiss him. Leave him alone, he's just a kid! I rage futilely inside my hijacked mind.

She sighs, mock sadly, and waves a hand in the air dismissively. "Well, you might have more guts than I've seen in a while—" She flicks her eyes deliberately to Icarus...no...Cassius, forcing me to see his shredded stomach, hands stained dark as they feebly try to keep his guts inside. He looks dead, except for those twitching fingers. "—in a manner of speaking, of course. But I'm afraid I don't have time to pull them out of you." Smirking still, she flaps her hands at Jake dismissively, sending an incredible stream of power straight at him, hauling him into the air and smashing him back to the ground.

But no. Her anticipation, her image is not the truth.

Jake doesn't move. Gritting his teeth slightly, he moves forward, with no more difficulty than if he were wading through water. Then he's airborne, flying toward me at a pace faster than I have ever seen. Cassandra knows one moment of pure incredulity, and then his hand is shattering into my jaw and darkness whirls through us-me, dragging Cassandra and me both under.

"Autokinesis, you dick" echoes in my ears as I disappear. "No one moves my body but me."

Chapter Four

TOBY

I can't see anything, but my power is returning, seeping back into my twisted body like a blessing, relaxing tormented muscles and soothing my strung-out mind.

Suddenly, hands are on me, and focus returns with a rush. Jake's scared, concerned face is hovering over me, and he shakes me gently again. There's a hint of panic in his voice.

"Toby, Toby you gotta wake up. You gotta help. C'mon."

I feel like I'm underwater, but I manage, with his help, to half sit up. My twin is slumped in a pile, eyes closed.

"I knocked her out. Serena Slam, right in the face. I think I broke my hand. I didn't know what to do. She was killing you."

I cough, dragging air into my heaving lungs, and gather the energy to lift an arm, pulling Jake against me. He collapses gratefully into the hug, and I try to look around. As my power returns, draining out of the body in front of me, I start to feel more alert, and realize the danger we could still be in.

We haul ourselves to our feet. Nothing seems to be in our immediate vicinity, save the various slumped forms I can't bring myself to look at yet. I drag myself over to my twin, using Jake as a crutch. I'm tired to the bones. There's still the faint popping sound of Zaps in the distance. I hope our remaining lines have it covered. I lift my gun, flick the button on the side, and shoot my twin in the neck.

The red dart sinks into her flesh with barely a whisper, and I bend to lift her slight form up. Jake helps me as best he can with one hand, silent, his eyes red-rimmed. Once I have her settled in my arms, we trudge to the bodies of our friends.

Serena's whole side is a mangled mess, so I take her unhurt hand in mine and wait. I can't do anything for her, for any of them. I'm barely alive myself. Jake sits next to Cassius, gently moving his blond head to rest on his thigh. He's not moving, the blood spilled over his hands is so red I can't look at it. The ground is cold. People start arriving, running and shouting around us, but I can't bring myself to care. I deliberately do not look at the remains of Johan, my friend and mentor, where they lie mangled on the bright grass. I can see his necklace, the one he's always worn as long as I've known him. If it wasn't tangled around the shreds of bone and meat, I wouldn't know who it was. I wish I didn't.

It starts to rain, gray skies reaching to the horizon. I can't remember the last time it rained.

There are so many missing, so many dead, in the chaos of the streets and the targeted attack on ARC, that it takes days for a full casualty report to come in. My twin is kept sedated; no one knows what to do with her. I hear many arguments hushed in the hallway that stop when I walk past, heading to visit Thea, or Serena—who's awake now but still undergoing bone repair and other treatments—or Darcy, her hand crushed and broken into a dozen extra pieces.

I am relatively unscathed, if I discount the exhaustion that has me sleeping eighteen hours a day, eating my own body weight, and then collapsing again. I look like a skeleton, and I feel like a ghost. I used to wonder how my twin could stand to be so quiet, but now I understand. There are so many words inside me that there's no room for any of them to come out, and no one who wants to hear me apologize for whatever part in this was my fault.

It was all my fault. My power.

Andrea is missing; no one knows what happened to him. He was on the grounds when Darcy realized Cassandra had taken over my twin.

And then, five days after the battle, he's seen on camera by a lab tech who used to play cards with him, and my twin disappears without a trace.

It's like she evaporated, as if she was never there. Every surface in her prison cell is clean of residue, both physical and Psionic. The ARC tech team actually requests Thea to scan the room, and I don't know whether to laugh or cry when I see the mission brief on her datapad, which I've been holding onto in case...I don't know, something happens.

She's gone, and I don't know what to do, so I just keep doing the things I can. I visit the injured, help with what I can, while recovering from having the life sucked out of me. Avoid the gossip mill as much as possible and try to remember what it's like not to feel empty, hollowed out. All the purpose I thought I had has looked at me and found me wanting.

I'm supposed to be so strong, so why do I feel so weak?

"You're not even trying," Serena complains at me, as I try to straighten my shaking legs under the weight of the heavy iron plates pushing down onto the bar over my shoulders. I *am* trying, but maybe not that hard. All there is remaining are regimented days and the ever-looming knowledge that my twin is missing, possibly dead now, and my near imprisonment at ARC headquarters, while I "recover" from the two power drains that left me able to see every vein and tendon under my skin.

Serena has nominated herself my jailer. The first time I tried to leave ARC to find my twin she caught me before I made it down the corridor outside my dorm room. I think she'd be sleeping in the small room with me for extra security if it wasn't for Darcy.

Darcy's hand was broken in fourteen places, and even with the incredible medical technology available to us, her injury—not life-threatening and therefore not a priority— is extreme. Serena's recovering well from the dislocation of her arm, yanked out of the socket as she tried to throw power at my twin and got caught in the shockwave. As soon as Darcy knew, Serena knew, I found out later. Their connection isn't as intense as mine and Thea's, but it is potent, built on years of trust and intimacy. She's still wearing a sling, and the cracked ribs she received when she landed on another soldier's boot mean she's restricted to light activity, but apparently harassing me isn't too tiring.

She promised me we'd go after Thea, just me and her, as soon as we're medically cleared. She held my hand when she told me, and I knew she was thinking of Damon...Demi. That takes a bit of getting used to. There was a kid in my elementary school who shaved their head and started going by a neutral name and pronoun after the summer I turned eleven, so it's not as if Demi is the first person who's switched names and pronouns ever, but it's still strange. I have to reprogram myself and the language I'm used to using, and apparently that's always an adjustment.

Leaf says it took his adoptive father a year to get his pronouns right all the time. Sometimes I forget he's not a Reader; he always seems to know what people are thinking. He misses her too. I can tell. I don't think he'll let Serena and me go alone when we look for Thea. He's been out almost every day since the battle into the desert, slipping silent and invisible through the land he grew up on, trying to find her.

He says she's vanished.

I know better. I can feel the string that ties us together, tugging at my spine, pulling me toward her. I can feel the fangs of Cassandra in her head sometimes, when I'm deep asleep and the space between us shrinks.

I wish I could talk to her, over the bond we share, but whenever I try, it feels as though I'm shouting down a canyon, only the echo of my own voice coming back to me.

It's as though I'm waiting for her to disappear entirely. Every morning, when I wake, I check the connection between us, twang it like an elastic and hold my breath in case today is the day I'm left holding one end of a link that leads to no one, to nothing.

I'm desperate to go after her, but as Serena points out, with an annoyed tone in her voice, as she helps me lower the bar back to safety with her good hand, I can't even lift fifty pounds right now.

She flicks me in my shoulder blade, the sharpness of her fingernail knocking against bone that's never been so exposed.

"Moping doesn't help anyone," she snarks, like I haven't seen her crying when she thinks no one is watching. Like her eyes aren't red-rimmed and constantly flicking to Darcy's casted hand when we're all together, sitting in broken silence. She told me once that before they started seeing each other, Darcy had drawn a picture of Serena that she'd accidentally left in the canteen. Someone had handed it to Serena thinking it must be hers, and Serena had scanned it to see who had drawn it. Without going into too much detail, I got the impression that's when she realized Darcy had feelings for her.

Sometimes when Serena's skin brushes mine as we set up weights or walk side by side or watch a movie in a pile with the rest of us—Aly, Darcy, and Leaf—I catch her fear that Darcy will never draw again, and that without art, Darcy won't ever be happy again.

We don't hold hands to pass thoughts anymore, really. We're all too broken and sad to want to share our pain.

I've walked into Johan's training room looking for him seven times in the sixteen days since Cassandra tore him into dogmeat. My feet take me there when my brain isn't paying attention. The small, octagonal room used to represent bruises and stiff muscles delivered with a grin and a quip, but now it's a grave.

And we're all trapped here, knowing that outside the city walls, the number of Eaters continues to grow.

The City heaves at the seams, packed to the brims with refugees from the slums. Citizens rail and panic against the newcomers; some set off overland to try to make it to the safety of an unbesieged city. While the Eaters prefer the brains of the Talented above all else, we've learned the hard lesson that they won't turn down meat of any kind.

If you're unlucky and the wind's high and in the right direction, you can smell the cooking fat.

Shuddering at the unwanted memory, I trudge to the incline bench and swing my leg over it, hook my toes under the bar and lie back to try to force out some sit-ups. If I work hard enough today, maybe I'll sleep the night through.

I don't. I haven't since the Eaters came. I wake up, gasping, dreaming of gel in my lungs and monsters in my head. There's a knife blade of light slicing over my floor, over the end of my bed. Above me, Jake stirs. The door is open, and there's a shadow waiting, silhouetted against the hall lights that never go out.

I slide to my feet like a warrior, silent and even. The tiling is cold under my bare feet, I pad to the cracked door and pack my hands with Talent. I'm still as strong as I ever was, here, but my body is so fragile that to use my power is like trying to drag lead through my veins.

I can't see who's waiting outside until my eyes adjust, and I blink in shock. Leaning against the white wall, as pale as the material behind him, is Cassius.

The dark bruising under his eyes matches the blood flowering on his hospital gown. His flanks, visible through the plastic ties at the side of his paper thin outfit are heaving and marred with spidery stitches over unhealed, angry red wounds.

His face, when I finally meet his eyes, wears a hard-edged but genuine smile. "I'm going to help you kill my—" He blinks, shakes his head, twitching his cheek violently like he's bitten it on the inside. "—*his* mother."

Chapter Five

E17

I wake up with a head full of cotton. It's not overly unfamiliar, and I thank whoever might be listening for my hard-wired, hard-learned skill of shutting everything down as soon as I am aware, before I'm aware, even, because when I manage to peel my sticky eyes open the first face I see is straight out of a nightmare.

Pollux grins at me. "Hello, cousin," he greets politely, with stained teeth and grit in every crease of his face. There's a piece of ragged flesh caught between his canine and his cuspid; his breath reeks of old blood.

"Pollux," I say, as calmly as I can, and within me, Cassandra squirms like a python in a sack, roiling under the glassy surface of my power. Somehow, while I slept, after Jake hit me and whatever has passed since then, we've traded places again. Somehow, I am here, and she is back in her cage.

But I am not safe at ARC to tell them I'm back, to have Kion thwap me on the shoulder or Darcy hold me to her soft chest and tell me I'm safe.

I'm not safe where my brother can find me and stand beside me so I don't have to face the dark alone. I'm not safe where Leaf can brush the backs of his knuckles against mine and smile lopsidedly at me so I can see his crooked dog tooth and open heart.

I'm not safe.

I'll never be safe.

I should kill myself now. I can see the hilt of a dagger on Pollux's hip, see the prints of two more against the cloth over his ribs.

Pollux follows my eyeline, cocks his head at me, and I force a bored expression, yawn. I try to do what Cassandra had been doing to my people, to my life. I steal her underthoughts and feelings, paint them on myself like a canvas. I've had more practice than her, but Pollux knows us both.

"My son?" Her thoughts are always of Icarus first.

Pollux grins, delighted, laughs, sits back on his haunches, finally getting his bloodstained breath out of my face. "Is very well! I'll send one of the lizards for him." He gives me a last smile, strokes my cheek with affection in his grimy fingers, and turns away.

I exhale, relaxing a little. The tightrope I walk feels more dangerous than it did at the Institute, even. There, all I had to face was the possibility of my erasure, or death. Here, well. I saw the meat in his mouth. I know what the Eaters do. It would be worse.

He ate his brother alive, Cassandra whispers to me, but it has the ring of a lie, and I ignore her. I could stun him, hit him in the great arteries that run the neck and in his moment of dizziness take his blade and drive it into my skull.

Within me, Cassandra sighs, almost bored. She's not concerned about our switch of dominance, here among her family she thinks it is only a matter of time until she regains control. *You won't kill yourself, so why pretend? It's only the two of us, here, and I know you better.*

She wants to tell me I'm weak, afraid; she wants to mock me, but she's also a little afraid that doing so will give me the strength to prove her wrong. I should kill us both, end it here, but as I uncurl myself from the hard bedroll I've been lying on, I see I cannot.

I am in a valley behind a hard crust of ridged rock reaching for the sky like teeth, and I am surrounded. There are Eaters everywhere I look, thousands of them, enough to blot out the stars above us with the lights of their fires. It is an army.

"Beautiful, isn't it?" I recognize the voice first, then the face, and then the fact the person speaking isn't Andrea. Icarus, mahogany-skinned where before he was milk white folds gracefully next to me. "They flocked to Pollux, to me. They think he's their prophesied leader." He laughs, his boyish face hard and colder than I've ever seen. I can see Icarus in the tightness around his soft eyes, the angle of his jaw. My heart freezes, little by little.

I never knew Cassius, not how it mattered, not that I remembered properly anyway. But Andrea—he was quiet and gentle, friends with Darcy more than the rest of us, although I know he spent time with Serena's younger friends, Jue and Young Shannon.

"Impressive," I settle on as my response, rubbing my temples as though I have a fierce headache, trying to mimic the way I've seen Cassandra do it, felt Cassandra do it when she walked in my skin.

I wonder if Andrea is still in there, or if he's gone. I wonder if I'll be able to leave without knowing if I could have saved him. I have to leave, have to get back to ARC and tell them what waits outside their doors.

"They're still coming." Icarus sprawls his stolen legs out, digs his toes into the dirt, and sighs. "I wish you'd chosen someone taller," he complains. Andrea is barely five six, Cassius was tall, and Cassandra knows her son's first body was six foot even.

"You'll adjust, and later we can choose someone better for you." I let Cassandra's thoughts guide me. "Maybe the brother. That has a certain fit to it."

"Oh, you'd leech him of his power and let me ride the shell," Icarus scoffs. "I thank you, Mother, but I think I can do better."

"The girl is strong—Serena." I'm needling him, or Cassandra is. It's hard to tell which of us thought that first.

Icarus snorts, clearly choosing to interpret my comment as a joke. I let it slide.

"So none of these...Eaters...would be suitable?" I press.

He rolls his eyes dramatically, throws his hand out to encompass them. "Riddled with tumors, they spend most of their gifts just keeping themselves alive. Most of them don't even speak, only mind to mind, with all the intimacy that encompasses. More of a hive than a collection of individuals. And their bodies have been ruined by a lifetime of privation. At least at the Institute we made sure the meat would be fit to wear."

He pauses, picks at Andrea's nails with his knife. "Also, they refer to themselves as the lizards."

"Hmm," I try to remember Cassandra's poise, the effortless way she has of sitting, when my shoulders want to slump, and my spine wants to fold. If I can get some time apart from Icarus and Pollux maybe I can get a message to my brother, warn him of what's to come. Maybe if I can get Icarus alone, I can pull him out of Andrea and send the boy back across the desert to the City.

"How far are we from the Wall?" I ask, trying to seem idle.

"Five days on foot. Far enough that they won't sense us. And we have chopper killers." He sounds delighted. "Lizards with technopath power, like the boy you tried to bring in from Second City. They'll drop anyone who tries to fly near us."

"They don't seem to have any kind of technology," I observe. I saw them attack the City, after all.

Icarus sighs, "The ones who headed in couldn't resist the lure of power. They're the least disciplined, the wild ones, the dregs." He holds out his knife for me to see, presses a button invisible on the hilt, and I watch as a spark of blue-white energy flows down the metal blade. "Zap knife, stab 'em and stun 'em. They have few ranged weapons because material is hard to come by, but this charges on motion and solar, more efficiently than our Zaps do, I wager."

It's beautiful, the crackle of energy, and I want it. I debate for a moment about how Cassandra would request such a thing and then decide she wouldn't. "Give it to me."

Icarus snorts air out of his nose and rises fluidly to his feet; for all his complaints he's adapted to this body well enough. "Once we're sure you're...quite yourself, Mother."

He pads off, his feet bare and digging into the soft sand and crumbled rock. I try not to shiver.

They leave me alone for a while, which makes me nervous. I'm not restrained, but I'm in an army, surrounded. I decide to see what kind of restraints they're willing to place on me and get clumsily to my feet. My muscles are weak from lack of use, from lying in a bed for however long it's been, but no worse than waking up from the Tank.

I stretch, run through a brief yoga routine I know was a regular part of Cassandra's day, and then crack my neck, looking about.

It seems I'm in a narrow gulley of rock, although it's hard to be sure in the dark. A valley sprawls downward, widening as it veers away from my feet. The remnants of an old river, maybe two kilometers across at its broadest and hundreds long. Dotted with bonfires and smaller camp setups. The cliffs that frame it aren't steep, except at my back, soaring above my head into the sky. Unclimbable. I've seen this ridge on maps, and orient myself accordingly, as best I can. With no clear view of the stars and no idea what time it is, I'm left to guess blindly for direction.

I do have a good excuse to wander, though. I let my increasingly pressing desire for the bathroom flood my thoughts, and a heap of rags near my left side pops up to reveal one of the Eaters, a lizard.

Forty down, seventy left. He means paces, and his instructions are stained with extra information, details of the broken rocks I'll find under my—also bare—feet.

I nod my thanks and carefully walk away. I can't tell if he, or another, follows as I pick my way down the narrow path. The "facilities" are little more than a crater with poles balanced over it for sitting on, and I lament my lack of ability to pee standing up. I know Ria can; she's bragged about it before, and having seen her naked, I know it's not that we have wildly differing biology. If I get back to ARC, I should ask her to teach me.

I take care of the necessary and decide to explore a little farther instead of retreating back to my sleeping pad. There are few Eaters up here, but I hear the rustle of cloth on stone behind me and assume I have company.

Ah well, hopefully they will learn nothing from me, but it's certain I will learn little from them if I return to my previous location.

"Now, cousin—" Pollux slips down a scree-covered slope in front of me. "—where are you going?"

"To look at the camp." I make sure the "idiot" that finishes Cassandra's sentence is clear, although silent.

He eyes me; it's disconcerting in the moonlight. His face looks like a skull, worn and sharp and only bone. His eyes are pits reflecting nothing. The metal casings that drill into his skull, for the phenolum—once he was too far gone for anything but direct to brain cell application—have been shaved down, I notice now. They're almost level with his skull.

He sees me looking. "Nice, aren't they? They have telepathic toolworkers, as well. Impressive. Held the tubes steady so as not to break my squishy bits." He smirks. "Better job than the Institute ever did."

I wonder how it is he seems so sane, here. How his power isn't smashing people against rocks with the anger that's roasted him since his brother left him and snapped his mind.

Either catching the thought from the air or from my face, he grins widely, looks more like a person than I've ever seen him. "Crazed is as crazed does. I'm the king here, so nothing I do is crazy."

"I'm not sure that's how it works, cousin," I say dryly, cock my elbow for him as I see Cassandra doing once, long ago. "Walk with me, show me your world."

He gives a mockery of a courtly bow and takes my arm. His fingers are wet in the crease of my elbow, and I know if I look down there will be bloody smears left on my skin. I don't look down, nor do I flinch.

Chapter Six

TOBY

Cassius looks as if he'd be hard pushed to kill a spider, but I don't laugh. Have I laughed at all in recent memory? I don't know.

Down the corridor, another noise, and then Leaf slips out of the T-junction at the end of the hallway.

He jerks his head at me, like "shut the door," so I do. No point in waking Jake, after all. And then Leaf pads down the corridor, giving me a lopsided grin.

"You can't," he tells Cassius softly, seriously. "You're barely capable of standing. Toby's killing himself every time he tries to use his power. Both of you need to heal, and then we can go after her."

"You've been looking," I point out, and he nods.

"I can't get far through the crowd, not where it gets packed at the foothills. I've walked among them a bit." He shifts; his face changes; he holds himself differently, hunched in and hollow-cheeked, and suddenly, I see an Eater in him. I flinch back, and he grins, Leaf again. "Doesn't fool all of 'em, but enough to let me shuffle about at night. They have their own Blanks, or near enough. I haven't heard talk of her; they don't speak much. But I will. And you—" He jerks his head at Cassius. "—will learn to walk without bleeding through your stitches."

He's right, I realize abruptly; there's fresh red blooming on Cassius's stomach. He looks down, shocked, sways a little, and Leaf catches him, moving like silk.

"Help me," he grunts, Cassius being probably half his weight again, even injured and skinnied down from months of desert living. I nod, bustle forward and almost drop Cassius on his ass as I try to alleviate the weight over Leaf's narrow shoulder. He rolls his eyes at me, but in an affectionate way, and together we maneuver the now half-conscious Cassius down the corridor back to his hospital bed. When we drop him off, he grabs my hand.

"Promise me"—his voice is faint and garbled—"Promise me, on your twin's life, you'll take me when you go for her."

Leaf wraps his brown fingers around Cassius's wrist, tugs gently. "We promise, man, even if you can't stay on your feet and we leave you to bleed out in the slums." His voice is soft. "We won't go without you."

Cassius nods, seemingly satisfied, and lets me go, fading into sleep as we watch.

"How can you promise him that?" I hiss, furious. Cassius won't be fit to walk for weeks, maybe months.

Leaf laughs softly, heads for the door, and glances back at me before he slips out of the room. "'S just words, big man. I dinnae mean them." I'm shocked, and I try to go after him, but he's disappeared somehow before I get to the door.

I trudge back to my room. Just words, a hollow promise; he didn't mean it for a moment. I don't know how anyone could lie that way, let alone sound so sincere. That promise rang like a bell. I shiver, unnerved, and pass my door, heading for the gym in my pajamas. I'll find gear there, rather than wake Jake. He's always worrying about me or about Demi. The kid is twelve, and sometimes I feel like he's my older brother.

The clothes I find are old and worn, washed so many times it's impossible to tell what color they started as, a miscellaneous beige now. I hook a chain to the weight bar on the bench, so it won't crush me if my arms give out, and start lifting.

My muscles wasted away when my power was taken, but they remember how to be strong, and I'm building them back slowly. It's all there is to do, anyway. I'm not cleared for any duty except the lightest, and everyone is busy or recovering from their own injuries.

Aly escaped without a mark on her, except in her eyes. They're darker than they used to be.

It's three a.m. when my body tells me *no,* and the thought of returning to my bed fills me with swirling anxiety, prickling my skin. I'll only dream again.

If Serena slept alone, I'd go and wake her up, make her hang out with me for a bit. I don't know why Leaf was awake, what he was doing prowling the corridors, but I also don't think that he's a person I can be calm with right now, or that I could find him even if he was.

In the shower, I remember Aly's roommate is still in the infirmary, and once I'm toweled off and back in my pajamas, I find my feet taking me to her door.

I don't knock. I don't knock, and then I do.

It takes her a moment to get to the door; she cracks it slightly, sees me and frowns, steps back and yawns. "What's wrong?" Her body language isn't panicked; she can tell nothing real has happened, just from my face.

I shrug, suddenly feeling useless and hopeless. "I just didn't want to be alone."

Her face softens, and she picks up my hand, pulls me into the room and shuts the door. It's dark inside, the only light coming from the very top row of tiles, dimmed to almost nothing.

She pulls me toward the bed, pushes me down, and crawls in next to me, resting her head on my chest. "I can hear your heartbeat," she says, muzzily.

It makes me smile just a little, the corners of my mouth jerk like they want to go bigger. "Means I'm still alive, I guess."

"It's gonna be okay, Toby." She lifts her head up and presses her lips against my cheek. I feel the soft hairs of my soon-to-be very manly beard shift under her touch. She smiles against my skin and then rests her head on my chest again. I carefully put my arm over her warm, solid body, and then she stuffs her hand into my armpit, making me yelp and flinch. "Shhh," she says, leaving her fingers wedged between my arm and side. "'S warm."

It is warm with her pressed against my side, her hair tickling my neck. I don't remember falling asleep, but the room lightening to day level is the next thing I notice.

Aly has migrated farther on top of me, and my body has reacted exactly as you might expect a teenage boy who hasn't had sex for almost a year and a half to react. I try to shift away, not wanting to wake her into awkwardness. My cheeks are so hot they might be glowing, and I'm focusing all my mental powers—the regular kind, not the Talent kind—on trying to convince my body to think about cold showers, mold growing on ceramic tiles, and the disgusting mouths of those bacteria called water bears when Aly squirms, presses closer, and says, "Oh."

"Sorry," I mutter, sure my Talent screams of embarrassment would be heard around the block if I wasn't so drained still, but Aly just grins.

"Sorry like... That's not for me? Or sorry like you're not sure if it's a present I want?" she inquires without moving.

My spine turns to syrup, and my mouth works uselessly, flailing for an answer. But then I don't have to say anything because Aly swings her leg over my hip and leans down to kiss me.

Sending up a silent prayer of thanks for the empty room and the Talent drain that means no one's gonna be bursting in to check why I'm having a heart attack, I make a mental note to ask Serena how to shut yourself down in situations like this, and I kiss her back.

We almost miss breakfast, which would be fine if Jake didn't immediately ask, "Where *were* you last night?" and Aly hadn't enthusiastically bitten my neck too high for a collar to cover.

I blush bright red, again, and bury my face in my eggs, while Aly coolly says, "He was with me," like she doesn't give a nuke what anyone thinks at all.

Serena smirks at me and waggles her eyebrows dramatically when I eventually have to look up to pour myself some water. "Looks like you had fun." She drawls the last word and Jake pulls a repulsed face.

"Gross." He looks at me reproachfully. "I thought you were better than that."

He looks so personally affronted I can't help but laugh a little. "Sorry to let you down, buddy."

"Give it a couple of years, Jake," Serena snickers, and Darcy elbows her, so she amends quickly, "Or not, if it turns out that's not your jam."

Aly puts her hand on my knee under the table, and I narrowly avoid jerking my leg up hard enough to crush her fingers.

Serena laughs uproariously at me, and I give in to my own grin reluctantly. It's almost, almost normal. I wish Thea were here to tease me. The thought washes through me and makes me sick to my stomach. How can I, how can *we* sit here like everything's okay when she's out there alone?

Darcy reaches for my hand over the table, curls her fingers around my now white-knuckled grip on my fork. "She wouldn't want you to be hurting, Toby. And it doesn't mean you care for her any less if you manage to take a moment for yourself every now and again."

"Speaking of not getting to do that very often"—Serena says as she gets to her feet—"you and I are expected at the lab, invisi-boy. We have to work out how the Eaters are all able to flicker, even the low levels." Flicker is the verb that seems to have caught on around ARC for the ability to pop in and out of visibility.

I nod, shoveling the last of my food into my mouth, and get to my feet. For a moment, I don't know what I should do, if I should kiss Aly goodbye—but I'm still swallowing—or hug her or something. I panic, because that's usually how I handle things of an emotional bent, and freeze, half in and out of my seat.

Serena takes pity on me and grabs me by the ear. "He'll see you later, Aly, and he's very grateful for last night."

My ears are so hot I feel like they definitely must be sending up little waves of distorted air above them, and I struggle free of Serena's grip, shoving at her to make her let go of me.

"You're welcome," Aly calls after us, setting Serena off into enough of a giggle fit that I manage to yank free.

When I glance back, Aly's still looking, and she winks at me. This time my smile is completely real and uninhibited.

Serena, of course, ruins everything by swinging her arm around my waist, almost knocking me over. "Does this mean you're over me now?"

"I've been over you for a year," I lie easily, bracing my legs and dropping her over my hip. Gently, though, because she's injured too. She lands easy and rolls to her feet, cackling.

"You have good taste in women, Tobes. Darcy is, of course, the number one babe, best on campus with me a close, close second, but Aly is very cute. And not engaged, or too old for you."

It takes me a second.

"You're *engaged?!*" I yell, squealing to a halt.

Serena gives me a broad grin, nods. "Yeah, I asked Darcy right before...everything. And then, well. It all went to shit, and we didn't wanna tell anyone. But now I guess I told you, and you screamed it loud enough everyone in ARC is gonna know in thirty seconds."

She gets the distant look on her face that means she's communicating mind to mind, with the soft expression she only has for Darcy, we walk in silence for a moment while she chats and then she grins at me. "Darcy says she's gonna punch you for letting the cat out of the bag."

"You surprised me!" I point out. "This is definitely your fault."

"Lies, I'm perfect and you're in trouble," she smirks. "Also"—her voice takes on a more serious tone—"I, uh, I wondered if you wanted to be. I mean, if you will—" She swallows, looking uncharacteristically self-conscious. "—be my best person?"

I grind to a halt; my heart feels big and tight in my chest, my ribs are too small. I try to make words happen, but I feel the wash of Talent stream out of me as if it was never gone. Serena takes a step back and blinks in the wake of my power.

It's gone as soon as it comes, leaving me sagging against the wall, but it leaves a tingling, sparkling sensation through my whole body, my veins singing.

"Well...if anyone didn't hear you yelling, they definitely heard that. I take it that's a yes?" Serena says wryly.

I grin widely, feeling better than I have in weeks. "Yeah, that's a yes."

They're not going to get married until everything is under control—until Thea is back, Serena tells me, while we wait for the techs. Darcy wants Thea to be her own best person, and I'm pleased by the thought of standing up for our friends together, once everything is settled and safe again. I'm glad we won't do it in the midst of war, but rather, as a new start when it's over.

I don't know how it will be over, though. How can it be, when the Eaters are outside our walls, and they appear amongst our citizens every few days. When we're all constantly on edge and waiting for someone to take us down. People don't spend much time alone, these days.

We get wired up, and I again go through the process I would to become invisible, if my power was available to use. This time, I feel it twitch inside me. Taking a deep breath in through my nose and out through my mouth, I close my eyes and try to find it, try to coax it into fullness. When Serena taught me to meditate, she showed me how to contain it, but now I need to blow the sparks of my power until they can return to me.

I can feel sweat forming on my lip and forehead, hear someone speaking to me distantly. My power glows, familiar and welcoming, a bank of coals where it used to be a furnace.

I breathe.

Toby?

For a split second I think it must be Serena, her hand warm on my neck, but I feel the shock of the contact career through her as I recognize my twin's power, my twin's inner self.

Thea!

I almost choke in shock and excitement. I haven't felt anything from her, besides an alluring certainty that she's still alive, still out there, taken by Cassandra or not, but still alive.

Toby. Her inner voice is thick with relief, with fear and anger and a massive jumble of other emotions I can't sort through that make my eyes sting and my throat pull tight.

Me too, says Serena. *Where are you? Are you okay?* I'm so grateful to her for being on top of things, again, for being so strong and quick and brilliant. She pinches my arm affectionately.

I'm alive, Thea replies. *I'm over the rock formation to the north of the City. Pollux and Icarus are here.* She sounds sick and tired and afraid.

We're going to come and get you, I cry, filling myself with positivity to mask the crawling fear that drenches me in cold sweat at the mention of Pollux.

Icarus is in Andrea. I won't leave him. And there's too many. You'd have to bring the Institutes from every city to stand a sliver of a chance. She paints her words with the thousands of Eaters, tens of thousands that surround her, that blanket the sands around the rocks as far as her eye can see. *They think I'm her.*

How long can you keep that up? Serena is brusque, businesslike. *Is she still in you? They'll kill you if they can save her.*

She's here. I'm...using her memories to fool them. I think I have it under control. Thea doesn't sound completely convinced. *They're both strong, but...distracted. I have a little time, at least.*

Or they're letting you think that you do, Serena chimes in. *Any messages for anyone?*

I accidentally think about the engagement and about being best person, and Thea standing up for Darcy, and a feeling that's uncomfortably close to a controlled sob spills down the wire-thin connection between us.

Tell Darcy... Tell her I'm sorry about her hand. I tried to stop it.

No one blames you, Serena says, bluntly.

And I know it's true as much as I know that Thea should have trusted us more, told us more, about what she was dealing with.

I love you, I send, because I don't have anything of much use to add. I just want to storm out, rage through the Eaters, and grab her. If I were at full strength, I might even try. I could shield, surely, for that long. Flicker out and they'd think I was one of them.

You'd never feel like one of them, Toby, Thea tells me. *They only live to take.*

And then she's gone.

Chapter Seven

E17

Toby twinkles into existence somewhere far, far southwest of me, feeling his leaden exhaustion in my bones is an unwelcome distraction. He's unconsciously siphoning off a little energy from our link; it straightens his spine and makes him clearer, but I know it will only be moments before Pollux feels him on me, so I cut the connection with a blade of our power.

It's comforting to know he's there, to feel his existence and shine. He's lost some of his happy glow from the days when I used to run in his head while the Institute sent needles through my brain tissue, but he's still optimistic to his core. It's part of him as much as his ribs.

I'm grateful that Serena told me no one blames me. I don't see how it's possible, but she felt truthful when she spoke it. I don't know how anyone could watch this body cut down dozens, squash Cassius like a bug under a rock—and I caught the echo of him in Toby's head, I know he's alive and held together by little more than a wish and a prayer—I don't know how they could watch that and not blame me. I blame me. If I'd left, they'd be safe.

Safe? Cassandra laughs at me from deep below my surface thoughts: *You were safe in the Institute.* She flashes thoughts meant to daunt and dishearten me, make me slip. I watch myself as a four- or five-year-old determinedly trying to escape the rubber straps that hold me down as they fit me with a new implant, attuned to my developing power. There was no pain—they wouldn't want to sit through the screaming—there's only helplessness and anger and fear, and the imagined sensation of instruments poking the secret tissue in my head.

That was never safety, I snap at her, careful to keep my face interested and my thoughts small, as Pollux leads me down a near invisible path between ravaged gangs of Eaters. As we move through the crowds, it becomes clear that those closer to the large bonfires in the center are more impressive. They hiss with power under my mind's eye but are also dressed in more durable and stronger fabric, have more equipment. I see several laser knives similar to the one I coveted so badly.

I want to be away from here, back with my friends and family, but since that's currently impossible, I try to make myself useful by estimating numbers—Eaters, in what ages; weapons, what kinds; supplies, little that I can see but the Eaters have made no bones of their ability to bring meat with them, walking on two legs. I wonder how they decide who lives and who dies, or if it really is just a case of grabbing whoever is handy.

Hunger already roils in my guts. I'll have to eat eventually. *Would you eat them?* I ask Cassandra, silently, but she just sends the impression of a smirk. I wonder if she would. If I should. Eat a person to survive. I wonder if I even could, and the squirm of my stomach tells me I'd have to be a lot more desperate than this.

Does Icarus eat like you, like them? I ask Pollux, thinking perhaps the mention of her son will make

Cassandra slip and reveal some of her likely actions in this place.

Pollux sneers at me, *No, your young prince won't touch the sullied.* He pauses to step over an Eater who could be sleeping or could be dead. It's a young woman, maybe the same age as me. I haven't seen much younger.

They're in a different camp. Pollux informs me, catching the unguarded, floating thought with ease. He's stronger than the Shepherds ever were. I wonder if I'm even fooling him at all. I daren't dip into him to find out, but I haven't felt the greasy fingers of his mind touch mine either.

It's impolite. Cassandra sounds almost bored. *He won't, until you give yourself away. We're not animals.*

You're worse, I tell her, nodding at Pollux in thanks for the information. *Some animals eat their young, but not many torture them.*

She snorts dismissively; she thinks me naive. Thinks I have no idea what I'd be capable of, given the right motivation. But her motivation is only greed, greed for power and control and more lives than anyone was ever supposed to live.

The floating thoughts on the wind from the Eaters are enough to make me want to claw my own skin off without her input, so I do my best to tamp down further on my Reader sense.

All around me, the camp looms, faces distorted by firelight, smeared with blood and filth. Many of them hold the sand to their skin even though there's no use for it now, in the dark among their kind. They've forgotten it's even there, have just become part of the desert. Its gaping maw.

The cliffs loom up, a prison fence greater than I've ever seen, but with the mass of Eaters thinned on the lower slopes and not spreading high. Partly for discretion; they don't want the City to see their firelights, but also because the ground is hard and sharp, slicing even their leathery feet to bloody mince if they tried to go too far.

I have shoes, now, though. Good boots. They'll hold up to the shale, if need be. I can take survival knowledge from the Eaters, the same way I've stolen so many skills before. I'll have to be careful, sly, snatch thoughts from different places and leave no trace of myself to follow back to my meat sack before I get clear of them.

Find a nice piece of rock to drive into your skull, Cassandra suggests dryly. I squash her as best I can.

"Hungry, cousin?" Pollux asks me, in normal speech, as we pass a firepit that has chunks of meat on sticks being turned by a scrawny man with no shirt on. I could count every one of his mangled ribs if I so chose.

"I'll have what Icarus is having." I try to sound cold, unfeeling, and Pollux laughs uproariously, swinging his arm around my shoulders so hard I stagger with the weight of it.

"Rock lizard it is!" He sounds delighted.

I half expect to eat around a fire with the Eaters but to my surprise I'm led to a kind of pavilion, open-sided but with a roof built of lightweight canvas and ropes weighed down with rocks. The ground has been cleared of debris and has several seating areas which at first glance appear to be lumps of furs until I realize they're spread over mounds of dirt and rock cleverly shaped to support one's back. There's a low table covered in dishes, and Icarus-in-Andrea lounges next to it.

He has the careless grace I've come to associate with him, none of Andrea's awkwardness and nerves, the constant almost flinch of expecting sharp words or sharper blows. Icarus doesn't carry any fear like that, and without the fight Cassius apparently gave him, he's steadier. There's not as much spinning confusion in his eyes; the mix of power that made him so unsettling to me is muted with his new body. He's not alone at the table.

"Mother"—he inclines his head—"this is Karan-Bathad and Up-Shup Benay," the names are unfamiliar sounds, thickened with a glottal swallow and a hiss over the top of the *th* and *sh* sounds.

"A pleasure." I nod to them, my heart in my throat. Their power is nothing I'm familiar with; this mass of people who can turn invisible at will. I daren't spread my power to see if more of them follow or are near me. Even when using the facilities, I must be on my guard, constantly. The Institute prepared me well for this, though. Perhaps more than anyone.

In a rare bout of talkativeness, Kion once said I was like trying to read a glacier. He said you could slide over my mental surfaces for hours and barely find a foothold or a crevice to try to curl mental fingers around and peek inside. And I learned to keep my face the same way, hard and flat and unknowable. The thought of Kion, however, makes a sharp ache curl and stretch in my chest, driving knives of regret and sorrow so vicious I think I might fold with it, and Pollux grabs my arm, steadies me.

"Are you quite well, cousin?" His sick politeness makes my skin crawl.

"She tries to speak with her brother. It's distracting," I tell him, painting the words with thick sweeps reminding everyone of the bond between this body and the boy we left behind.

"We have ways of cutting links like that," Karan-Bathad unfolds in a graceful wave, sliding to her feet and allowing me to get a decent look at her in the firelight. Her teeth are sharpened points, as I've come to expect. Tearing through raw human meat and ligaments requires fangs. She sees me looking and bares her teeth in a facsimile of a smile.

I don't flinch. I've seen worse. Her skin is a shade darker than mine, although it could easily be sun exposure rather than nature. It glows bronze in the flickering firelight, stained in places by smoke and other grime. Her clothing makes sense for the desert, a hooded shawl attached to loose, light clothing, with leather straps holding weapons. I've seen many camels in flashes of memory around us, so I surmise the beasts are used as food, transportation, and clothing.

Her hair is shaved close to the head, barely a half inch of bristle to show its coppery color. She has rings in her ears and other metal adornments on her fingers and wrists, which have the shape of trappings that show her power. A chief or leader of some kind, which makes sense for her to be here, with Icarus, in what is clearly an area reserved for the most important.

"I thank you, but I can manage her," I respond to her question. "The thread between the twins should enable me to siphon off his strength when we capture him." I have a thought and raise an eyebrow the way I've seen Cassandra do myself when she doubts someone. "That is the purpose of this gathering? We will take the City?"

"We will," Karan-Bethad tells me, and I'm suddenly struck by the question of how she learned the Common tongue. There are still other dialects thriving among academics, and I heard other languages when we were in the inn in the slums, but how is it the Eaters have this knowledge?

I let my thought drift up, judging it harmless enough, and she smirks at me with shark's teeth. "They haven't showed you." It's not a question. She laughs lightly, and Pollux joins her, a raucous bark he doesn't try to smother.

"Eat the brain, take the skill." He tells me, smirking. "We made sure that we grabbed some locals for the leaders so we could all communicate."

"How many of you are there?" I take a seat on a small cushion next to the table, and Icarus stalls my fingers as I reach for a dish.

"Allow me." He starts to plate some sort of heavy bread, a sauce, and some slices of meat that match what he has on his own plate. They've been lightly cooked, the edges of the white-pink slabs darkened with grill marks but the flesh inside milky and almost translucent. *It's lizard, only lizard,* I tell myself, and then I recall the Eaters call themselves lizards also and have to hide my shudder.

"Fourteen thousand primes." The word is laced with multiple meanings—primes are warriors, powered, and untouchable by their peers. They're not in danger of being grabbed and cannibalized. "Seventeen thousand unders," she continues, and the word tells me that unders serve the primes, are on their first body, and aren't protected by the decree of the leaders. Less than people, seems to be the implication. Slaves and servants like those we fought under the tube.

"And you're all Talented?" I inquire, using the bread to mop up some sauce and lift it to my lips. The flavor is sweet and heavy, and I force myself not to wonder what's inside it.

She makes a spitting noise. "Those with no voice we add to the heart of the tribe." She means eat them. They eat any babies that show no skill for telepathy.

And you wondered why we hid you, and you thought that we were the epitome of evil, Cassandra points out. *We protected you.*

And robbed us of our lives, I mentally throw at her, ducking my face to my food. The meat is good, salty-thick with a flaky texture.

"Efficient," I reply dryly when I have the mental control not to slap my broken heart all over the words.

Pollux laughs again and joins Up-Shup Benay at the end of the table. From the way they fold their legs against each other, I surmise there is a more physical component to their relationship. Up-Shup Benay reads as neither clearly masculine or feminine and they sit straight-backed with the hilts of many weapons visible against their baggy clothes.

"Is this a council of war?" I inquire, when my hunger is finally sated. I sip a cold, sweet and milky drink that a silent Eater delivered to me after I filled my plate for a second time.

"Of sorts." Icarus drawls. "There are summits that must be held with the smaller groups of Eaters. Up-Shup Benay and Karan-Bethad are the heads of all, but they operate with a kind of council."

"There is still much to be spoken of, many maps we need and plans to be hammered out among the war council," Up-Shup tells me. "We seldom work as such a large entity, and old rivalries must be settled before we can fully unite the clans."

"Settled?" There was violence in the word, and Karan-Bethad shows me all her teeth, again.

"Tomorrow we start the war games."

"And I fight for my right to rule the clans," Pollux adds, as though he talks of having a picnic.

Chapter Eight

TOBY

After Thea cuts me off, Serena has to catch me to stop me falling off my stool, and I don't remember going back to my room. When I wake up again, I'm starving, and I can feel my power tingling in my blood like it was never gone. It makes me realize how much I missed it, how much I relied on that fizzing feeling to protect me and mine, and even when it couldn't, it still made me feel safer.

I can feel my tie to my twin properly, although only vague shadows of fleeting emotions are coming down it. I'm a distraction she doesn't need, although the lack of communication makes me feel lonely. I send a burst of pride in her strength, love, trust in her, and all the other good stuff I can manage, and feel a shiver of gratefulness twang down the connection between us.

So she still feels me, and my recent sense of hopelessness isn't what I want to share with her. If I can be a safe space again the way I was for her when they drowned her, maybe she'll have the steadiness to fool them all, the whole army, and escape.

The army!

Serena? I throw her name out and wince when I realize it's late, and I've just roused a gaggle of sensitive Readers from their sleep and meditation. I send a pulse of apology and shut my power back into my body.

Serena takes ten minutes to arrive, and I spend the time cleaning up a bit and brushing my teeth. Thankfully, when she does barge in, she has a tray of food. I fall on it like a starving wolf, and grin at her through my mouthful when she flops down on my bed and pushes her feet up into the mattress above.

"Don't worry, I told the bosses about the stuff Thea sent. You should be working on your control," she points out, poking the mattress until it raises in a mound. Good job Jake's not up there, I think, and then realize I don't know where he is.

Serena rubs her forehead. "He's with Demi, having a sleepover so you can get some rest, and because your dreams are so loud everyone has a headache."

"Shit, really?" I frown. I don't feel that out of control.

"Really." Serena smirks. "And my advice to you would be to sort that out before you pay Aly another nighttime visit, or you'll be sharing some very intimate thoughts that no one, especially not I, wants to hear."

"Nuke," I grumble, seeing days of chores, meditation and weights yawning out in front of me.

Serena grins. "Well, it's not like they have much use for you on the planning committees. You're not exactly a military genius. More like...a weapon we can point at whoever we want to explode."

I'm unwittingly reminded of the mess that remained of Johan, *my* power, stolen though it was, turning him to chunks. Serena flinches.

"I didn't mean that," she apologizes. "It's not your fault, either."

"Isn't it?" I grumble. If it wasn't for my link to my twin, would they ever have found and toppled the Institute?

Serena kicks me, not gently either. "One, do you think anyone could have stopped me from finding Demi eventually? Two, are you so idiotic you think that kidnapping children is the lesser of two evils, here?" Her impatience for my self-pity is clear in her words.

"If it's a choice between being kidnapped and being eaten, I know what I'd choose," I reply, and Serena rolls her eyes.

"And you think Thea would say the same?" Shame-faced, I shake my head, knowing she's right.

"What are we going to do?" I ask, helplessly. We're fighting three wars at once.

Serena lifts her shoulder, kicks me more gently this time. "Meditate."

My power feels weird, and I miss Johan furiously as I try to sink into it. He could always explain things in a way that made sense to me or put his hand on my shoulder and show me what he meant. But Serena's right, I need to get under control, and the blending of our powers last time was a disaster that took months to undo. This time, I know what I have to do. Sort through the threads for what is mine, and what is Thea's, and send them in the right direction.

I take a deep breath in for seven, sink into my own bones, let the glow of Talent guide me to my center. I start scanning myself, looking for the scraps and strings of power that aren't mine, that belong to Thea.

I can't see any, so it must not be as bad as Serena thinks. The surface of my Talent is all mine, the indigo color I associate with it shining clear in my mind. I go deeper, sliding through the shell that holds my Talent inside. It has holes, the shell; I haven't meditated since my power was sucked out, and that's probably the issue.

Breathing rhythmically, I fix the gaps I can see, leaving only one: a space that marks the thread of my twin's power joined to mine. It's not until I finish that I realize the color of her power and mine are identical, that it's impossible to see where they become one.

I come out of my trance like I've been yanked out of the Tank, coughing and choking on the air that feels liquid in my throat. Serena bangs me on the back until my airway clears, and I lean forward, breathing frantically.

"What the nuke, Toby?" Serena asks, her hand gentle on my sore back where she smacked me to remind me to breathe.

After I get my breath back, I explain, and Serena thuds her head back onto the bottom bunk, swearing. "And without Johan we don't have any Psi-scientists," she groans. "But hey, at least you didn't yell all that stuff out. And I can't hear you right now."

"There were holes in my shell, again," I tell her, propping myself against the bunk next to her. "I think that was why I was loud again."

"Here's hoping," she responds wryly. "Meditation, every day, morning, noon and night; in fact, every time you have a spare ten minutes. I could do without knowing what you feel like when you're having an orgasm."

I blush instantly, top to toe, and Serena eyes me with a grin. "You're worst at shielding when you're embarrassed, and I didn't even get a peep from you. Good job."

"I...hate you," I grumble, trying to rub the heat out of my cheeks; from miles away I feel what seems suspiciously close to a slight giggle from my twin.

"Have you meditated with staves?" Serena yawns widely after she finishes speaking, doesn't bother covering her mouth, the slob.

"Johan used to hit me with sticks all the time," I complain. "Said it made me split my attention."

"Yeah, it's good for you, and the movement will help you with your skinny-ass self." Serena pokes me in the ribs. "That way, you can meditate and exercise at the same time."

"With you?"

"Nah, I'm shit with staves; not much good with weapons in general. My body's my weapon of choice." Serena snickers, and I smile at her brag.

"What, you learned the Serena Slam 'cause you couldn't keep up with weapons?" I tease, and she pinkens, wrinkling her nose at me.

"Well I was eleven, and I was always getting nasty bruises from my *shield* whacking me. I figured if I could wrap my bones it would be easier, and I was right. And now the whole damn army uses my technique, so mind your manners." She finishes with her nose in the air.

"Yeah, yeah, I know. You're a big shot."

"And don't you forget it." She smirks. "Anyway, Darcy's waiting up, so I'll see you later now you're not screaming about dragons in your sleep." She gets to her feet.

I snag her sleeve between my thumb and forefinger. "Thanks," I tell her, and she grins.

"You won't say that when you see what you're gonna wear at my wedding." She flicks my ear and grabs the door handle, firing me a mental image of a suit with so many frills and ruffles on it I'd look like a meringue.

You're kidding, I tell her flatly, but she just laughs and lets herself out.

When I wake up again, morning this time, there's a message on my datapad for me to report to the gym, and when I get there I'm—surprised is too small a word—shocked to see Kion waiting on the mats, twirling a stave in his hand in complicated patterns. He waves me over without turning, clearly picking up my presence without any need for an announcement.

I go to pick up the second stick from where it lies on the floor next to him and freeze when he shakes his head. I wonder why he's taking an interest in my training, and he cocks his head at me. "I need the exercise," he replies to my unspoken question. "Take your ready stance."

I know he's trained Thea extensively, but I was trained by Serena, and she never really showed me a ready stance so much as a guard? I turn sideways, raising my hands like a boxer, and he sighs, shakes his head. "The open hand," he instructs, and sends me a blazing image of himself, standing face-on, arms and legs slightly bent, palms hovering over his thighs. His projection burns like the sun in my mind, and I do my best to mimic the pose. He nods, then rearranges my limbs with gentle hands that could tighten until my bones snap.

He flicks me in the ear. "Serena said you were easily distracted," he grunts.

Did she tell you to flick my ear, or did you teach that to her? I keep my thought as locked down as possible, but from the slight twitch in the corner of his mouth, I'm not overly successful.

Moving back in front of me, he takes my wrist and tugs my arm gently until I lift it, following his guidance and turning my arm so it's at a right angle, with my palm facing inward. My body is slightly turned to support the block. He nods and gestures for me to return to the "ready" stance.

"The breaking waves," he says, and I assume that's the name of the block, but he's already showing me the same slow, even turn of my left arm. "Now you. Practice," he tells me, stepping back.

While I slide through the easy, repetitive motions, he shows me myself, corrects my stance and weight and the twist of my elbow. I think I've done more than a few hundred repetitions before he holds his hand out over his staff, which rises hard and smacks into his broad palm. Then he hits me in the shoulder with it.

It's not hard enough to hurt, but as he easily spins the stave and thwaps me in the other shoulder, I realize, after a few hours of this, I'll be lucky if I can lift my arms. He smirks at me. "Close your eyes, count the sevens." He hums a rhythm softly and steps back, holding his stick in both hands, pointed out at me.

He hits me on the even numbers with a break in the pace when it turns from seven to one. It takes me a few rounds to get used to the movement, to do only that, not to try to predict the blow, but to anticipate it with the rhythm he's handing me and the sureness of his teaching style. There's no aggression in the taps, and when I catch them on my forearms, the blow is soft enough I barely feel it. As I find the pace, the speed to move and keep moving and breathe and keep breathing, I feel the same meditative calm settle over me as I sit cross-legged on the floor with my palms open and up.

"Let it become your skin," Kion instructs in a voice so low and slow it curves through my even inhale-exhale without disturbing me.

I feel the shape of my power move within me, twist and coil in my body. It's usually a ball of power, but suddenly I wonder if it's a ball only because Serena told me it should be. I keep moving, and urge it into the shape that is *me,* my meat-shape, like I do when I am urging a hard shield between myself and danger. But there is no danger here, no need for hardness. My power tingles into my skin. I feel every grain of the wooden staff as it softly presses against my skin.

Kion speeds up. I move faster.

He turns around me. I feel the whisper of movement in the power that hums through everything, and I turn to follow him.

He sweeps low. I lift my foot over the stave, without losing the rhythm, the pace, the peace.

Then he hits me in the head hard enough I flinch back, open my eyes, and lose the control over my power. It roars out of me, and Kion throbs golden in my Talent-sparkled vision as he sheds my inadvertent wave of energy like water.

He nods, the corners of his mouth turning down in a thoughtful expression. "You Read now. That's good."

"It's not mine," I point out, rubbing the throbbing welt behind my ear. It's smaller than I expected.

"It is what it is." He shrugs. "Once you were Blank." His thoughts say *to live is to change.* He's the calmest person I've ever fought with. Serena is all sparking movement and quick, jagged reactions. The other soldiers don't have the...depth of those two. "We are warriors," he tells me, reading the thoughts I'm not trying to hide. "We feel it differently. Thea too."

"But not me," I finish for him. I don't need to be a Reader to know that the level of concert Kion and Serena have with their bodies is not something I can aspire to.

He grins, and it's like seeing the moon jump out from behind a cloud. "No." *You're not bad,* he tells me. There's a lot more in his words, there's a thickness of will to conquer your own body, your own weaknesses. There's years...decades of work to one end. Thea hasn't had the time to become what Kion is, what Serena is, but she has the drive for it. The desire.

I nod, and he lifts his staff again.

He teaches me two more types of block—one to shield my head and one to protect the thick muscles of my legs. When Serena teaches me to fight, she focuses on aggression, on attack. Kion tells me with his heart that the stillness of the warrior-who-waits is what I need to learn, what will help me rein my power. Once I've learned the new blocks, he picks up his second stave and uses both to tap at me.

He works with me until I'm sweating and wrung out and then lightly thumps his fist against mine. "You'll do," he tells me, and it's like being praised by a mountain. A force of nature. The swollen feeling of pride and excitement lasts until he jerks his head at the shower. "Ria will hit you at eighth hour tonight, Sanay eighth morning hour, Delia eighth evening."

Fried, I nod and head for the showers. After I've scraped myself clean, I stumble back to my bunk and pass out, remembering to set an alarm for lunch since missing a meal right now isn't a good idea. I can still see the sinews holding my bones together; it's disconcerting, and I want to bulk back up.

Chapter Nine

E17

My sleeping area is close to the pavilion we ate in, and I think they kept me on the outskirts until I woke in case I turned out to be...me. I wonder a little why they haven't subjected me to deep psychological analysis, and Cassandra laughs in my head as we settle down into our blankets. *You think I would let them. That they would dare to risk dipping into* me?

That her hold over them could be so strong, and that my act could be so convincing, seems unlikely. But the alternative is that they know or suspect I am me and they're stringing me along, waiting for me to give myself away. There are guards around my bedding.

The desert night is cold, and I am grateful for the thick blankets. They aren't soft, more a carpet than a sheet, all things considered, but they keep me off the increasingly icy sands. Beetles the size of the palm of my hand scuttle across all surfaces, me included. They seem to be avoiding the fire, but they don't bother me that much. I hope they don't run over my face while I sleep, but only because I need the rest.

There's a tingling feeling in my veins, adrenaline, maybe. I'm both hyperawake and exhausted simultaneously, as though I've run for miles and drunk gallons of the strong black coffee ARC brews in the mess.

Sleep doesn't come easy, but I appreciate being out under the stars. If I keep my eyes straight up, see only the sky above me, I can pretend I'm in the gardens of the City Hall.

When I close my eyes, the whispers of thoughts around me assail my senses, and they're all stained and dark and grubby, grabbing kinds of thoughts. I close my mind as fully as I can and hunt for soft blackness to take me away from here. Maybe I'll dream of Toby's life, again.

Something grabs my shoulder; it has sharp teeth and thinks only of its hunger. I thrust it away, yelling, and a wash of power sweeps out of me, blasts the aggressor away from my pile of bedding. For a moment, I am Toby, thick with power, rushed with it.

The Eater I threw through the air slams onto the ground eight feet from me, air squeezing out from broken ribs with an awful hissing sound.

Another leans over him; there's a flash of light, and I know a Zap knife has sunk into his heart. My throat tightens. I shoved him away telekinetically; how can that be? Am I stealing my brother's power, still? At the end of our connection, distant and dazed, Toby sits up in his bed and smiles; next to him, Aly mumbles something and rolls over. *It's okay. Me, too,* he tells me, and I shiver as he shows me what happened to him in the gym today. A rush of jealousy swamps me at the normalcy of his day. It makes me sit up and look around for anything to distract me and hide the feeling from my brother. It's too late, and I feel his apology and sorrow sparking down the wire that strings us together across the desert.

Mind-to-mind communication is so fast that the second Eater is just standing away from the body and flicking the blood off the laser blade of her knife before dragging it back into its own hilt, a turtle pulling into its shell but lethal and fast.

The standing Eater bows to me. "My sorrow. I was away for a moment. Your power is strong; it calls to them." Her hair is cropped short on the side, a fat braid holds the rest, pulled back from her forehead. Her skin looks dark, darker in spots, which it takes me a moment to see as tattoos.

I swallow, clearing my throat, and swipe my hands over my head, the soothing scratch of my short hair grounding me. She doesn't mention my flare of telekinesis. Perhaps no one told her I shouldn't have it.

Breakfast is a porridge-type dish with some sort of flatbread tasting of fire, and I scoff it down as fast as I can. I'm so *hungry* since I woke up.

The Eater who appears to be my guard clicks her fingers while I am licking mine clean, and I'm presented with a new plate, heaped with a rice-like substance that I shovel into my mouth, sighing in contentment when I finish.

"There are more." My carer cocks her head, squints for a moment, and then nods like she's remembered. "Maggots, if you are still hungry."

I carefully swipe my finger around the edge of the dish for the last of the meal. It tasted good, whatever it was, and I won't let them see me weak even if my stomach did squirm momentarily. "This was enough, thank you." I look up at her, and she squats down, splays her hands to me. She has thick scars crossing each pink palm in a raised X.

"I am Hepeh-Ganuh," she tells me, "and I am bound in your service."

I try to forget that if she speaks my language it means she ate one of the people who learned it themselves. "Cassandra," I tell her. It's the first time I've used the name and it sits in a cold lump in my stomach, threads razor wire through my rib cage.

"The fights begin in an hour." It's dawn, pink fingers spreading through the skies behind the mountains.

There's the germ...the seed of an idea in the back of my mind, but I can't lay fingers on it. "How many fights?"

She shrugs, baring fangs and throwing a hand around. "The leaders of each nation will send a champion to see who will lead the armies."

"And Pollux."

"The lizard whose head is open to the skies." She nods staidly. "He will fight last, the champion only. It will take many days."

And so, the City will be safe a while longer.

The hour before the fights goes fast, enough time to wash and to drink more of the sweet, milky liquid I was given the night before, and then Hepeh-Ganuh takes me through the emptying camp.

They've left their belongings, scrappy tents and bedrolls, pans and pots, and odd things I don't recognize. Bones carved into shapes. The Eaters are also going to watch the fights. We join a trickle of bodies, heading toward an escarpment of stones reaching to the skies like the spine of a giant, dead thing.

I feel the drums before we're close enough to hear them. The camp is huge, and we cross most of it before the dull *thump-thump* I can feel in my chest coalesces into a drumbeat instead of my heart.

The ground rises under our feet; my breath comes in shorter pants. I'm in good shape, but the going is rough and treacherous, and then we're at the top of the spine and looking down on a semicircle of rocky, sandy dirt that's been painstakingly carved into stairs that curl all the way around inside the curved ridge.

"The unders have been working for weeks." Hepeh-Ganuh tells me, and I catch the floating thought she shows me of skinny, sweaty Eaters digging with sharpened rocks to make the flat levels that are now filling with Eaters. We are at the center of a line, unmarked, but no one sits here, a staircase slicing down the slope, and Hepeh-Ganuh leads the way through the packs of leather-clad wolf-people.

Apparently, as a guest of honor, I get a nicer viewing spot than most. We join Pollux, Icarus, Up-Shup Benay, and Karan-Bethad in a rock-bordered square a few rows up, giving us a nice view of the valley floor. It's an amphitheater of sorts, and presumably why they camped here instead of further north or south.

I nod at my companions, as regally as I can manage, and lock my thoughts down as hard as I can. Sitting next to Pollux and Icarus, sensitive Readers who know Cassandra so well, I'm suddenly hit with the fear that the telekinesis leaking from my brother will let them read me. The fear stills me for a moment. I'm frozen as I sit on the rubbed-smooth ledge, wondering if my charade might be over.

But no one grabs me, no hands or ropes of telekinesis fasten around my shoulders. I gradually relax, remembering how I read from Toby that open kind of telekinetic power is an invitation for someone stronger to hijack your power. Their fear of each other's theft protects me. For now.

Pollux grins with all his freshly sharpened teeth, the metal stubs of his old phenolum headgear silhouetted against the sun. "What a lovely day for a picnic."

The heat is, of course, oppressive, but I don't notice it too awfully; the gear they dressed me in when they snatched me was the same as most ARC soldiers wear, my usual clothes. They're UV proof and have cooling wires that are powered by my own movement, so they won't run out. I'm covered from toe to nape, leaving only my head feeling the true heat of the sun.

"Perhaps I could trouble you for a hat," I inquire of my keeper, and Hepeh-Ganuh bows before walking two rows forward, snatching a hat off the head of a settled woman, cuffing her sharply around the ear when she protests, and then presenting it to me with a flourish.

My skin crawls when I put it on, not just because it was taken from someone right in front of me. It's leather, smooth against my fingers, stretched over a frame of worked bones. The sense that it is human skin hits me strongly, and I have to work incredibly hard not to throw the garment far, far away from me.

My hands are shaking only a little as I settle it on my head, and I curl my fingers around one another lest anyone see. My heart is thumping, but the general excitement pervading the arena is excuse enough for that.

"There are eleven fights today," Up-Shup Benay tells me. "The first fighter is my...offspring?"

The words are accompanied by a sense of kinship, of familial ties. I don't look too deeply to how a family is made when people can jump between bodies and take the flesh of whoever they choose once their body is worn out. It's against the natural order of things, but worse, it reminds me of the dislocation of Cassandra inside me. She seems content enough that I am in this place, not pushing me for control, but it's only a matter of time. They welcome her, in my body, in a way that makes me feel sick and dizzy, like the world could fall out from under my feet at any moment.

I try to smile as I nod, and Icarus lolls in his chair and grins at me. "Maybe I should fight Pollux for the right to lead."

Pollux narrows his eyes and sends a band of telekinesis to squeeze at Icarus's throat; Andrea's face darkening until Icarus slashes the tie with a surge of his own power. They both use open lines, and I wonder if they've learned the skill these Eaters have but don't use it. When Pollux fights, it should be clear.

I roll my eyes at Up-Shup, and they smirk in response. "I'll be rooting for your kin, then."

"This time," they reply with a wry smile. These Eaters treat death as almost nothing, even after grabbing on to every method they can to survive. It's a strange dichotomy. It must float out of me enough, or show on my face, because they shrug in response. "The weak are always eaten. It is the way. No feeble will ever lead me or my people, so if he dies, it is right."

"Why don't you fight?" I ask, curious.

They lick the point of their canine until their tongue produces a welling drop of blood before replying, "I would not win, but I hold the heart of my clan. Maybe Renu-Dasat will try to take it from me when this is over, if we both survive. And I can beat him, because I kept a few tricks back when I taught him."

I'm not sure if the laugh that comes out is mine or Cassandra's; we're both kind of amused by the idea of deliberately holding back your best secrets in order to ensure your continued survival.

"I like this meat, though." Up-Shup slaps their thigh heartily. "It is strong and whole."

I want to ask how long they've had this body, if they enjoy the androgyny of it or if their pleasure is mostly in the lack of tumors. Cassandra snickers in the back of my skull. *Would you take another body if it suited you better, felt less* female? *You're not so different from me.*

Ignoring her, I wave a hand at the still empty arena. "What are your rules?"

Up-Shup shows me all their teeth. "If you stand, you fight again."

"Isn't that a bit...stacked against the fighters who start at the beginning?"

"They take strength from the fallen. The stronger their opponent, the stronger they rise." Up-Shup shrugs. "It is the way of things."

"And I fight last, because I am the Starman, Eater of Worlds." Pollux intones with a serious air, ruined by the ridiculous gestures he makes, dragging his fingers through the air as if he's molding something.

Eater of brothers, Cassandra points out dryly.

Up-Shup and Karan-Bethad laugh quietly, a hissing kind of sound through their sharpened incisors, but my bodyguard, Hepeh-Ganuh does nothing. With the hat on my head, the heat is more manageable, but I still drink gratefully when a server comes around with more milky liquid.

Before I've drained my cup, a roar rumbles through the crowd, and two figures emerge from the masses of standing Eaters who didn't merit seating on the sloping end of the arena floor.

Up-Shup points to the man on the left, a large, hulking brute who's naked except for his loincloth. His skin is stained dark from sun exposure, a carved teak statue.

His opponent is whip thin and twitchy, jerking their head from side to side. When they turn, I see breasts swinging behind a manky leather jerkin. A woman then, most likely. They're both weaponless.

"From the Aru-Gal-Uh in the North. She'll wither in the heat," Hepeh-Ganuh says decisively, and I wonder if she is a great fighter, if she'd be down there with the champions if she weren't bound to me. I wonder, also, what that binding means. If she would be mine still even if she knew my secrets.

But for now, I have only to watch the fight.

A drum peal sounds, and the crowd falls silent, the thick absence of sound settling over everything like a heavy feather blanket. The smell of them is raw in my throat, but if I close my eyes, it's as though I'm alone apart from that. Even their thoughts are quiet for one, beautiful second of peace.

And then it shatters. Renu-Dasat blasts a swirling ring of power out of himself. I see it with my mind, lights sparkling in the air as the molecules change form for a moment, becoming something new. Something hard enough to dash the Northerner to the ground.

She doesn't flinch, though, crosses her arms like the woman from the comics in Toby's room and crouches, breaks the wave of energy and slides forward in its wake like a knife. The fight is swift and bloody, telekinesis and blows traded indiscriminately. It seems impossible for a woman so small to beat this man-mountain, but she worries at him, a wolf around a moose, nipping and prodding until finally she swings herself in the air and comes down double fisted on the side of his neck, and he topples like a tree. To his knees, and to the ground.

The woman bites out his throat while he gasps for air, his hands working uselessly.

I try to imagine it's a television show, that none of this is real. The blood stings the air though, sweet sticky in my nostrils. "Why doesn't she take his body?" I judge Cassandra would have no sympathy for a woman who watched her kin be half eaten in a dust bowl in front of thousands.

"It takes time to get the...motor control," Up-Shup does the pause I have noticed the Eaters do when searching for the right words in Common. "Her reactions would be slowed. She knows this meat."

"She fights well," Hepeh-Ganuh observes. "But she will tire in the sun."

"She'll have his strength, now, his sun-born skills." Karan-Bethad disagrees it seems. "She's a contender."

She is, but she only makes it through four more fights, each bloody and exhausting just to watch, before a slightly built male Eater with dark skin covered in raised pink welts destroys her. He pulls her heart out with his fist, and the crowd roars, bloody and violent.

"Still confident of your chances, old man?" Icarus ribs Pollux.

"I will crush them like the sea rolls over the pebbles of a beach," he replies haughtily, but I see shadows in his eyes, feel greasy spots in his projection of confidence. He's afraid.

The Eaters are skilled fighters—the ones who get in the ring anyway. The man who beat the Northern woman stays alive for two more battles, each more vicious and efficient than the last, before he's cut down by a blonde female giant. She's the largest woman I've ever seen; her hands could crush my skull with ease. Bizarrely, I'm reminded of Kion, although he's short and stocky, brown-skinned and long-haired. In appearance you couldn't ask for two more disparate athletes. It's the feel of her that's like him. The calm in her heart when she fights.

Chapter Ten

TOBY

I sleep the day away except for eating, and my dinner is followed by enough bruises that I wish I'd waited to eat. After my second bout of training—Ria is a *lot* more violent than Kion—I'm wired enough that I drag myself down to one of the small lounge areas to see who's around. I want to message Aly, but I don't know if texting her so late would look like I'm trying to booty call her.

When I get down to the lounges, though, I'm happy to see her curled up on a couch next to Jake, showing him something on her tablet. On the chair opposite, Darcy is frowning at her own datapad which is balanced on her knee. When I get closer, I see she's trying to sketch with her unbroken and nondominant left hand.

My face creases in sympathy, just in time for her to look up and catch my wince, and she gives me a tired grin. "One day at a time."

I nod, flopping down by her feet and stretching aching muscles. "My days now consist of getting beaten with sticks."

"Serena told me." Darcy smiles affectionately, knocks her knee into my thigh. "It's good for you."

"Why is everything good for you *terrible*?" I joke, belatedly noticing that Serena is sitting on the floor under the window, with her arm around Demi. They're obviously talking mind to mind. Demi is wearing a red skirt, the first time I've seen her in "girl's" clothes, and I make a mental note to tell her she looks pretty when she's done with whatever emotional sharing is going on.

"Because how would you know it improves you if it wasn't?" Darcy leans her head on my shoulder, setting her datapad aside. "We should do something horribly not good for us."

"Like what?" I shift to make a more comfortable spot for her head, and she gives me a Darcy grin that says: "I see you do a nice thing." I poke my tongue out at her.

She raises an eyebrow slowly, and I grimace. "Gross, Darcy." I complain.

"What's gross?" Serena inquires. She's holding hands with Demi as they walk back to the group, and Aly shifts to make room on the couch for Demi to sit next to Jake.

"Your girlfriend hitting on me." I jokingly shove Darcy off me, making space for Serena to sit down. "She doesn't realize you'd snap me in half."

"Damn straight...not straight." Serena snickers, wedging herself between us and using me as a back rest while throwing her legs over Darcy, careful of her hand. "I thought we agreed that men are disgusting?"

"Mmm," Darcy agrees in a way that means "No, we definitely did not," and Serena flashes me a bright grin.

"Loser."

"Hey," I protest, before trying to change the subject. "What bad for us thing were you thinking, Darcy?"

"I don't know. Everything's been so serious. We should...steal some ice cream and make sundaes and stay up all night watching terrible movies."

"And getting drunk," Serena adds and then waves a hand at Jake and Demi. "Not you, obviously. You're much too small."

"When I was four, you were thirteen, and you threw up on my bed and made me tell Dad it was me..." Demi pipes up, and I laugh so hard Serena moves her head off my shoulder.

"You're a terrible influence," Darcy teases her.

"Well...you're only almost twelve, so no booze for you." Serena recovers gracefully. "Now to figure out how to steal some supplies."

"We should ask Leaf," I chime in. "Because, well, he came here with Thea, and now he's sort of on his own, and he's an amazing thief."

"Somehow, that was both moral *and* immoral." Aly laughs. "I like this plan. I'll find Leaf and steal some booze with him. I'm much sneakier than any of you." This is true, especially me.

"Darcy and Demi and I will get ice cream and sundae stuff." Serena decides.

"What about me and Toby?" Jake asks.

"You boys go and procure blankets and pillows and a projector, and you—" She points at Jake. "—stop him from picking any awful action movies, where no women exist, let alone speak."

"Okay." Jake grins brightly. "You can carry stuff, Toby."

"Brilliant, thanks," I grumble with a grin, wriggling off the sofa. "ETA?"

"Back here in forty minutes." Serena checks her datapad. "And *break!*"

Jake and I definitely have the least exciting job, but my body's exhausted, and I don't mind the fact that we're curled up on the sofa playing Tetris before anyone else makes it back. We have five movies for everyone to vote on, all of which are suitable for a wide age range, and have lots of female characters, which is a requirement for this crowd.

Darcy, Serena and Demi return first, carrying boxes and giggling. Demi shuts the door behind her, and then they reveal their spoils.

I am midway on making an ice cream sundae as big as my head—yes, I know it's wartime; yes, supplies are in high demand, but I've missed ice cream with a fiery passion, and it's not a dietary requirement for injured soldiers—when the door opens again.

We all freeze with various expressions of *uh-oh*, but it's just Leaf and Aly. Leaf has his ever-present flatpack with him, but right now it's bulging. "Wotcher, gang." He gives us all a once-over. "Cute skirt, little 'un."

Demi wriggles like a puppy that's been petted and gives him a blinding grin. I should have said something before, but I'm glad someone did.

Leaf opens his bag, after shutting the door, and holds up two transal bottles, one filled with dark brown liquid, one clear. "Aly's a natural con, if y'all don't need 'er after this'z done, I'm takin' 'er back ta Secon' City." He grins at me, nudging her with his elbow.

Aly looks pleased and dims the light switch before plopping next to me on the floor and grabbing a spoon. "Chuck us the rum, Leaf." She gets a bit more of an accent when Leaf's around, and it's really cute. I watch, fascinated, as she makes some sort of rum-soda-ice cream concoction.

She proffers me the bottle, and I douse my chocolate-vanilla-strawberry sundae with rum, and then Aly passes me a can of cream soda and I finish it off, laughing as the cascading bubble-explosion tries to make a break for it over the side of my dish, and I have to frantically slurp at it.

When we're all set up with alcoholic or nonalcoholic ice cream disasters, we clamber up onto one of the two couches—that Jake and I arranged to be end to end in a triangle shape—and get the movie rolling.

It's a good one, full of silly jokes and very lighthearted, a sci-fi space comedy about a team of misfits thrown together, and I laugh so hard my stomach hurts. Or that could be the ice cream extravaganza. I'm buzzed by the time the credits roll, and Jake and Demi have fallen asleep in a pile at my side.

"We should put them to bed," I stage-whisper at Serena, who is listening to Darcy and looking a bit too interested in her mouth. Aly's tucked in against my left side, under my arm, and she grins up at me, a smear of chocolate ice cream on her cheek.

"Yeah, you do that," Serena instructs me, without looking over. "We're gonna go to bed as well."

"I'll give ya a hand." Leaf slides off the couch next to Serena, where he's been sitting just a bit apart from her and not under the blanket at all.

I haul Jake up gently and prop him over my shoulder while Leaf grabs Demi and we pad down the corridor as quietly as we can. It's late, now, the lights all switched to "night" and the hallways mostly empty. I have to fight off a fit of the giggles when I realize neither of us know Demi's room code, and she won't wake up enough to tell us. In the end, we throw Demi in my bunk, with Jake in his own top bunk, and then head back to where we left Aly.

She's sipping a mixed drink, sprawled out on the couch, with a pillow wedging her shoulders, watching a cartoon and giggling.

Leaf stops in the doorway and gives me a look, and I realize I must be making oh-no-it's-cute face when he claps me gently on the shoulder and rolls his eyes. "I'll see ya." He's off before I can reply, leaving me to head back into the cozy lounge, which suddenly feels a lot smaller than it did before.

Aly grins widely at me before I'm through the door. "C'mere, you big lummox." She holds her hand out, and I gratefully head over. She tugs me down into the couch with her and wriggles her head onto my thigh. "Hi."

"Hi, yourself," I say wittily, with great amounts of coolness. "You have ice cream on your cheek."

"I know. I put it there so you could get it off." She smirks up at me, and I feel my face go soft as my stomach flips over.

"Oh."

Nobody messages me to tell me my shields are down and that I need to stop what I'm doing immediately and meditate, and even though we fall asleep partially clothed on the couch, with alcohol bottles and ice cream debris strewn about, it's Darcy who wakes us, so we don't get in trouble.

"Wakey wakey." Darcy's annoyingly cheerful, and I bat weakly at the direction her voice is coming from. "Toby, you have meditation in forty minutes, and judging by the amount of rum you drank, you're gonna need at least a shower, and possibly some carbohydrates before you go," Darcy continues, unimpressed.

"Nrghle," Aly complains from where she's tucked into my chest. "Go 'way."

"You can go back to sleep in your actual room," Darcy cajoles, and I peel my eyes open, immediately regretting it because the world is very bright.

"Tell them I'm sick," I moan, hiding my face in Aly's morning-messy hair.

"If I tell them you're sick, you'll have to go to sick bay, where they will take a *single* sniff of you and know exactly why you're sick, and then Kion will hit you with sticks." Serena's voice comes from somewhere near the doorway. "And believe me, he has very little sympathy for hangovers."

"I think he's immune." Leaf pops his head around the door, looking none the worse for wear "Ain't never seen the big man miss a beat, day after a boozin'."

"Up you get, Tobes." Serena tugs my ear gently. "You smell like a dive bar."

Attacked on all sides, I scrape myself off the couch and abruptly remember I am only in my boxers. Aly, however, is wearing even less, so I can't pull the blanket off her over me. I panic and end up grabbing a half-empty bottle of rum to hold over my lap. Serena laughs like a hyena and chucks me my pants.

"Smooth."

Embarrassed and hungover, I yank them on, followed by a shirt stained with all kinds of ice cream smears, and shove my feet into my shoes. The good-natured sound of cleaning follows me out the door as I stumble down the corridor to the showers. I don't have time to eat, because I throw up instead of going to breakfast, but when I emerge into the gym, Sanay—I only vaguely recognize him, but he's holding the staffs of doom—thrusts a greasy sandwich at me before turning his back on me and starting some warm-ups. Thank you, whichever of my lovely friends made sure I had food. It was almost certainly Darcy, thinking about it.

I'm worse this morning, or at least, it takes me longer to get into it, but once I do, the feeling of sinking into my power is refreshing, and by the time we're done, I feel better, as if I've been in the cold pool. Which actually sounds like an amazing idea.

I text the gang "Going swimming," with a selfie of me by the rock pools that feed into the back of the Hall and then pile my kit up on a convenient rock and slide into the coldest water.

The pools are natural ones that've been reinforced with concrete in places. There's a transal ceiling above, letting muted sun in, and the area is surrounded by luscious plants. It was clearly a place for showing off wealth and prestige before ARC took over, and now it's more like a spa, military and civilian. There are two cold pools, a medium temp one, where you can often find people having swimming lessons, and a hot one for sitting in. They're all sort of interlaced with one another so you can socialize across temperatures.

I've yet to go in the medium pool. I put my toes in just once and had a panic attack that left me flopping on the slippery rocks next to it with my hands clutching my head. I think I'll always be scared of drowning. But this cold pool, the one I prefer, isn't deep. I can stand up in it easily at the deepest part. I think it's probably a kid's pool, really, but I don't care. The medium temp pool feels like blood, feels like nothing, the temperature so close to my own it's like touching the gel that bound me, the gel they drowned my twin in. I'd prefer the goose bumps of the cold and the scalding of the hot pool over that, thank you very much.

Leaf joins me first; he pads around the edge of the pool, squats down, and puts his hand in, and pulls a face. "Didn't know yeh folks even 'ad a swimmy place. This one's real cold."

"They're all different." I lean back on the framing rocks, letting my feet float so I'm scooched down on my bum with my shoulders just under the surface.

"Huh." Leaf leans over fluidly and dips his fingers into the closer midtemp pool. "This un's better." He peers at me through the water. "Where d'ya get your swimmies?"

"The chute in the change room." I point in the general direction of the men's, and he grins at me.

"See ya in a mo, captain." He unfolds and heads for the changing rooms, his already bare feet carrying him over the rough rocks with confidence. While he's changing, I wonder if he's bored hanging around here. I know he goes out into the desert a lot, trying to gather intel, but I don't know if he's doing that formally, for ARC, or just for himself. Kion knows him. I know that, though, so I guess probably he's at least being listened to. Not that I could do much if he wasn't.

Aly, Darcy and Serena turn up in a little herd, already changed, and they chose to get in the warmer pool, so I slide around the side of the cool one until we're kind of in the same place, a convenient feature of the interlocking structure of the pool designs.

Leaf plops into the water next to Serena, splashing her, and then she splashes him back, which devolves into a small fight that Darcy and Aly swim out of the way of. Watching with amusement, I realize Leaf isn't wearing a brightly colored short-sleeved tank top, as I'd initially assumed, but that his upper body is largely covered with tattoos. I can make out red roses in full bloom curling across just under his collar bones, with thorny stems behind them, and other flowers I can't identify wrapping around his shoulders and arms. When he turns, I see the tattoo doesn't continue far down his slender back. I wonder if it hurt.

Serena gets a face full of water and sits back, gasping, and Leaf catches me looking. "Yeah," he says.

"What?" I'm confused, and he grins at me.

"Yeah, it bloody hurt. This's seventeen hours of work, 'ere." He flexes, making the stems of the roses twist and shift. I can see the faint lines of scarring where he had chest surgery, but they're worked into the flower image so naturally they're almost invisible.

"It's really awesome," I tell him, honestly, considering getting a tattoo all of a sudden.

Darcy props her elbow on the side. "Can I see?" she asks quietly, and Leaf slops through the water and sits next to her, letting her get a close up, and me too a bit. The detail is really impressive.

"Mah brother did it," Leaf informs us. "'S a bit awkward sometimes fer being sneaky, like, but I don' en' oop naked very often. I'm more of a short game guy."

"Didn't you infiltrate the Watch once?" Serena asks, also checking out the ink for a moment and then getting bored and sitting back.

"Yeah, bu' tha' recruit died in a tragic acciden', and fortunately, the tattoos 'e 'ad made it very easy ta identify the body bits tha' were left after the whole station mysteriously besploded."

"You've been around, eh?" Aly snickers, her wet arm brushing mine on the rock.

"Yeah, some," Leaf agrees, somehow not sounding at all arrogant answering the question.

"But you grew up in the desert, like Kion?" Serena hauls her wet hair out of her face, looking interested.

I carefully swap pools, gasping as I get into the hot one and work my way around the side, so I can hear the conversation.

"Yeah, he's laike mah cousin's cousin, yanno?" Leaf drags his fingers idly through the water, making abstract patterns. Darcy has her casted arm propped on the ridge between the hot pool and the medium pool, so I stop just short of the space she needs to be comfortable.

"Our clans go' wiped abou' the same time," he states, as if he's not talking about his entire family being murdered, and the water ripples around me for a moment until Serena half climbs out of her pool and pinches my ear hard between two fingers. "Ah'm touched," Leaf drawls at me as I concentrate on breathing until I'm calm again. "Anyway, I ended up in Second wi' me new da'; him's in charge o' the slums so 's a pretty good life. He liked the way I coul' do impressions. 'Dopted me later."

"Oooh, do an impression of Toby," Serena demands, and I pull a face, but sit forward anyway, interested.

Leaf looks at me for a second, then does a sort of sitting wriggle and suddenly changes everything about the way he's holding his body. Somehow, he looks larger where before he wasn't taking up much space, his shoulders look broader, and his face takes on a slightly dopey expression, which I immediately try to make sure I'm not making. Leaf copies my half smile, which embarrasses me into ducking my chin and looking away, and he does that too. It's surreal, looking in a mirror that resembles me only on the inside. We look like...family, at least.

"Wild," Serena sighs. "Do me, do me!"

Leaf snickers, runs his hands over his face as if he's rubbing the skin back into his normal, slightly sharp-edged, quick-witted looks, and then does the wriggle again.

Now he's feminine but strong, sitting with his legs tucked in and his shoulders at an angle that somehow says "come at me," capturing Serena's constant aura of challenging everything that clings to her, regardless of what she's doing, unless she's looking at Darcy. He smirks, flicks an eyebrow, and it's Serena's expression under his now-hooded eyes, "I can punch through walls, and practically fly. You wanna go, shorty?" he drawls in a perfect impression of her speech patterns but pitched lower instead of putting on a fake-high voice. It's *very* convincing.

"Shit, I thought *I* had superpowers." Serena grins.

"How about me?" Aly curls her little finger over the back of my wrist, and I feel it all the way down to my toes.

Leaf snickers, ducks under the water for a second, and slicks his face when he emerges, again like he's washing his old impression off. He shifts until he's sitting with more easy grace. Aly moves like a dancer, her limbs are more flexible than most people's, and somehow Leaf manages to embody that. His face looks more delicate, but he's still settling into the impression when Aly splashes him with a face full of water and he splutters.

"Sorry, too weird!" she exclaims, giving an exaggerated shudder. "I didn't like it."

"Neh worries," Leaf smirks at her. "Am ah off the hook, or yeh go' more people yeh wanna see?"

"Kion," Serena whispers, looking absolutely thrilled.

I lean forward, excited. "Yeah!"

Leaf wrinkles his nose and casts about the room, like he's checking Kion didn't magically appear in the open space, and then he runs his hands over his face, does the little wriggle I now associate with him changing character, and suddenly he's Kion.

It's *creepy*. Leaf got the look so quickly—brows lowered, shoulders up, keen intelligence with an air of "I know exactly what you did, and you're in so much trouble" in his eyes. I reckon he must have done Kion before, he steps into it so naturally, and then he speaks, and I physically jump.

"What are you *doing?*" If he'd thrown his voice, I'd have looked around for Kion immediately—it's so spot-on, deep and raspy with a hint of a growl under the mild accent Kion still carries when he's speaking Common.

"Yikes," Serena says exactly what I'm thinking. "That is...truly horrifying."

"I used ta leave mah bros voice messages all the taime pretendin' tah be our da'," Leaf is back in his own voice, sounds smug with it. "Took 'em ages ta figure it out. I can still ge' the little ones sometimes." He looks a little sad for a second and then shakes it off, and I realize that he left his whole family behind to help Kion and Thea, and that he has no idea when he'll be able to go back. The overland journey is treacherous at the best of times, let alone when the sands are crawling with Eaters. I wonder what they'd do with Leaf—if they'd eat him or take his body.

Serena hits me. "Gross, dude." She frowns. "Don't be such a mess."

Darcy gives me a sympathetic look, which means she caught my thought as well, knows that I'm worrying about Thea again, and I force a half smile.

"Sorry!"

"Sorry!" Leaf mimics back, even though he can't possibly know what we were talking about, cause he's Blank and can't get my thoughts, and the tension breaks when Aly laughs.

We laze around in the pools for a while longer, until we're wrinkly and pruned with the water exposure. This stuff's no good for drinking, full of minerals, but it feels good, and my skin is all soft and glowy when I'm done drying off.

We find Demi and Jake already at one of the long tables in the canteen, sitting with Ana, the shy girl who was with them the night of the Eater attack, and another kid, Geronimo, who's a redheaded, freckled little guy with a big scar down his neck that looks fresh enough it has to be from the recent attack.

Leaf excuses himself, after grabbing a sandwich from the cooks, saying he has to check in with Kion before heading into the desert again, and we all say goodbye. I snag his sleeve when the others are chatting at the table. "Hey...if you see her..." I don't know how to finish my sentence.

"I'll letcha know, man." He gives me a half grin and claps me on the shoulder. I let go of his sleeve and raise an eyebrow. "F'reals, I'll tell ya."

He still could be lying. I'd have no way of knowing, but I decide to believe him. "Thanks."

Chapter Eleven

E17

The next fight doesn't start for a while; there's a delay while torches are lit around the arena, casting coronas of violent light over the jagged earth.

Hepeh-Ganuh walks four steps behind me when I excuse myself from the viewing benches to find some peace. There are booths around the arena, selling various meats and foods, and I see a stall hawking slabs of meat from rat-like creatures as big as my torso that squeak as they're hauled from the crate next to the stand. I belatedly realize I have no idea what they use for currency. "How can I pay?" I inquire quietly, while a silent argument between a seller and a customer rages telepathically in front of me. I don't listen. I've had enough of the swarming thoughts of the Eaters. Out here is the loudest place I've ever been, a cacophony of telepaths screaming about various unpleasantness.

"With power," she replies, as though I am an idiot child, and I suppose in many ways I am in this world. "As a Reader, you don't have much to contribute, but if you can siphon a little from the boy, you can use that. Or, if you cannot, I can pay. I will be reimbursed."

A world where people pass power between them like a tool they can gift, so different from both the world I was raised in *and* the world I discovered outside the Institute's walls. "I can bring some power here." I breathe in, tug at the string between Toby and I, take a second to relive the memories of him training with Serena, and then shiver as a little power fills me from toes to scalp. My hair stands on end, and around my feet, dust puffs into the air slightly.

Around us, silence falls, and everyone turns to look at me. I ignore them, with my best haughty Cassandra face, and Hepeh-Ganuh smirks at the crowd. "Anyone who didn't know you before will do so by the end of the night," she predicts. "I don't know if you should work on your control or if the raw power is impressive enough that the advantages outweigh the costs."

"Hopefully the latter, as I feel it will be some time before I have an opportunity to practice at my leisure." I pay more attention to the currency exchange ahead of me and watch as the customer passes a puff of tethered power to the stall owner, who squirms as though feeling great pleasure and then cuts the power thread with a knife of his own telekinesis. I grit my teeth, unwilling to open a link to a stranger—what if he sucks the strength out of me, out of Toby, and we are both compromised? What if this is all an elaborate trap?

But the bustle of the war-party-gathering-cum-festival around me is more convincing than any charade could possibly be. I would have read a trap on this thousands-strong band by now, surely.

I shuffle forward and offer my hand to the greasy man behind the improvised table, the metal drum holding coals smoking next to the hung sheet of canvas, covered in dripping meat on sticks. He flares his nostrils at me, sniffing the air. I don't know what he could possibly smell past the charring fat and general, animal aroma permeating the air.

He grins, showing the classic sharpened teeth I've come to expect from the Eaters, but with added decoration scratched into the surfaces with red ink staining them in cross-hatched lines. Or blood, I belatedly realize, if he's just eaten. He says something in a hissing, sibilant language I have no comprehension of, but his thoughts say, "How many?" and I hold up two fingers, assuming that's universal and hoping that it isn't some sort of rude gesture.

Behind me, Hepeh-Ganuh shifts in a way that sends a wave of aggression through the air; I get an impression of her hand on the hilt of her blade and an expression that tells the stallholder to serve me without comment.

He deftly picks up two sticks of dripping meat chunks, twirls them over the fire to reheat them and sear the fat just a little more, and then holds his hand open palmed toward my chest. Understanding from the gesture that it's time to pay up, I twang the power I siphoned from Toby and thread it toward him. He yanks on it immediately. It *hurts,* having something torn out of my chest. I'm not prepared for the way it will feel and stagger slightly, but Hepeh-Ganuh has her arm on my elbow immediately, steadying me. The Eater slices the link between us just before I find out what happens if I drag on the other end of the connection, and Hepeh-Ganuh releases me as soon as I'm balanced, holding her hands up as if she expects some sort of punishment for her actions.

The skin on my elbow tingles, reminding me that the bare contact between us could have given her any sort of glimpse into me, but she doesn't sound an alarm or look at me differently. Her eyes are still flat and hard, and her primary attention is still on the world around us, ready to protect me from any threat she perceives. And I didn't see anything of her past, which I'm thankful for.

When I don't move, shaken, she steps forward and takes the proffered meat from the stallholder and gestures for me to move out of the way from the front of the queue. "You adjust to it," she tells me quietly.

"It gets better?" I ask, feeling slightly out of breath. The smell of meat, which made my mouth water before, is now turning my stomach, but Hepeh-Ganuh is offering the spears to me expectantly. I take one and gesture for her to eat the other. Originally, they were both for me, but I don't think I could manage them now, and she's probably hungry. If she eats this rat beast maybe she won't eat a person later. It's hard to reconcile someone I feel connected to, like she's actually trustworthy and more on my side than the rest of this mess, with the fact that she eats people.

"You adjust to it," she repeats, glazing the words with the knowledge that no, it doesn't get better, it just becomes part of life. I shiver. It's a violation to allow someone to pull your power through you like that, I don't want to adjust.

Hepeh-Ganuh is smirking at me, and I roll my eyes, tearing off a mouthful of meat. It's tangy and potent, thick with an herb I don't recognize, and the grease makes my insides roil in protest as I force the flavorful mouthful down.

We eat as we push through the crowds, eventually finding a space to sit near a low burning fire. We sit in silence for a while, but I have so many questions, and Hepeh-Ganuh is my best chance at answering them. "What do the X marks on your hands mean?" Maybe not the most tactically useful piece of information, but the way of life out here is so different, sometimes it seems like if I understood them a little better I'd be able to figure out some way out of this.

"My power is bound in your service." She basically repeats what she told me when we first met, and I shake my head, exasperated.

"And what does that mean?" I finish the last scraps of meat on my stick, place it down on the floor and jump when an urchin skitters out from behind a rock to grab it.

Hepeh-Ganuh sighs. "If you would agree to let me share with you, it would be easier."

I snort. "I know we have lived different lives, but I can do without seeing you eat children, if it's all the same to you." It's so surreal, to sit here and float on the surface of this violent cesspool and pretend to not be disgusted by it. Like all choices, even these, are valid. They are not, but I can't openly disapprove in case that results in exposing my secret. I am not who they think I am, and I must play this part to the hilt. I'm sure Pollux would love to take my powers if he knew the truth.

"I bled on the great rock and promised myself in service to you," Hepeh-Ganuh intones in a way that sounds like she's repeating scripture. "My highest loyalty is no longer to my kin, or my clan, but to you. As such, I am exempt from certain rules. Until you die, my only service is to you. And if you die, if I survive it, I can have your power and be bound only to myself." She bares her teeth at me in the smile-that-is-not-a-smile of her people making jokes that are not jokes.

"And that's why you pledged yourself to me? In the hopes you can take my power when I die?" I ask, genuinely interested.

Her pale eyes spark in amusement. "No, I was bound in service to Sanep-Bolin, who still fights today." An image of the dominant, huge blonde warrior who won the last fight floats to me. "She was...unkind. I was glad when she chose another to take her service. I was a gift to her, but not to her tastes. It was better to be released, but this is not a good world for one who's marked—" She holds up her X-scarred palm. "—and untethered to a strong owner. I chose you when Pollux told me of your coming, for I knew you wouldn't have a marked one of your own." She spits like that's something dirty. "He spoke well of you."

"Why not him?" I inquire, beginning to see the shape of things.

She gives me a lopsided grin. "He said he would refuse my service, and one twice unbound is as good as dead. But he placed his seal on my scars to protect me while you adjusted. As soon as you're ready to take my service fully, he will remove them."

"His seal?" I ask, and she holds out her hands, palm up.

"Look," she says, and she doesn't mean with my eyes. I soften my vision to Reader sight, and see, finally, what she's talking about. Her power is opened, the marks on her palms were made...somehow...with telekinesis as a cutting blade, and the line to her strength is still shimmering like it could drift out of her into the air, as if it doesn't belong to her body and skin anymore. Over the open wound in her power, a thick slab of telekinesis rests, forcing her Talent to stay where it belongs, inside. If Pollux removes the seals he's placed on her, her Talent will burst out and out and never be available to her again. She'll be powerless, in a world that eats the weak.

"To take your seal, officially, would be a great honor. When I bled on the great rock for the second time"—a black monolith, a night so dark it's impossible to see the true shape of it, the glassy edges shining like knives, the power being dragged from her skin and sealed by a swatch of Pollux's telekinesis that he must always, always hold there or let her power all be drawn out immediately—"I knew that it was the right choice." She sounds more fanatical than anyone I've ever heard. "I knew that you would be a worthy leader." She pauses, trying to find the right words, I think, and then looks right in my eyes. The firelight turns her skin gold and orange, her eyes to purple moons. "He's the strongest I have ever felt, and he quakes with fear of you. You locked him in a box."

Inside me, Cassandra howls with laughter. *Is that what he remembers?*

Chapter Twelve

TOBY

After lunch, Serena and I volunteer for inventory, since it's one of the few tasks we're cleared to do. Serena seems mostly back to normal, but she winces when she turns sometimes, and her shoulder is much weaker than it used to be. She uses telekinesis instead of her physical strength to haul the boxes onto the floor to be sorted.

"Darcy's cast comes off tomorrow," she tells me while somehow not losing count of the Zap packs she's riffing through. I painstakingly write down sixteen on my tablet before responding.

"That's good." I try to be enthusiastic, but I can see how worried Serena is, and she rolls her eyes at me.

"Yeah, unless it turns out her hand was too mangled to fix."

"They'll fix her." In this, I do feel confident. "I knew a kid who got hit by the monorail when he was thirteen, broke like forty bones, and he was on our Rizkball team the year after." Serena raises an eyebrow at me, and I shrug. "It's true! I saw his scars; they were super nasty."

She relaxes a little, packs the batteries back in the padded case, slams the lid on, and starts to stand up, but I beat her to it, hauling the sealed case back onto its shelf with a grunt.

"What?" I say to her unimpressed look. "I'm not being a gentleman; you're injured, and you're supposed to be taking it easy."

"So are you," she grumbles at me.

I grab the next crate and carefully ease it off the shelf, grunting as I take the weight and lower it to the ground. "Nah, I'm supposed to be doing exercise and eating a lot. This is like going to the gym; it's probably good for me."

She holds her irritation for a second and then sighs. "Ugh, I hate when you're right."

"You hate when anyone is right except you or Darcy, because you think everything she does is amazing, even if it's embarrassing you." I point out.

"True. She is the best." Serena smirks at me. "What about Aly? I haven't had a chance to grill you properly."

"I...don't know." I join her in yanking the crate lid off and removing the top layer of sponge padding, the raspy material scratching at my newly soft skin and making me wrinkle my nose at the sensation. Aly...is confusing; there's so much else going on I hardly have time to think about what this all might mean, or if it has to mean anything other than what it is.

"You're ridiculous." Serena sighs, taking the first tray of magazines out, checking they're full and laying it to one side. I copy with the second, not bothering to argue with her statement.

"Do you like her?" Serena prods, after a minute. "Wait, of course you *like* her—you like everyone—you're basically a nuking cartoon character," she grumbles.

"I don't like everyone," I complain, checking off the magazine trays one by one on my datapad.

"Name one person you don't like." Serena snarks. "You even like *Johan.*"

There's a moment of silence where I can't say anything, and Serena stares at her hands. "Shit."

I don't really have anything to say to that, so we sort in silence for a while.

"I dunno if I *like* her," I break the quiet after I can't stand the weird awkwardness filling the small storage room. "I mean, yeah, I like her as a friend, and I like...you know."

Serena snorts. "Reenacting famous battles with her?"

I scowl.

"Flower arranging?"

I growl.

"Umm, you like carefully handcrafting holiday cards together?"

"You're a dick." I can see that she's willing and able to go on indefinitely. "I like hooking up with her."

"So you're not sure how you feel about her, really? Have you talked to her at all?" Serena inquires, restacking the magazine boxes and dropping them back into their crates. I slide the lid on and get to my feet to return the box and get a new one, marking it with a red sticker that means "Inventoried" according to the harried woman who'd sent us this way.

"Not really, but it's only been a few days, and it's not as though we get a lot of peace and quiet. Also, not to make myself an even easier target, I hadn't actually thought about it at all until she kissed me." Well, until she sat on my lap. Close enough.

"True." Serena allows, scooting out the way of the next, bigger box as I lower it carefully, wincing as my knees creak. "Ask her to the wedding."

"You want me to ask her on a date for some indefinite time in the nebulous future, assuming we all don't die horribly in the next few weeks when an army of cannibals descends on us?" I ask wryly.

She gives me a shit-eating grin. "Yeah, why not? Give you something to look forward to."

"Only if you promise I don't have to wear that...whatever that thing was you were gonna make me wear." If I can get out of the meringue outfit with this, that would be ideal.

"You're not gonna ruin my wedding aesthetic, are you, Toby?" Serena is terrible at puppy-dog eyes; she always looks a bit murderous.

"Uh," I hedge, wriggling backward in case the look is based in reality.

"We've been planning for entire *days*, Toby. I don't expect this kind of attitude from you!" Serena yells and then telekinetically throws a bunch of sponge padding, she's been surreptitiously assembling, at my head.

I manage to shield them all and bounce them back, and soon we're having a full-on foamy pad fight in the tiny storage room, trying desperately not to knock shelves over while we bash one another with foam sheets. It's the most fun I've had in a while, and I'm laughing so hard I can barely stand up when the door opens, startling us both.

"Productive," Kion drawls from the doorway, and we simultaneously drop our foam weaponry and sit back down, sniggering and pretending we never stopped inventory. "You're pushed till nine, Toby," Kion says, and the door shuts behind him, setting us off into proper hysterics.

We roll around on the floor for a bit, until I have a vicious stitch and have to hide my face under a foam sheet while I get myself under control, in case I meet Serena's eyes and lose it again. It's a *good* feeling, for once, like everything is a little bit lighter, brighter than it's been.

Training with Kion goes better than it has before—I settle faster, better with this kind of meditation, I think. There's more for my body to do than ignore the discomfort of sitting still, which I've never been very good at. Serena can calm herself to utter stone in seconds; it's equal parts impressive and impossible-looking, and this new kind of meditation makes me understand that a little more. The power I have sits inside my skin and with Thea's Reader power staining mine, at the right angle, with the right focus, I can see it sparkle on me without having to close my eyes and look *inside*.

I need to train, Reader-wise. There's war on the horizon, and any skills anyone has have to be honed. I've come to realize, though, that Serena isn't actually a very good teacher, so it's Darcy I turn to. I knock on her door after meditation. Serena is still in the gym, squared off against Ria and Domas in a two on one, so I know I have a little time.

She looks up from the bed, spies me through the transal panel on the door, grins, and beeps me in with her wrist pad. "Hey, Toby." She greets me when I'm through the door.

"Heya, Darce, how're you doing?" I pad over to the beanbag chair and flop down, glancing around the room. They've decorated it more since the last time I was here—there's a few hangings on the white walls and an open shelf unit that has some bits and bobs, pretty things like a small whale made of glass that catches my eye.

She sighs, shrugs. "Eh, I've been calmer." She lifts her casted hand, the white-blue material shocking against her brown skin.

I wrinkle my nose in sympathy. "Tomorrow, yeah?"

"Yep." She manages a weak smile. "At least I'll know."

I spread my hand out on the red fabric of the beanbag; the space where my finger used to be is glaring. "You'll figure it out." I try to sound encouraging, because I really think she will. Even if she can't draw the way she used to, she can still make art—she can use a huge touchscreen and her palm, or she can change mediums. She'll figure it out, somehow. I know it.

Evidently some of my thoughts make it across to her, and her face softens. "Thanks."

It's a bit heavy, so I change the subject. "I wanted to ask if you'd do some Reading exercises with me." I make sure to verbally capitalize the *R* so she knows I don't need help with a literature assignment that I don't have to do because I don't actually go to school anymore. Hopefully someone will give me an equivalency certificate when this is over, 'cause I really want to go to university.

She raises her eyebrows, and her eyes do the slightly distant thing I've noticed that people do when they're slipping into Reader vision, looking at energy as though it's something tangible. "Ah. Have you talked to anyone about this?"

"Not really. Serena, a bit. Kion knows, but I guess he's too busy to worry too much."

"Hmmm," Darcy does not sound as if she approves of people being too busy to deal. "I guess I'm the best you have, then." She grins, showing her dimples. "Not that that's saying a lot, but at least I know the theory."

"And, more importantly, you won't flick me in the ears." I point out, and then deflate when she gives me a look that implies she definitely will.

"Do you have time now?" She closes the cover on her ebook and sets it down on the bedcovers.

"Sure."

"Serena will be back in an hour, but that gives us a little time. Do you need to move to meditate, or can you do it the old-fashioned way?"

I take a deep breath, relax into the beanbag chair. It's easier than sitting on the floor. I'm not constantly distracted by shifting uncomfortably against hard tile. I'm still distracted by the tickle of something on the back of my arm, the slight breeze on the back of my neck, the way the beans squeak when I breathe, but I try my best to lock it out and sink into my power. I close my eyes, and let my Talent fill me.

"What's this?" Darcy asks quietly, picking my hand up and setting it on an object. It's large, cylindrical, and I try to move my hand to feel the shape of it, but she stills me. "No, use your power, feel the object, like you're touching it with your Talent, like when you hit something, but instead of pushing or pulling, listen."

I try, but I don't know what it is; it feels almost like plastic against my fingers, sort of oval, smooth and curved, with a notch and a ridge where my thumb rests. "I don't know," I say, trying to move the object in my hand, but Darcy laughs a little laugh and holds my hand still.

"You're not reaching. You're just touching. Don't listen to your fingers, listen to your Talent. Let the power tell you what it is. Tell me what you know."

"It's plastic," I say, and she hums in a way that sounds negative.

I frown, confused, the material is hard, warmed under my skin in a way metal just doesn't; feeling somehow almost soft in its hardness, it reminds me of something. I drape my power around it, trying to imagine a scarf or something, floating over the shape to give me the size and angles of it. It kind of works. I'm suddenly confident that it's longer than I thought it could be, balanced in a way that means it's hard to feel the weight. "Wood?" I guess and feel the truth of it in my bones; it reminds me of the sticks Kion's been hitting me with. Wood is precious and hard to come by, so chances are this is old. A weapon of some kind? I push harder to try to wrap my Talent around the item, and then Darcy grabs it away from me, shaking her hand out. In her lap is a smooth, amber wooden baton, a carved handle for grip.

"You made it hot!" She giggles, rubbing her palm against her pants.

"How?" I ask interestedly.

"Vibrated the molecules." She passes me the baton. "Here, have a look with your eyes, and then try again with your power."

"But now I know what it is," I point out, inspecting the gorgeous weapon. It's art, how it curves and balances when I hold it flat on my palm.

"You know *what* it is, but whose is it, where does it come from, what wood is it, how old is it, where has it been?" Darcy lists questions like they're obvious, and I remember Thea-as-Epsilon 17 going through my possessions to try to find me, back before everything.

"Oh." Feeling a little stupid, I run my fingers over the soft-hard surface, feeling the dents of time, the nicks of use. There's a smudge of darker color round the handle, and I waft my power over it, trying to remember how Thea reads, how she feels her power when she sends it out of her for information.

A spark, a flare—blood—it's blood, Serena's blood, but not from a force injury. Blood from hours, days of working with the baton, trying to use the lead-weighted heavy object to build strength in her back and shoulders, to catch up on weapons' work. Blood where her blisters flowered and popped against the handle.

"It's Serena's." But it wasn't always hers; there's other hands behind the shadow memory of hers on the grip, there's a broad, muscular hand—Kion—this was Kion's baton before he got too big for it, kept it as a memory of his family. This baton has seen the sun, been wrapped in oiled cloth to protect it from rainstorms, has bruised flesh and broken bones for a chain of a hundred years or more. There are so many memories, so many people. I sit back, gasping, overrun with it.

Darcy cocks her head at me, lifts the baton away from my hands. "You went deeper than I expected." She keeps her voice soft. I feel wild-eyed and wild-headed, like my skull's been opened. Information seems to be streaming around me, thoughts and shapes and feelings. I can't breathe. I press my palms to my forehead, trying to push out the noise.

"Listen to me, Toby—one, two, three, four, five, six, seven." She doesn't touch me, and I'm so grateful, I'm drowning in people, I'm choking on air made liquid.

TOBY, Thea screams in my head, rushes across the world to push the voices, the memories, the shapes and history of everything out of my skull. She shores my shield back up for me, the way Serena once did, back when I had nothing of Reading in me. *It's okay, it's okay.* Someone's holding me without touching, and my breath comes back with a rush that might break my sternum open. I'm gasping, and gasping, and there are hands on me but hands that hold no trace of time and memory.

Leaf blurs into my vision; he has his hands on my face. "Come on back, then, luv. You're okay."

Let it go, Toby, Thea tells me and pulls my power back into my skin, cutting me off from the everything.

Leaf grins at me, sitting back a little so he's not quite as in my face. "Boy howdy, yeh don' do thin's bah 'alf, deh yeh?"

Serena, behind Leaf, leans over to flick my ear. "What are you *doing?*" She's still in her gym clothes.

"It's my fault." Darcy looks shocked, but kind of pleased with herself somehow. "We were practicing his Reading."

"Mah cousin duz tha'." Leaf pats me on the cheek affectionately and lets go, plops back on his haunches. "Ge's too deep. Blank 'ands 'elp. Sorreh for the nonconsensual touchin'."

"Uh, thanks. You have my full consent to do whatever you did if I'm falling out of my own head like that again," I croak, struggling into more of a sitting position.

Darcy hands me a water bottle, and I drain it, swallowing gratefully. The sensation of water down my throat pins me back in my skin.

"Noted." Leaf fiddles with his sleeve.

"How did you know?" Darcy asks him.

"Ah wuz jus' back ter repor' teh Kion, so I wuz on mah way ter the gym when this un ran pas' me laike 'er tail were on fire, seh ah though' probly I'd see wha' wuz goin' on. An' then he were all white an' gaspy laike me cousin, with the mad eyes. If yeh pu' Blank hands on the temples, laike, i' 'elps cut the flow sometaimes." He shrugs.

"When I met you, you used to run away from possible danger," Serena finally sits on the end of the bed, looking a little shaken. "I heard Thea, Toby. She yelled at me. How's that possible?"

"We're...sharing." I shrug, dazed and punch-drunk. "I have the Reading now, a little. I guess she's got the Projection too."

Thea? I quest out.

Quiet, she tells me, but she feels safe. Feels okay. I let her go.

"She's okay. She can't talk right now." I hope she can talk later. I'm scared for her, but she's the only one who might be able to make me understand this new type of power. What it means. I can't imagine being able to sort through all that, to *hunt* with the information found. But that's what she does, what she's always done. It's so much. I feel like I've been punched, if I checked my torso there'd be the marks of memories bloody against my skin.

"No wonder Thea likes you," I mumble to Leaf, putting my water bottle aside. "Everyone's so nuking loud I don't know how she could *think.*"

"All that from a stick," Serena says cheerfully; she's holding Darcy's hand, for comfort and to pass the view of whatever I looked like while tripping balls on a piece of sweaty wood. "Just imagine how much fun you'll have when you try to Read a person."

"Let's not, and say we did," I whimper.

Sadly, no one agrees with my plan, and I'm shunted off to a quiet little Reader with a round, smiling face called Miyaki, who does a much better job than Darcy at explaining what I should do. She also doesn't pass me anything that's hundreds of years old with a violent history, and she explains that age and strong emotion make objects hold more afterthought.

We do a similar exercise to the one Darcy had me do, but with a child's plastic block that has only been handled by a couple of kids. The worst they hold is a memory of a wet and uncomfortable diaper, and a general sensation of indignation that I can't quite pin down. I do get the names of the kids who have touched it, though, and a little bit of basic information about their personalities and feelings. Miyaki says I've done well, and to come back tomorrow.

So my days fall into a pattern, waiting to hear from Thea, learning how to control the Reader power I now have access to, meditating with Kion or Ria or Sanay, and spending my free time with my friends, waiting to hear from my twin.

Chapter Thirteen

E17

The wash of Toby touching the baton, the echoes of memories reverberating off the inside of his skull knocked me off my haunches, I leave my body in the dust with Hepeh-Ganuh, hoping she'll guard my meat while I try to drag my brother back into his skin. I hope also that Cassandra doesn't manage to use this moment to lock me out.

He's with friends, and when I know he's safe, I drop back into skin with a shudder of relief. Cassandra recedes, washed away by the burning power I share with my brother. For a moment I think I can scour her out of myself completely, and then I remember I might still need her to fool the Eaters. I shove her violently back into the deep, dead space at the back of my Talent-mind and leave her there, cursing.

When I manage to open my eyes, Hepeh-Ganuh is standing over me, her knife emitting a dull orange glow like banked coals. As soon as she sees me stir, she steps back a little, offering her hand to me to get to my feet. I pull my sleeve over my palm before I take it, and a glint of what might be hurt in her face startles me before she sets her face into stillness.

It doesn't matter if she's hurt; she's a cannibal, part of an army here to destroy a relatively peaceful—child abduction and torture aside—community. She's not my friend. She's a source of information and a tool I can use.

I shiver away from the blankness in her eyes when she said that her previous owner was unkind.

A bell chimes through the air, and I flick an eyebrow in question at my bodyguard.

"The fights will start soon," she tells me. "We should return."

I wonder if she hopes to watch Sanep-Bolin die.

The short walk through the crowds of Eaters pushing their way back to the arena is undertaken in silence. Hepeh-Ganuh leads the way, a steady stream of power pushing those ahead of us aside, some snarl, but quieten when she shows them her palms. There's a lot I still don't...can't understand about what those marks mean, about the people who wear them, but they're obviously respected in some way.

Night is fully drawn in by the time we make it to our seats; the moon is low and fat on the horizon, providing a silvery highlight to shapes lit by fire. The shadows are long and monstrous, more beasts than men, like who the Eaters are is exaggerated by the darkness.

Pollux is lounging on a bench with his head on Up-Shup's thigh, eating what looks like grapes but smells like raw flesh. He grins at my expression. "Meat is life, cousin." The tone is mocking, and I wonder if he plans to kill me...kill Cassandra, even. I wonder what his real game is here. He takes command of the Eater army...and then what? Razes the City to the ground?

"Sometimes you set things on fire just to watch them burn," he tells me, flicking his tongue out to lap at the corner of his mouth. "You taught me that."

The mention of fire makes Icarus tense, and Pollux reaches his pale, spidery hand out to wrap around Icarus's wrist. "Not you, my love, never you. You were the only one who visited."

What would he have had me do? Cassandra would be checking her manicure disinterestedly if she had fingers to look at. *You should put a mad dog down,* I tell her.

Hepeh-Ganuh straightens the pad of leather against the back of the impromptu seating, and I sit down gratefully. I'm still dizzy from Toby's experience. I grab a cup of the white liquid and gulp it down, turning my attention to the flame-lit floor of the arena.

There are still three fights to come, by my count, and while I might wish I was anywhere but here, specifically with my brother and our friends, this is the situation I'm in, and it's not the worst place I've ever lied through my teeth in.

Yes, you're a marvelous liar, Cassandra snarks.

Well, I was trained by the best, I reply internally.

Hepeh-Ganuh glances at me from the corner of her eye, and I firmly quash Cassandra down, momentarily distracted by how used to her living in my thoughts I am. Like I've adjusted to this being how I live now. But no, I'll find a way to get her out of me, and frankly, I doubt there's anyone at ARC who's as much of an expert in body-stealing as the Eaters.

Maybe I can get Hepeh-Ganuh to tell me more about their origins and ways after the fights. Maybe it will help me loosen Cassandra's hold on me. I remember how she dragged Icarus out of Cassius and plopped him into Andrea without missing a beat.

The crowd roars, snapping me out of my thoughts and back into the moment; people are on their feet chanting and whooping. "The next combatant is popular," Up-Shup drawls, as though we couldn't tell from the crowd's response.

Without the sun overhead, the air should be colder, but the close proximity of so many bodies dulls the cool. Still, one of my shoulders is slightly chilled, away from the brazier, and when Hepeh-Ganuh moves closer, to block the breeze with her body, I can't tell if she caught the thought on me or if she saw me shiver.

My Reader power lets me know I'm not drifting thoughts out, even with Toby's Projector strength woven into mine so tightly I can't tell which is which, apart from that the focus is different, passive and aggressive, internal and external. And no one has knocked me down or tied me up, so the chances are I'm still safe.

Or they're toying with you, Cassandra points out unhelpfully. *Waiting for the right time to play their cards.*

I refuse to respond.

The next fight is just as bloody and brutal as the rest of them, and at the end, it's still Hepeh-Ganuh's old master standing, blood on her fists. I think I see anger in the lines around Hepeh's eyes as the arena starts to empty.

"What now?" Pollux asks Up-Shup, stretching his body out and wriggling.

"The first day of the fights is over; there will be a celebration, music, dancing, feasting. You are, of course, welcome to attend," they respond after a moment.

"Sounds like a party," Pollux declares, getting to his feet.

"Yes, a party," they nod.

"Icarus?" Pollux pokes the boy with his foot. "You used to be a good dancer, as I recall."

"I need to work this body more," Icarus yawns, pulling himself upright. "I may not be fighting this week, but when we take the City I will be."

"You'll lead one of my regiments," Pollux agrees.

"You expect the boy to lead us without fighting?" Karan-Bethad interjects, disbelief thick in her voice.

"When I have beaten your champion, surely what I say is law if I lead your armies." Pollux stares her down.

"It is not the way of things. No warrior will follow an unblooded child into war." Karan-Bethad replies haughtily.

"Your people should know that the way someone appears and the way they are is not always one and the same," Pollux replies, an angry note staining his voice. "Icarus and Cassandra are my generals."

"And we are not your foot soldiers to die for your cause at the hands of untested, unproven weaklings," Karan snaps back. "There is a hierarchy, and if your followers wish to replace myself, or Up-Shup Benay, or any of the two hundred below us, they must show they are worthy."

"I'll fight, if I must," Icarus drawls, letting power radiate from him. Karan-Bethad makes a small, almost unnoticeable shift backward, "But surely killing all your great warriors just weakens your armies? On the arena floor today, you have lost ten champions who thought they were good enough to lead you all."

"And they were *wrong*," Up-Shup hisses. "But their knowledge and power was taken by their betters. Nothing was lost. You are ignorant of the truths of our powers, and you are fools if you think that a few weeks or months is enough to learn."

Cassandra would probably try to smooth things over, but I'm too interested in the conversation, and I have no intention of either leading a section of the army or fighting in it at all, so I merely listen in silence, trying not to interrupt.

"The strong lead, and the weak follow. You are strong; we all can feel how strong, but your power and our power are not...cohesive." Up-Shup finishes.

"Am I not your prophesied leader?" Pollux feels spitting mad now, like he'll throw something to the ground and smash it any second. Like it might be a person.

Up-Shup eyes him thoughtfully. "Many say not. We shall see. And if your boy wishes to fight for a lesser position, that will be arranged."

Icarus smirks, the expression strange on Andrea's gentle face, and I'm reminded again that while they may not be identical, the Eaters and the Institute have similar views on what does and doesn't count as violation. "Well, maybe when they've seen me train, they'll submit." He flicks an eyebrow toward me. "Mother will tell you I've been a weapon since long before I was a man." He's not so subtly letting them know that to call him "boy" is not something he will tolerate, and I shift in my seat, reaching for a knife that isn't there.

For a moment, the air hums with violence, tension and power rising off all parties in shimmering, Reader-visible waves. Something I'd noticed, but not registered, hits me with meaning for the first time—where Toby or Serena or myself show only one color of power, the Eaters are a veritable rainbow, and even Icarus has threads of green wrapped through his own bloody red. The power of those whose bodies they've taken, no doubt.

Another thing I had no idea about. But just two years back, telekinesis was a secret to me, I had no brother, no family, and I was alone. The tension hangs for a moment, and then Pollux throws back his head and laughs, breaking it with the true merriment that ripples out of him. "Come, brethren, we must not fight amongst ourselves while just nearby our enemies feast on fresh vegetables and sleep on warm, soft pillows. Tonight's a night of celebration."

Up-Shup relaxes first, and then Karan-Bethad, and finally Hepeh-Ganuh, who's positioned herself in front of me as if I can't protect myself, if necessary. She saw me throw the Eater with telekinesis; she knows I can pull it from Toby, that the muscles in my arms are hard-earned, but still, she tries to defend me. It's harder and harder to remember she's one of them.

We shuffle out into the crowd, which is gathering on the floor of the arena, a makeshift stage being constructed at one end, which fills with drummers before we get off the staggered stairs. I drift away from Pollux, who's being introduced to various Eaters, and Hepeh-Ganuh stays with me.

"How old are you?" I ask her. "How many lives have you had?"

"I'm bound," she tells me, like that means something related, and then sees my confusion. "You can only be bound in your first meat, when your flesh remembers your power. This is who I have always been."

"You've taken no bodies yourself?" I want to check, can't figure out why it's important to me.

"None. I was bound as a child, for a debt my kin incurred. I'll always be a slave, tied to the great rock."

"What if you… left?" I don't look at her, but I don't know how you could stay here with these people.

She laughs—it's hollow—there's no humor in it. "Where would I go?"

Chapter Fourteen

TOBY

"Let's go, Toby! War games," Serena announces, bursting into my room. "We're cleared."

I was actually cleared two days ago, finally to do more than cleaning up or inventory. I've been on a couple of patrols, but without Serena at my side, it never felt right. I never felt ready, even with my new Reader talents streaking glitter across my vision and showing me things I couldn't even comprehend before. It's a whole new sense, and it's taking a lot of work. I miss Serena making it easy.

War games means we're going into the new arena. "Teams?" I inquire, sliding out of bed and pulling a cotton shirt on and then gesturing for Serena to turn around while I change my skivvies. She's fully kitted out, a military belt around her waist and a shoulder pack bulging with weaponry over her arm. There's a handgun at her hip.

"You, me, and Leaf!" Serena emphasizes his name. "Ria, Kion and...Cassius."

"Cassius is cleared?" I'm shocked, vividly remembering the livid red of the fresh scarring holding his insides together.

Serena shrugs. "I guess? He must be, but I didn't hear anything."

I thread my belt through my jeans. "He was a mess."

"Well, Kion wouldn't let him sign up unless he was cleared." Serena states the obvious. "Are you decent?"

"Yeah." I pull socks on, hopping on each leg in turn, and then shove my feet into my boots. "How long do we have?"

Serena looks at her datapad and curses. "They might be in already."

Nuke, if they're already on the Arena floor, they'll be spread around the gate and we'll have trouble even getting in. But the fact I can hide Serena as well as myself pretty well should even things up a bit.

I bounce in my boots, checking I've pulled the Velcro straps tight and fully sealed my feet into the high-tech footwear.

Serena slaps me on the shoulder heartily enough it's probably going to bruise, and I shove her playfully through the door, jostling. "Leaf?"

"Waiting for us at the door." Serena grins. "When I worked with him before, it was wild. If you can't see him, you can't...*see* him, so, like, you just gotta trust he's watching and keeping up. Blanks, man. It's wild."

"I can't cover him," I point out, breaking into a jog to match her speeded up stride.

"Obviously," she snickers. "Don't worry though, I've seen Leaf disappear right in front of me more times than I've seen you do it."

"Or...not seen me," I put on a fake mystical voice and shroud myself in power, knowing I flick out of view in the corridor. Serena promptly kicks me in the back of the knee, because I forgot to also move, and I stumble forward, losing my grip on the invisibility.

"If we survive this nuking nightmare, I'm gonna shoot you with rubber shot until you can hold the invisibility while getting pummeled," she announces cheerfully.

"Sadist," I complain, and Serena snorts a laugh as we head out into the sunlit grounds, across to the sprawling, half-destroyed mess of buildings that were unrecoverable after the Institute attack and have been blocked off to use for training grounds.

It's nothing like the old Arena, which was shut in in the dark and gloom, where you could hide in shadows and trust that your black uniform made you barely noticeable in the visible spectrum. But the war has changed now; we're aboveground and that has to be reflected in the simulated battles we fight.

Serena jostles me, clearly full of energy, delighted to be let back into proper military training, and buzzing with excitement for the chance to pit her skills against some of ARC's finest. And Cassius.

Three on three is much fairer than the qualification run new trainees used to have to do. These days, it's more like anyone who can hold a gun and wants to is expected to train, but when us old hands—I laugh at myself—ran the Arena, we did it against a full squad, by ourselves, alone in the dark.

This should be a lot more fun.

I doubt we'll win—Kion himself is basically a one-man army, Ria the only person who can keep up to him in hand to hand, and Cassius an unknown but trained by the Institute. He must be pretty good if Kion chose him. Or...pretty bad, I guess. Maybe Kion's just being nice.

"Not really his thing," Serena answers my idle, unspoken thoughts that I wasn't trying to shield, "I mean, yeah, he's a good man, but he doesn't do stupid things to be nice. If Cassius is on his squad, he's a threat."

"They're all threats." Leaf appears out of thin air, or more to reality, a narrow path leading between two outbuildings. "Bu' they're also street soljas, and them are usually easy ta fool."

"You got something in mind?" Serena asks him as he falls into step, and we stride into the shadow of the ruins we'll be fighting in. There's a small crowd gathered, watching the projector screens set up outside the buildings, cameras dotted inside that respond to motion will keep the crowd entertained by any ruckus. I watch the screens for a moment, looking for anything that will give us an edge. I can't see any of Kion's team right now, the cameras showing a steady stream of nothing as they cycle through automatically, not drawn by any motion. So they're hiding, then. Right inside the doors is where I would be.

"Well firs' off, yeh shoul' never walk' inter a trap," Leaf cranes his neck, looking up at the side of the building It's pockmarked with remnants of explosions. "'Ow's yer climbin' these days?"

"We have to go through the door." Serena twists her mouth in thought. "Or it won't start the timer."

"Welp, are we doin' this teh be the quickes' or wha'ever, or teh win?" Leaf asks. "Cuz if yeh go through tha' door I'm no' comin' with yah. Neh wish ta be pasted by three folks wi' guns, fer no reason."

"He's right." I lick my lips. "Do we all have to go through? I might have an idea."

"Whatcha go', Tobes?" Leaf inquires, getting some white powder out of one of his numerous pockets and rubbing it into his palms.

"What if you guys head up—you're better climbers than me anyway—set a diversion in one of the early rooms, move on fast, and I'll rush through whoever they leave on the door when they split. Serena can track me, and we can reconvene. I can watch the feeds from out here for a minute and make sure I know where they are. Cloak and run. I can move faster if it's just me, and I can take a couple of rubber pellets."

"They hurt like nukers." Serena sounds like she agrees. "But yeah, sounds like a plan. Luck." She claps me on the shoulder, and I grin at her.

"Same." I nod at Leaf. "Don't fall off."

Leaf snorts. "It's jus' five storiez, mah man; we'll be sound." He spits on the ground and Serena flashes a grin at the crowd before setting her hands into two of the chips in the wall and pulling herself off the ground. She's an excellent climber, spends a lot of time on the gym walls, can do the overhangs I always drop off from. Leaf makes her look like an amateur, though; he spiders up the wall with no more effort than if he was crawling across uneven ground, tiptoes and fingertips taking his weight with no sign of strain.

I watch them head upward, see Leaf helping Serena navigate a few of the trickier areas, but they seem to have it well in hand, so I, instead, close my eyes and use my burgeoning reading skill to see if I can tell what's going on inside the building.

I can't, as it turns out, but that's really not that surprising. I could get Thea to help me if this was for real, but it's just a training exercise. The screens remain unhelpful, and then I see Sanay smirking at me with a controller in his hand. He must have turned off the motion sensors until I'm inside. I roll my eyes at him, draw my power through me and cover myself from head to toe.

A ripple passes through the crowd as I flicker out of view, and I debate whether to go immediately, even though Serena and Leaf aren't at the top and haven't done anything distracting yet—if I were Kion, I'd definitely have placed one of my crew so I could see the outside world—I might be able to take them by surprise anyway.

Serena and Leaf vanish through a black maw of a gaping, transal-less window, and I press myself up against the wall of the building. It's cold through my shirt—I should be wearing armor, but there's no rule on it, and I hate the way it constricts my chest. I edge forward, trying to remember everything Serena ever taught me about stealth. Heel, then toe, breathe through the mouth, slow and even, every movement deliberate, every muscle working, everything in balance, like wading through molasses.

I hear a whisper of sound milliseconds before the crack of a firing weapon, and I throw my power into a shield without dropping my invisibility. The rubber bullets skim the extreme edge of the protection over my cheek, but not enough to disturb my shielding *or* alert whoever fired to the fact that they were extremely close. I assume the next move is going to be to splatter the area in the hopes of pinging me, so I drop, as silently as I can, cushioning my fall with puffs of tightly controlled telekinesis. Thanks to Thea's power, I can see my structures are good, nothing escaping to alert people to my presence.

As predicted, a battery of rubber splits the air over my head, not low enough to impact me, and there's a ridge of broken wall close enough I think I can belly crawl to it.

Far above, an explosion shatters the day, a puff of dust spewing out of a window when I look up. The grenades Serena's carrying will only be concussion, nothing actually explosive allowed into the damaged buildings. They've been inspected, with a few closed off even for the military, but no one wants to deal with an unexpected building collapse. I shudder, remembering being in the barracks that day, crushed under tons of concrete and steel.

But I don't have time to fall into recollections. I have to use the distraction. Hopefully, the combination of obvious incursion up the top and the lack of hits on me down here will draw them off. I tentatively belly crawl toward the protective spine of broken wall. Making it without entering a world of pain gives me courage, and I slowly move to my feet, overly conscious of how clumsy I am, how large. Serena would move like silk over this rough ground, but I have to move slowly, cautious of every tiny rock.

An idea hits me, and I thread my power into the ground, keeping it close and locked, I grip the shards of gravel and even dust under my feet, holding it still as I move across it, making sure it doesn't slip and slide under my weight.

I get through the door; no one shoots me, and I can't tell if there's anyone there, so I just stay invisible and silent, creeping forward like a thief into the dark room.

Chapter Fifteen

E17

The next days pass in a similar fashion: we watch the fights, which get longer and harder every day, and at night we join the shuffling dances and display fights that are the Eater's prime entertainment. I'm reading, reading all the time, and I'm starting to understand how their power differs from ours, how they draw it from others. It's more a learned skill, I believe; their transactions and everyday lives are all based around the sharing, stealing, and exchanging of power. It is natural to them in a way it isn't to ARC or the Institute, and that gives them the insight needed to snatch someone else's power away from them. I think I could do it, if I needed to. I got to practice on Toby, after all.

On day nine of the gathering, the huge blonde who used to own Hepeh-Ganuh, the one called Sanep-Bolin is still standing. Pollux has watched fewer and fewer fights as she mows down opponents, has spent his days training with loaned warriors and studying with Up-Shup's kin.

Pollux has always been wearing Eater style garb—unlike myself who's kept the clothes from ARC, dusty and dirty as they are. Hygiene is not my top priority at the moment, and the familiar, military style outfit makes me feel more like myself—but today he's wearing gear that matches that of the best fighters I've seen. Studded leather, sewn with pieces of the black, glossy rock that Hepeh-Ganuh tells me is numbstone, the same material as the Great Rock which can leech power if one knows how to rouse it. I assume Pollux has learned, rather than it just being for show.

His teeth are stained red, he's wearing a sort of helmet that will protect the stubs of metal emerging still from his skull, and his hollow cheeks have been dusted with sand that sparkles and glows golden in the right light.

Sanep-Bolin has plowed her way through thirty-nine opponents, gathering strength and power from each of them. When I look at her with Reader vision now, she's a rainbow titan, it's impossible to even pick out single colors in her Talent.

Pollux, standing across from her, is a lamb about to be slaughtered. She's a half-head taller than him, and her shoulders make his look brittle and snappable. He's never been a large man, even in Cassandra's memories of him, when he was whole and hale, not eaten away by the loss of his brother, his mind, and his freedom. But the months in the desert have been good for him, darkened his skin to a healthier golden shade instead of the insipid white he was before, and hardened his muscles into ropey lines standing clear on his bare arms. Even from here, maybe two hundred meters away, the definition is clear.

Sanep-Bolin is a tree trunk, her thighs are as thick as my torso, and she's sheer muscle from top to bottom. The slabs of her flesh aren't delineated, but they don't look fat, only strong. And she has the Talent of dozens swirling in her, filling her with prismatic light that hurts my eyes, so I have to tone down my reading.

Pollux throws his head back and howls to the sky, an animal, undulating sound that washes over us, boosted with his Talent to vibrate with power. The crowd roars back in kind. They love him already, I realize. They want him to win, want him to be the one that was spoken of. Maybe they just want to feel like there's hope for something different in their lives.

I still don't know what the best outcome for the City would be, for the friends and family I've been sending scraps of intelligence to when I can. If Pollux wins, he will use this army to raze the City to the ground and rebuild it in his image. I've seen it on him; he cares nothing for the fact that his army, these people, will never be content to take the livelihoods of the city workers on. Who will run the factories and work the desalination lines and tend to the farms when the citizens are all bleeding out on the ground? No one, that's who. Pollux will end the way of life that is—while not ideal and definitely in need of adaptation to provide more equality inside and out—at least self-sufficient and supportable.

I don't even know where the Eaters are getting water or the sweet white liquid from, how they're able to have this gathering. It must be an oasis, but I've yet to see any plants or animals or water that didn't come with the group.

Another ripple travels through the crowd, a drumbeat starts the death count. The sound will continue until one of their hearts is stopped, the longer someone lasts, the more respect and reward their kin will get. The betting is all based on the drumbeat.

I didn't bet, although I was offered the opportunity to do so. I don't want to either donate my own Talent or receive someone else's, it's still a violation to me. I remember Johan's face when he talked me through separating my power from Toby—for all the good that's done us now—how the idea was such a wrongness to him.

And of course, ARC is infallible and knows all, Cassandra announces cheerily, so clear that I start, wondering if anyone else has heard her. Icarus doesn't twitch, though, and I think he'd be the first one who would notice. It's hard to remember who he is, wearing Andrea's face. I'm only glad I didn't know Andrea well enough to falsely remember "friend" when I look at him.

Pollux offers his hands to the sky in some sort of salute, while Sanep-Bolin faces him calmly, no emotion on her pale face. She looks to have been carved from marble, the sun bleaching her white skin even further.

"How doesn't she burn?" I ask Hepeh-Ganuh quietly, and she raises an eyebrow at me.

"We are from the shadow-rocks. Usually she would hold the sand armor on her skin to protect her from the sun, but today she will need all her strength. We have good medicine for the pink skin." She shrugs.

I'm about to answer with another question, maybe where the shadow-rocks are, how far they have traveled to be here, but I'm cut off by sudden movement on the arena floor.

The drums have signaled the start of the death match.

Pollux spins away from an arc of multicolored lightning that leaves spots in my "vision," and I dull my reading even further, trying to find a balance where I can see what they're doing, but don't have dancing afterimages printed on my brain.

The wave of power lashes out, flicks around his ankles; he gracefully sweeps an arm through the bulk of it, and it shimmers to nothing. His gauntlets are embedded with the black rock and I watch as it leaches the energy into itself, rainbows skittering across the surface and flickering out as if they were never there. I suddenly want to get my hands on some numbstone very badly.

Pollux sends a burst of energy soaring out of himself; his power is a sickening, dizzy greenish yellow, and there are stains in it from the others he has taken. Not enough to drown out the putrescent shade of his natural Talent. *It used to be pure,* Cassandra tells me. Again, I wonder why she's helping me, giving me useful information. Is it because I'm so laughable to her she can't see me as a true threat, or for some other, more troubling reason. *I'm bored,* she sighs after a moment. It feels like the truth.

Pollux's Talent strike mows into Sanep-Bolin, Pollux hasn't kept it linked to himself, so she doesn't have to sever it, just withstand the power. He's stronger than I thought, and she rocks back just half an inch, barely enough to see the dust puff up from her heels. And then Pollux is on her.

He's fast, as well, like a striking snake; he has a blade in his hand without me seeing him draw it, slashes it once, twice, thrice, wide, gaping movements that open his guard, but when she tries to repel him he bats her hands and power away with puffs of telekinesis that remind me of Kion, the way he seems to have more hands than he should.

There wasn't a lot for him to do, locked up. We let him train, because if we didn't, he took to battering his way through the shields of anyone nearby and making them smash their heads into the wall. Cassandra sounds eager, aroused by the violence in front of us.

Why didn't you kill him? I've asked her this before but have never been given an answer.

You don't throw a weapon away just because it misfires every few shots, she tells me, superciliously.

It's too stupid a reply for me to deign to answer. If the weapon that misfires explodes in your hand every now and again, you damn well should throw it away.

Sanep-Bolin is fast, too, but not as fast as Pollux. Because of her size, I'd wager. She's much stronger, though. The fight begins to take shape, Pollux attacking and scoring a few, light blows, leaving more red streaking down Sanep-Bolin's arms each time he is thrown back. And I do mean *thrown*. Sanep-Bolin smashes him through the air to the ground, to the back of the wall. If he wasn't shielding well, his ribs would be shattered, but as it is, he still has enough energy to laugh maniacally as he attacks again and again.

He's still light on his feet, but now he's conserving energy, where before he was dramatic and over the top. He's not cut, but he must be bruised, even with reinforcing telekinesis wrapped around himself. Sanep-Bolin takes the small cuts like a machine, not even flinching, but the blood is flecking the ground around her feet and eventually she'll feel the loss of it, especially in this heat. Pollux has chosen a clever method, not even trying for a killing blow which might give her the opportunity to crush his spine—if she gets ahold of him it'll be over in seconds—but choosing to commit to a lengthy fight. It appears he has the stamina for it.

It's almost as if there are more Polluxes than one, the way he throws his power out to shove her in the back, bash her in the head. Those blunt blows—making a blade from telekinesis is almost impossible and involves a level of concentration beyond most people's ability, Serena has told me—aren't especially threatening to her; with the power she has available, she doesn't have to skimp on shielding, but they're distracting enough that he slips past her tree-trunk arms again to leave a red slash on the thick slope of her trapezius.

And it seems she can't shield against his knife. It takes me a while to realize why, and then I register the oily blackness of the blade, the effect it has on Sanep's power. It's made of numbstone, also.

"A clever trick"—Hepeh-Ganuh whispers, sounding shocked—"a blade of the Great Rock. Gauntlets. I've never seen this."

"That's why he'll win," Icarus says smugly. "You people haven't updated your fighting styles since you figured out how to slash one another's power and suck it clear." There is an undertone in his mind that tells us "only animals don't use tools," and Hepeh-Ganuh bares her teeth at him, which doesn't exactly refute his statement.

"It's allowed?" I ask, pulling her attention back to me before Icarus can say anything else.

"You're allowed anything in the arena, but most weapons are useless." She shrugs helplessly. "This will change the face of battles for the rest of time. But it is sacrilege."

Now that they've seen it, will every Eater try to make themselves a weapon of numbstone, or will their reverence of the rock itself mean that most will be too afraid?

"How big is the Great Rock? Are there other sources of numbstone?" Icarus sits forward without removing his eyes from the battle on the arena floor. Sanep's bloodied across her cheekbone, dripping down the side of her face in a red river of tears. Pollux is cradling one wrist close to his body; maybe he's been hurt while I wasn't paying attention.

"I'm not bound to you," Hepeh-Ganuh answers Icarus calmly, and Up-Shup hisses through their teeth as Pollux goes flying again, rolling smoothly over his injured wrist without letting it hit the ground. It costs him his knife, though, and Sanep-Bolin reaches out with telekinesis to grab it, only to have the blade—and handle, it seems—deny her grip. She lumbers forward, trying to place herself between Pollux and the weapon as he struggles to his feet. She doesn't have time to scoop it up with her hand, and they circle each other warily, each with an eye on the knife. Whoever reaches it will almost certainly win the day.

"The Great Rock stretches for many thousands of miles," Up-Shup replies to Icarus's question, ignoring Hepeh-Ganuh. "It marks the world's end."

I saw a map, once, at the Institute, that showed the edges of what is known. The ocean, out to the east, and to the south, land shaded black. The Eaters came from the south. Could the Great Rock be there?

Hepeh-Ganuh growls so quietly I think I'm the only one who hears and then lifts her voice to respond. "The Great Rock will chew you up and spit you out, city-dweller. It wouldn't even notice as it hauled your power from you."

Icarus laughs heartily, throwing his head back. "Maybe one day we'll find out, slave."

Hepeh-Ganuh's jaw muscles bulge, and without thinking about it, I lay my hand on her wrist, trying to prevent her from leaping over the low table and attacking Icarus.

Our bare skin touches, and I'm assailed by images, feelings, in the split second before I can pull my hand clear.

Darkness, fear, so much fear, the sun on my face, the joy of the wind dragging through my hair. The shadow-rocks Hepeh-Ganuh called home are far to the southwest, crevices and valleys dug by long vanished waters. Small farms carved into the sun-facing surfaces, the feeling of earth between my fingers. Strong hand curling into my hair, dragging me back; it hurts, my back scraped and savaged by the violent rocks. It hurts more, later, back in the dark. Sanep-Bolin watches me from across a fire, her eyes flat and hard like the iron she branded me with. I feel the agony of healing skin in a moment, and then I'm back in myself, and Hepeh-Ganuh is on her knees in front of me, prostrate, eyes on the ground.

Up-Shup smirks at me. "Something pretty?"

I'm breathing heavily. I haven't accidentally sucked images from someone without trying since... Well, I don't really remember ever doing it like this. Another side effect of Toby's power spilling into mine? Or something to do with the way the Eaters use their power.

"My apologies." Hepeh-Ganuh sounds stiff, but also, under the formal tone, is fear of a kind I haven't experienced for a while. "I wasn't prepared. I forgot myself."

Instead of answering, I lean down and touch her shoulder with the tip of my finger, sharing a memory of lying in the grass outside ARC headquarters. I'm careful that nothing except the feeling of grass tickling my skin, the sunlight warm and gentle on my face gets shared.

Hepeh-Ganuh inhales and I see the muscles in her back relax. *Thank you.* She sends me, and she looks up. I smile at her and move my hand.

When I look up, Icarus is staring at me with a sneer on his face. "You're going soft, Mother." He mouths, and

I smirk at him, forcing a casualness into my thoughts and face that I don't feel.

"She's mine," I tell him haughtily, allowing the possessiveness Cassandra feels for everything to stain my words. If Pollux dies, his hold on her power will dissipate, and she could die of the leeching. But either way having him have a hold on her is no longer acceptable.

Sit, I tell Hepeh-Ganuh, and she straightens up slowly, sitting next to me again after a moment. *Tonight you can show me how to seal your power.* A feeling of relief so strong it makes the hairs on the back of my neck stand up pulses out of her before she controls it.

If she must be a slave, I suppose it's better to be mine than Pollux's. Especially if he dies in the arena.

Ignoring Icarus's clear disdain, I turn my attention back to the fight. I can't see any new injuries on either of them, but they're both clearly tiring. Sanep's power is flickering unreliably, and Pollux has lost a lot of his too. His bones are still wrapped, but he's given up on his skin, and he's scraped and bruised enough that I can see it from where I'm standing. It's impossible to call who'll win, and I have to take a deep breath as I realize either way, the respite is over. The armies will march, soon.

Suddenly I'm desperate for some genuine, friendly contact. *Toby?* I quest lightly, threading my power down our private line.

Thea! He responds eagerly, immediately, I can feel how delighted he is to hear from me. He's sweaty, hiding, adrenaline up but not afraid. Training of some kind. The Arena, I register, finally.

The fight is almost over. I let him see Pollux, sweat-streaked and cautious as he throws a sloppy punch. The knife is still on the ground, almost as though they've forgotten about it.

Fear pulses down our connection. *And then they'll come.* He says, heavily. I don't have to confirm; he knows that's the case.

Are you ready? I ask, just because I want to keep him on the line. I make sure my eyes stay focused on the fight, that nothing shows on my face.

Of course! He thinks brightly, pulsing "No, how can we be ready, how could anyone be ready?" behind the statement.

How can you gun down an army when it's invisible? How can you hold walls against people you can't see, people who fight just to survive. The City will fall, how can it not? It's just a case of when.

What about evacuation? I know it's a lost cause, I just want to talk some more, just for a moment.

To where? You think Second City is gonna welcome thousands of refugees? You think the citizens are going to happily walk for days over a desert full of people trying to eat them? To arrive to closed doors and nowhere to live? Toby sounds even sadder than I feel.

You could always turn the Wall on. Cassandra sounds highly amused. *If you wanted to stand any kind of chance.*

What?! Toby and I demand at the same time, and Cassandra laughs at both of us.

She won't say anything else, almost like she didn't mean to say that at all, and I wonder for a moment if she's going mad, trapped in my head with nothing to do except try to trick me into relaxing my guard, no power or autonomy. Cassius certainly didn't come out of the same thing hale and hearty. She sneers at me. *He was fourteen when Icarus took him. I've been myself for long enough I'll never lose that.*

How many years do you think you'll manage? Toby yells at her. *Get out of her head!*

She snickers at him, but Hepeh-Ganuh's gasp distracts me, making me look down onto the field. Senep-Bolin has the knife, and Pollux has a huge, gaping wound in his thigh. He's trying to hold the blood in with telekinesis, but he hasn't much left. He's finished, dragging his leg along the ground as he backs away from the huge, bloodied woman.

She lurches after him, injured enough to be graceless, holding the knife in her upraised fist, she's going to smash it down into the top of Pollux's skull.

First rule of winning, Cassandra tells me, Toby fading away as he's snatched back to his own reality by someone flicking him in the ear. *Never let your opponent see all your cards.*

Senep-Bolin has Pollux pinned against the rock wall at the back of the arena, the black knife flashing in the fading light as it descends, falters. She staggers back, gasping. Her power flicker-flicker-fades, and Pollux staggers away from the wall.

Senep falls to her knees, drops backward, and Pollux leans down and pulls something thin out of her neck. Blood roars after it, a dark tide spreading across Senep's chest and the sand around her fallen, massive body. The crowd boils to its feet, screaming in triumph and despair.

Pollux holds his hand up to the skies, the needle-like second blade is so thin it's hard to see. He must have hidden it somewhere, and Cassandra smirks in my head.

He staggers slowly to the edge of the arena, the crowd roaring his name. It hits me inside and out like a drum, and I hazard a last send to Toby. *It's done. Pollux will lead them.*

Chapter Sixteen

TOBY

When Thea's second message comes through, it's not at a good time. Ria drives her fist into my face, through my shield—she's not expecting my loss of concentration, and it's only her quick reflexes that save me from some truly stupendous brain damage as she pulls the punch at the last possible moment.

I'm left gagging on blood with my nose so flattened I can feel it sickly rubbing against my rapidly swelling lip, but I'm not dead, which is a victory in and of itself.

"Shit, Toby!" Ria wriggles off me, where I've been pinned to the floor after messing up a stealthy entrance to one of the last rooms between my team and victory. Serena let go of me as soon as I was shot, and I don't see her or Leaf, so I assume they're still "alive." The young kids train with beanbag guns, which don't hurt that much, but the qualified personnel play by different rules. You're still in the game until you can't continue.

I lie on the floor for a moment, trying to scrape my brains back together, the shock of a blow to the face disorienting me unpleasantly, but, eventually, I manage to sit up, gingerly touching the bridge of my nose. It *hurts*.

Kion, I yell mentally, not bothering with any formalities, *Pollux won.*

Timeline? He asks me, his inner voice calm and not bringing any traces of where he is or what he's doing.

How long? I send out to Thea.

She doesn't reply immediately, in a way that makes me think she's speaking with someone. *Three days until they move. Eight until they are at the Wall.* She tells me, and then our connection withers again as she pulls away from me. I try not to feel hurt. I know she can't be distracted. I know she's in danger all the time. It makes me think of what it was like for her growing up, and I squeeze my eyes shut to feel the pain of my face and drive out the things I don't want to think about.

Eight days. I dutifully let Kion know.

Game's still running, he tells me, and I barely shift out of the way in time as Ria drops her casual resting pose and dives for me, trying to get my wrist so she can twist me into a submission hold.

I roll out of the way, dragging my power over myself again and scuttling clear. I'm making enough noise that she's able to track me, and she grins wolfishly as she hauls her handgun clear of its holster, swinging the nose through the air level with my torso.

"Give it up, Toby, save yourself the bruises," she drawls, but I'm already moving.

Her first shot misses me by a centimeter. I flick a loose piece of stone off the floor with my toes, hurl it at her with telekinesis, smash another puff of energy into her chest while she's distracted by the rock, and then fling myself through the nearest doorway into a roll.

I lose some skin on my knuckles, to the ground, plus poor shielding, and a rubber bullet clips my calf, sending a wave of agony through me that I have to bite my tongue to hold in.

My whole face throbs in time with my heartbeat, my poor nose is aching angrily, and my right eye is swelling shut, but I'm limping away from the immediate danger.

Someone drops off the ceiling behind me, and I whirl with my arms extended, power rushing through me and bursting into Cassius as he raises his own empty hands. Good, I'd rather fight power than bullets.

Our energy meets, smashes into each other, and I have to brace my feet to keep from being forced backward.

He's strong, too strong for me with the pain I'm in, but a ghost whisper *here* lets me know Serena's in the room, and I just have to hold him for a moment. I bare my teeth, push with all I have, and then suddenly the pressure is gone, and I'm falling forward, into another roll, as Serena slams her elbow into Cassius's jaw and drops him.

Ria bolts into the room, and I throw power at her legs before I'm up, dragging them out from under her a bit before she gets a grip on the walls, and then I'm tussling with her hand to hand and power to power while Serena and Icarus face off against each other.

"Now, kids, don't do anything stupid." Kion sounds very, very smug, and I see why as a glow stick hits the floor, illuminating our shadowy forms in violent green light.

Leaf has his hands up, fingers laced behind his head, and Kion's gun is pointed at the back of his neck as the big man moves into the room. We're maybe forty paces from finishing the simulated run, and I'm trembling with the desire to smash my fists back into Ria's torso and finish this. But, if this were real, that would be sacrificing Leaf, and probably Serena and I wouldn't make it out alive anyway.

Leaf's two paces ahead of Kion.

"On your knees," Kion growls, and Leaf obediently drops, but as he does so, instead of hitting his knees in a submissive kneel like Kion clearly intended, so he could gloat for a minute before making us admit his victory, Leaf rolls.

I don't even know how he does it, but he twists himself, avoiding the discharge of Kion's bullets, by the grace of Google, which conveniently slam into Ria's arm, making her drop her gun, and then I'm a bit distracted trying to keep her from caving my skull the rest of the way in.

By the time I've used my superior physical strength—it is definitely that and not the fact she's just been shot three times in the bicep—to get Ria pinned face down against the dirty rock, it's over.

Leaf is whistling quietly, with Kion's gun pressed right between Kion's legs, while Kion has his hands up and a look of extreme confusion mixed with some clear *wow* on his face. I wonder how often he fights Blanks.

Serena, however, has somehow been disarmed by Cassius, who has a gun in each hand, one pointed at me and one pointed at Serena, his attention split between us.

"Yeh think yer faster'n me?" Leaf asks, sounding genuinely interested.

"No, he doesn't," Kion says with an air of finality. Cassius huffs out a breath, spins the guns in his hands and then holsters one, offering his hand to Serena.

"Not fast enough to save his balls, fast enough to take you all out, yeah," he says. "But it's just training."

Serena takes his hand and clambers to her feet. There's an impressive gash forming under her left eye, her earlobe's been ripped enough she's bloody down her whole neck, and she's holding one arm in over her body. I can't believe Cassius took her down. Ria taps the ground, and I clamber off her, letting her uncurl.

Serena growls at me. "I saved your slow ass you stupid loser," she huffs.

"It's true. I was about to shoot you in the back," Cassius agrees, breathing unevenly.

"Bu' I think we cin all agree i' were me tha' save' the day for our team," Leaf declares cheerfully, and I laugh, regret it, and lean over to rest my hands on my knees and get my breath back. Ria got me a couple of good ones in the ribs.

"You got caught!" Serena points out, snagging her gun out of Cassius's unresisting hand and stomping toward the door.

"Part of me master plan!" Leaf lets Kion up and gives me a grin. "'Sides, if it were real, I'd a shot the big man in the nads an' then save' yer skinny butt."

Serena turns to give him a look, and he cracks up laughing. "Alrigh', alrigh', I guess i' were more like a draw all thin's considered. Bu' yeh, and Tobes nee' a trip ter the medicos, and I'm golden, so I'm gonna coun' tha as a victory."

I help Ria up, and she slings her good arm around my shoulders, cradling the other in. "Is it broken?" I ask quietly, very hopeful that it's not. It's hard to remember when your blood's up that every injury you inflict on someone now could cost them their fitness for the war that's coming.

"Just bruised." She flexes it and hisses. "Nothing a few hours under the laser won't fix."

"Good," I say, fervently, and Cassius and Kion fall in behind us, both walking with a heaviness that implies some minor injuries, at least.

Leaf hangs out while Serena, Ria, and I get seen to. We play a couple of video games while the medicos do their work, none of us able to find the mental concentration to meditate.

When Serena suggests we wander into town for dinner, Leaf and I agree immediately, and we buzz Darcy and Aly to join us.

It's a fairly quiet affair; the boisterous, over-confident energy that we've all kind of been floating on for the past few days has disappeared with the announcement that Pollux will have the army to our gates in eight days.

We still have no plan, as far as I'm aware, and no way to organize against enemies who can disappear at will.

Something's nagging at me, like I'm missing something important, and then halfway through a mouthful of pho it hits me, and I snort broth up my injured nose, which still stings even after being unswollen and straightened. The bone knit they can reproduce is fragile, and my head will ache for a day or two before it settles.

Hacking violently, I manage to breathe past the hot liquid and groan as Serena thwaps me on the back enthusiastically.

"Cassandra," I pant, when I can make the word form. "She said something about the Wall. She said we could turn the Wall on."

"What?" Serena's eyebrows draw in. "What did she mean?"

"I don't know! I don't think she meant to say anything." I gulp some water, wincing.

"You ever hear that, babe?" Serena looks at Darcy.

"Nope," Darcy has her datapad out and Aly is only a second behind her, their hands flicking swiftly over the keys.

"Nothing in the Central Library," Aly murmurs, her white teeth caught on her bottom lip. I can't help smiling slightly at the look on her face; the fact she went for the library first; the fact we met there so long ago.

"University archives don't spin up anything obvious," Darcy frowns. "Run it up the flagpole."

Serena drops her utensils enough to hold her arm across her body and type a message on the almost invisible curve of plastic riding her left wrist.

Leaf props his hand on the table, his mouth working for a moment like he's trying to say something.

"You know something?" Aly asks him, looking up when he moves forward.

There's a pause before he answers, and then he exhales. "My cousin used ta tell me stories. I mean, my whole clan use' ta tell storiez, bu' she was our wordkeeper." He looks around the table and rolls his eyes. "Storyteller. Yeh couldn' ge' tha' from contex'?" I wrinkle my nose and then regret it as a wave of pain wriggles through the bones. "Well anyway, there's stories of the Wall bein' black. I dunno how or why, bu' ever since I saw the firs' Wall fer the firs' time, I remember bein' confuse' when i' were all white and shiny." He shrugs. "Might be summa' there."

Chapter Seventeen

E17

The rebonding ceremony is surprisingly straightforward. Pollux, drained and exhausted and manically triumphant, lifts his telekinetic seals with barely any interest, and I slap a bit of Toby's power over the leaking streams of energy, following Up-Shup's hissed instructions as to how I should link the fibers of my power to Hepeh's scar tissue, and how to leave a connection between those seals and my power. A mere seed is enough to support the seals once they're in place; it's not something that even requires conscious thought or attention. Unless I die, the last flicker of my power will keep Hepeh-Ganuh's Talent intact, and she will be forced to obey me, lest I leech her power and use it to punish or kill her.

I keep myself locked down, and so does she. We don't share anything during the ceremony, and for that I'm grateful. I don't want to feel anything for her, wish I didn't already have traces of sympathy and protectiveness stirring in me.

Afraid and angry, I excuse myself from the celebrations and go to bed, hoping no one will really notice I'm gone. A contingent of guards follows me, however, and I deduce that Pollux is displeased with my decision.

I wake up with a hand over my mouth, and Toby's power coiling through me. I recognize Hepeh-Ganuh a millisecond before catapulting her through the air, as she tells me, *Quiet.*

I quiet, feeling in my bones that she's not a threat. She can't be a threat, not to me, not now we're bonded.

We have to go. She slides her hand down, against my neck. I can feel my pulse against her warm skin. The ridges of her scar tissue are swollen and thrum with my power, I feel them buzzing. When I sit up, as quietly as I can, I see my guards all sleeping around the small fire in my area.

It takes me a moment, and the sight of Hepeh-Ganuh's dripping blade to realize they're corpses. *They'll kill you when they find out what you are. And that will kill me. So. We have to go.* She sounds infinitely practical, but I'm disoriented and shocked.

My confusion echoes through our skin-to-skin connection and she snorts almost silently, sitting back on her heels and taking my hand. *Anyone who links to you can tell you are first meat. I killed the shopkeeper you paid already, now it's only me that knows. But I don't know if he told anyone, so we have to go.*

You killed him? And these guards. Well. None of them innocent, all of them an army here for slaughter, but it still makes my skin crawl.

She gives me a lopsided grin, showing off her sharpened teeth. *We will die when they discover you. If your kind knew how meat works, then you wouldn't have fooled the Starman or the Broken Boy for a moment.*

She tugs my hand, using telekinesis to push my furs off me and make a pile. I wriggle clear, get to my feet. I sleep in my clothes and boots these days, so I don't have to get changed. Hepeh-Ganuh passes me a knife, hilt first. I tuck it into the thigh holster I've worn since I arrived at ARC, and the weapon pressed against me makes me whole again.

If we go to your people, you'll protect me. She declares it as fact, and I nod, agreeing. If she can get me out of the army, then she'll have earned forgiveness for whatever crimes ARC would try her of. And they have more to worry about now, anyway. If she fights with us, they'll probably extend as much trust to her as they do to me. Plus, the intelligence she brings could be invaluable. We still have no real idea how to fight these people.

She's killed the entire contingent of guards, silently enough that I didn't even stir, nor did the other Eaters, sprawling out in little piles. They're all resting in the Eater style, having dug holes for their hips and shoulders to rest in. They didn't move when she killed them; the control and silence she must have worked in is undeniably impressive. We slide around the groups, no light, no weapons out; we're heading for the toilet pit, and once we're behind the canvas walls, out of view of the majority of the army, tucked between a stinking pit and a towering rock wall, Hepeh-Ganuh takes my hand again.

I need to show you how to lock yourself, become nothing, or we'll be dead before we're halfway up the cliff.

Oh, Google. *We're climbing the cliff?* It's a stupid question, because she just told me that we were, and since I have no chance of making my way through the ground—packed with Eaters all of whom know I'm not one of them since everything about me from my clothes to my teeth give me away—I have to bow to her expertise.

If I die, she dies, after all. It's in her interests to keep me alive, and she's never seemed overly attached to her people.

They treated me like scum, she tells me. *Why would I be attached? Enough thinking. Now listen.*

I do. I let her thoughts press into mine, let her lay invisible hands on my power, on the thread between Toby and me. It's a kind of trust I never thought I'd be able to give, but the bond between us bolsters me. She yanks on our power hard enough to wake him, tells him to hush when he protests, and ignores his attempts to communicate further, slicing the connection in a way we have never been able to. There's none of the caution of Johan teasing each thread of power out back where it belongs. I'm left with a decent store of power that feels like Toby's, enough telekinesis to make me strong and dangerous.

Hepeh-Ganuh hisses through her teeth at me and makes me concentrate on what she's doing. She drags the power into my skin, handling it with such skill and finesse it makes me feel like an idiot. She shows me how to lay the power into hexagons, strong enough that even if one is shattered the others will survive while I replace it. She treats it like a material that can be anything she wants. She just tells it what to do and it's done.

And then she tells it to hide me. My hand, in hers, shimmers, fades, leaves a ghostly outline in my Reader vision like I'm made of smoke.

Tighter. She tells me, and somehow, I draw the smoke in, until it, too, is under my power shield, and I am gone. Hepeh-Ganuh nods approval and blinks out of view.

Her hand is warm and strong in mine, though, and she doesn't let go. We lace fingers as she leads us, silently, around the base of the cliff.

I marked the best place to climb, Hepeh-Ganuh informs me; it's disconcerting, not being able to see her, but she doesn't let go of my hand, and I'm grateful. *We need to make a thread. Very small. So I can show you the route.*

A tiny, delicate filament, the kind I used to read with when I was locked underground in the Institute, weaves out of the center of where her body mass must be. *You!* She demands, impatient for the first time, nervous maybe, and I send a matching fiber of my own power. She knots them together somehow, lets go of my hand.

Stay close, or they'll see the link, and we'll be killed. She matter-of-factly tells me, and then yanks on me, and I'm watching through her eyes as she places her hands on the cliff face and starts to show me the basic movements that will take me up the cliff.

I'm not a good climber, not good enough for this climb, but my shoulders are strong and she teaches me the holds, the grips, how to make a hook from my power and hide it with my body as I use it to anchor me to the cliff.

How not to die.

We climb. The surface is jagged and rough, cuts my hands until I start shielding them individually, not just from sight but from the sharpness of the rock. Pieces crumble, and I flinch every time a pebble drops down to clatter unbelievably loudly at the base of the cliff.

My fingers are swollen and painful, even with the shields, the wedging into cracks, swinging my body weight off my fist alone as I scramble for a foothold. Hepeh-Ganuh saves my life more times than I can count on the vicious hours we spend crawling upward over the cliff surface. My back is stiff with the expectation of a blast of power from the valley floor.

I've never been in pain like this. Every muscle in my body is trembling, protesting, trying to make me give up. It would be so easy just to let go, I'd die; Hepeh-Ganuh would die; the Eaters will take the City, and everyone will die. But they'll probably die anyway, even if we make it over the never-ending heights and down the other side. *And then the desert,* Hepeh tells me helpfully, sounding stupidly cheerful for someone who could fall to their death at any moment. *I know it hurts, but pain is just a message from your body. You are in charge of your meat.*

I try to be, to follow her instructions, to force my shoulders to lift my arms, to force my legs to move, to force my meat to obey myself, but I'm not strong enough.

A rock shifts under my foot, and my weight shifts. My thigh muscle seizes, refusing to take it, and the world slows down as my bodyweight drifts backward. There's a moment of nothing, a moment of weightlessness, and then my throbbing fingers slide clear of their tentative hold, and I fall.

It's a relief, to be honest. A second where the sky above me is all I can see. The moon is fat and heavy, clouds wisped in front of its face, stars spangling the black velvet of the night. It's beautiful.

Cassandra screams *NO* inside my skull so loudly it shatters the illusion of peace, and it's Cassandra who swings my body back against the cliff face, who drives telekinetic pegs into the soft, crumbling rock, and who holds me there until my muscles are ready to obey me again.

She lets go without a fight, drifting back into the smallest confines of my power. Not prepared to die today, but too weak to fight me for control?

Above me, Hepeh-Ganuh feels concerned. *Come,* she tells me. I inhale until my ribs might pop, and move one hand, then the other, one foot, and then the other.

Dawn is spreading pink fingers over the horizon, smearing black shapes to soft gray as I belly over the lip of the cliff. Tears sting my eyes, breaking the world into sharp prisms of light and shadow, and Hepeh-Ganuh crawls over to me, panting heavily, as exhausted as I feel. *Ten minutes.* She's even gasping internally. *And then we must move.*

The climb took us around four hours, by my internal clock, which makes sense for how late the Eater camp stays bustling, busy. Even with the minimal power we used climbing, we'd still have been spotted at the right angle by a Reader glancing upward, even with invisibility over us, the thread between us would have been visible. You can only tie your power to your meat and things you are touching enough to hide them. I've dropped my invisibility, I realize, probably hours ago, too weak and distracted to hold it.

I'm sorry, I tell Hepeh-Ganuh down our connecting thread.

You did well. She's quite cheerful about it, to be honest. *I thought we'd fall.* Her happiness is glowing, enough to spread to me and lift my spirits.

Then why try?

I wish I hadn't asked as she shows me a ritual fire and the screams of a blood-traitor being burned alive. *It's better this way. And we did it; we climbed the Spine. Not since Reaper has anyone climbed the Spine and lived.*

I'm too tired to ask any more questions, and all too soon we have to stumble to our feet, move away from the cliff edge and down a sliding slope of scree. It's impossible to be quiet on this kind of ground, but Hepeh-Ganuh tells me that the mountains split echoes strangely, and that our noise will be lost in the waking army.

All I can think of is that I'm grateful it's downhill. My arms are leaden twigs that might snap under any pressure. I can't even lift them to wipe sweat out of my eyes.

We stop for water, and Hepeh-Ganuh passes me a dried-up leaf. *Eat this; it will move your feet,* she tells me, and I'm too exhausted to inquire as to what it is, or what it does. I bite the leaf and bitterness bursts on my tongue, Hepeh-Ganuh laughs at my face, and then energy swamps me. My heart rate picks up, and my muscles relax out their state of trembling on the edge of cramping.

We move on. The downhill soon stops being a blessing and starts being a curse—the tension I have to hold in my body, the pull of gravity conspiring to knot my muscles back into vicious messes. I don't know how I'll make it across the desert when we're finally at the base of the mountains.

Another mouthful of the bitter leaf and a few gulps of water, not enough, the heat of the day basting down on us and we have to move. Hepeh-Ganuh brought a piece of material to use as a scarf, but even shielded from the sun, it's so hot my skin is drying out as I walk, like I'll crack and tighten until I crumble into dust.

My head's buzzing with questions, how long must we walk, how far before we can rest? When will we be safe? But I imagine that as soon as Pollux discovers us missing he'll send scouts out, and while climbing the mountain got us on a direct path to the City, it's not as though they don't know where we would likely be headed. They can run in the desert for days, live on almost nothing, and Hepeh-Ganuh is held back by me. Her loping, even stride fills me with jealousy.

She catches the thought on me and turns to grin, stepping smoothly over a broken boulder, "I was a desert runner, when I was too small to fight or fuck."

It's not funny, at all, but her pride in her skills here makes me smile slightly. "You should see what I used to look like." I throw her an image of my old, underground-pale and slave-weak self, and she stiffens, turning back to the main path.

"It's not right." She tells me.

I laugh incredulously. "And what your people did to you is?"

"The strong eat the weak; it has always been so." She sounds tired, resigned.

The land is flattening, we're finally at the base of the mountain and blessed shade swoops over our head as we turn along the base. Somehow, I find the strength for words even though we're still jogging. "But you're not weak. I don't understand that. Your power is strong, and you fight well. You move like a warrior. You killed all those guards."

"I do not belong to myself, so I am weak." She shrugs a shoulder and looks back, sparing me a humorless grin, I barely even notice her teeth anymore. She just looks like herself to me now, not like a monster. I shiver with the realization. She licks her teeth like she caught the thought from me. "I was a child, and all children are weak."

"I was also a child when they took me." I don't know if I'm commiserating, bonding, or trying to explain myself, who I am now.

"They kept you weak; it was their job to make you strong. My master taught me, trained me, until I feared no one but her." She stops suddenly, sniffs the air and holds a hand back to me. I grind to a halt, grateful for the moment of peace before she sniffs again, hawks spittle into her throat, and swallows it.

She starts running again, and I struggle to make my feet move once more. *I made myself strong,* I think inside, without saying it. *You made yourself strong too.*

The day passes in run-run-rest-rest-run-run agony. I am numb, dead, nothing but pain and determination not to stop. Hepeh-Ganuh picks me up when I fall, feeds me snacks of dried meat I don't ask about the origins of, holds the water bottle for me so I can drink, pushes strength into my muscles with her power, and provides a running commentary about anything she can think of to keep my mind distracted from the constant agony of movement.

We don't stop until the sun is well over its zenith, and then Hepeh-Ganuh casts around a small rocky outcropping and flashes me a delighted grin. *We can rest.*

I sit down on the floor midstride, and she laughs at me, the loudest sound I've heard all day. She must feel safe indeed.

Not there, Two-Sides. I don't even have the energy to inquire where my new nickname has come from. *Come.*

She has to half carry me, sling me over her shoulder, still with strength in her legs and back. I am so grateful for her, in that moment, that it washes through me with enough strength to make her miss a stride. When she looks at me, she has a flush high on her bronze cheeks.

Here. She awkwardly eases me through a crevice in the rock that looks like a shallow crack from the outside but opens into a wider space, the black-gray rock running with water down its massive sides. There are pools filling on the uneven floor. I stumble toward one, desperate for the cooling wetness to touch my parched skin and Hepeh grabs me by the collar of my shirt like a child. Her inner voice is thick with amusement. *You should take your clothes off; if they get wet, they will dry stiffly and chafe your skin more. I will be back. The water from the red rock is clear to drink; do not drink from the grays, and I will bring food after I have covered our trail.*

She's going to run back across the path we've taken, brush away the sign my idiot feet left behind us, hunt for us, and then come to rest. I giggle at the very idea of it, lightheaded and silly with relief that we get to stop for a while.

Water, water, blissful water. I'm floating comfortably, naked as the day I was born, scrubbed clean of desert dirt and grit, when Hepeh-Ganuh comes back.

She has a thick, gutted lizard over each shoulder, a bulging pouch at her waist, and a grin on her face. I watch, interested, as she builds a small fire with moss from a dry wall and some small cubes she produces from the pouch. She arranges a rock next to the fire, and a small tin at the base of it, before breaking the lizards open at the rib cage and spread-eagling them on the slanted rock.

I see the fat sizzle and run down into the tin, and the scent makes my mouth water eagerly, my stomach growling for sustenance.

She strips off with quick, deliberate movements, folds her clothes neatly, and brings her knife and still mostly full pouch to the edge of the pool before sliding in. The firelight gilds her golden, and I avert my eyes as she settles in the water, snags her pouch with one hand and brings out a white, round object.

As I watch out of the corner of my eye, she uses her knife to crack a corner of what I suddenly realize is an egg. She grins at me. "Protein." She slurps the egg contents out of the shell with the ease of practice, and then hands me an opened, second egg.

My attempt to eat it results in egg on my face, hands, and a bit in the pool, but I got most of it in my mouth and the tangy, viscous fluid is so delicious I lick the inside of the shell, and then my hands, clean.

Hepeh-Ganuh is studiously watching the water streaming down the wall of the small cavern when I finally discard my eggshell and dip under the water to wash my face.

When the lizard meat starts spitting and hissing, Hepeh climbs out of the pool, her musculature is so pronounced I sigh, wondering what it would take to reach that level of strength, and she smirks at me over her naked shoulder as she crouches to deal with the meat.

"It is time to eat, and then sleep," she tells me, still smirking a little at the corner of her mouth. "Tomorrow will be long."

"How many days until we reach the City?" I ask, suddenly concerned.

She sniffs, peels a piece of lizard meat off the corpse with her bare hands, not seeming to notice the heat— power in her skin again, I note—and eats it with a sound of pleasure before responding.

"We can make it in four more like today. The army moves slowly, but they will send runners after us. They will have to come around the Spine, so we gain two days there. For today, tonight, and two days we are safe. Then they will be on us, and we will fight as we move."

My apprehension must show in my face, because she gives me a big, reassuring smile and pats the rock next to her. "Eat. You will feel better after meat."

I do, a little, but the rock is hard under me, and even the exhaustion written through every cell in my body isn't enough to let me ignore the discomfort of rocks poking and hard ground.

I'm halfway between true sleep and wakefulness, rolling against the rock to try to find some peace for my aching body when Hepeh-Ganuh reaches out, takes my hand and pulls me toward her. I curl up on her chest, grateful for the softness and the smell of her sweat-stained shirt.

We run.

Day two is worse; my muscles stiffened into boards. Hepeh-Ganuh has to pummel my calves and thighs to get them warm enough for me to stand, and it takes three hours of stagger running before they start feeling like legs again.

The second night we sleep curled up in a shallow dent with no fire, no fresh meat, and water only from a sip-well Hepeh-Ganuh digs with unerring accuracy that she doesn't care to explain, and I'm too exhausted to ask about.

Day three is better, my legs stronger, my body adjusting to the constant heat, the demands of the desert.

Night three has soft sand that is like a miracle blessing when I first lie down, and as hard as iron under my aching hips by the morning.

On day four, they come. The first I know about it, having no energy to spare to read the environment around us, is when a spinning blade cuts through the cloth at my shoulder as Hepeh-Ganuh pulls me to one side.

The fight is short, as Hepeh-Ganuh uses power and fists to destroy them in a fight I have never seen the likes of. She spits on the ground next to one of their corpses as she rummages through their pouches and pockets. "I beat Sanep, once. In training. I got fifty lashes for a prize, but it was worth it." She joyfully yanks a canteen clear and throws it to me. I take a mouthful. It's the white liquid they were always drinking at camp. It feels a little fizzy against my tongue.

"Do you think you could beat Pollux?" I ask, the idea that's been on the tip of my mind for days finally coalescing at her announcement—if we could send a champion against Pollux, to fight like an Eater, to beat him and lead their armies—maybe we could send them away from our walls without extensive bloodshed.

"It's possible, but not like that. A slave or an under cannot fight to lead, Two-Sides." That name again.

"Oh," I sigh heavily, letting the idea go.

Hepeh grins at me. "You or your brother could fight. But you'd die. Maybe there will be someone skilled enough who has left their meat, at your camp."

"You said anyone would know it's my first meat, but I'd be allowed to fight?" Maybe I'd die. Maybe not. I trained with Kion for a long time. He was proud of me.

"The Starman is also in his first meat. You only must leave the skin to be considered prime." Oh. I think of the times when I pushed out of my body, down the wire that threaded me to Toby, before I even knew it existed. I think of Toby's glowing form next to mine in the tube tunnel.

"Pollux had a twin, like me," I hook the half-full canteen against my hip, prepare to follow her as she straightens after moving the bodies into a crevice. She doesn't ask me to help, so I wait, conserving my strength until she's clearly ready to move on again.

She breaks into a light jog, feet scuffing small puffs of dust up from the sandy ground. In the distance, I can see a glint on the horizon that I think might be the Wall, and it lights me with hope.

"Kin makes it easier," she agrees.

"Is that why you call me Two-Sides? Because of my brother?" I still have enough breath to speak out loud, and it's somehow more comforting than internal speech.

"That, and the one who hisses in your head. And the two sides of self you hold. You are Epsilon 17 and Thea." She shrugs. "But one does not erase the other. Two-Sides. Slave and free meat." She grins at me. "When you fell, you lost your hold on yourself. I saw your secrets." She spits on the ground. "But I am yours, bound. They are safe with me."

I'm silent for a moment, my feet dragging against the softer ground, trying to find the right words. "I will never use that power against you. If you want to tell my secrets, don't hold them because you're afraid. I..." I don't know how to explain how sick the idea of her being tied to me for fear makes me, so I take two faster steps and offer her my hand, for sharing.

She takes it and I let my barriers down, let her see the insides of me. The marks the Institute left on my heart, the disgust at the idea that the connection between us is only fear. The fact that even if she left me in the desert alone, or left me at the gates of the City, I wouldn't remove the seals holding her power in. That that isn't in me.

She holds my hand for a long time after she retreats from the opening I've given her, and I carefully replace my barriers, bit by bit.

"Friends, then?" She says it like she's never heard the word before, as if it's something she's uncertain she quite understood, and I nod.

"Friends."

The moment is broken by arrows streaking out of the sky, Toby's power swirling out of me to knock them away. We fight nine more Eaters, back-to-back, but we are more than a match for them, and escape unscathed, with our supplies once again replenished. Night falls, cooling the air blessedly.

We run.

"Thea!" The glow of the City is fully in sight when someone hisses my name so suddenly I'd have died if they were trying to kill me, but when I hear them and spin, I'm only just in time to grab Hepeh-Ganuh's knife before she slings it at Leaf, intent on burying it in his heart.

"Alrigh'?" He grins at me so huge and happy, halfway down a sloping dune with his hand up, shielding his eyes, "thought tha' was yeh."

I'm already running toward him, up the hill, the sand weighing my feet down into a brutal slog before I crash into his chest and wrap my arms around him.

He holds me gently while I do some embarrassing crying in his neck, his hand curved around the base of my skull.

Hepeh-Ganuh watches us. I can feel her concern, her urge to move, her unsureness about this change of situation, and manage to pull myself clear, sniffing heavily and wiping my face off with my palms.

Leaf eyes Hepeh-Ganuh curiously but doesn't go for a weapon or anything; maybe the way we were running together, side by side, has shown him that she's an ally.

"Leaf, this is Hepeh-Ganuh. She's saved my life about four hundred times in the last five days. Hepeh, this is Leaf. Leaf has also saved my life a few times."

"Your bro's been losin' 'is shit, Thea. He thought yeh were dead." Leaf tells me, rapidly typing out a message with his free hand strumming the air.

"We had to cut the thread, or they would have known where to hunt," Hepeh says, her voice wary and overly even. She's drawn into herself, her eyes flicking around the desert. She's ready to run. I pull myself clear of Leaf and trudge down the slope to her, brush my finger against her wrist to share reassurance for a second, but she pulls away like I've stung her.

Leaf slip slides down the hill after me. "Any frien' o' Thea's." He gives an elaborate bow, which loosens the tension in the air a little. "I take i' we're in a 'urry."

Hepeh flares her nostrils, casts a web out so quickly I would have missed it entirely if we weren't so close our arm hairs are touching. "Yes. There are forty more coming. They'll catch us before dawn."

Leaf grins at us both, and I want to move closer to him, but I don't want to leave Hepeh, who is bristling and nervous. I can't tell what Leaf's feeling beyond his face, and his face is good at showing only what he wants us to see, but I have to hope he'll trust me. "Welp, I can call fer backup." He waggles his wrist. "Tobes says 'e loves yeh an' 'es gunna kill yeh."

Hepeh growls, steps in front of me, her shoulders up, "No one kills her, Numb-Boy."

"Tobes is Thea's brother. Is a joke. No nee' to call names." He stands, totally relaxed, until Hepeh uncoils slightly, and then he starts moving away, toward the City. "Nice nigh' for a run."

Hepeh looks at me, and I nod, and then we start running after him.

Chapter Eighteen

TOBY

Leaf's message comes through when I'm getting ready for bed, and the stone that's been living in my guts since Thea cut me off and disappeared melts into a sickening mix of fury, relief, and delight.

Serena, I find her with Thea's Reader power that I've been hoarding, dreading the day it's used up completely with no chance to refill it.

Tobes? She's sitting up, in bed. Next to her, Darcy stirs, rolls over, and Serena yanks her shields up before I accidentally get any impressions I shouldn't have.

Leaf found Thea; they're coming in hot. I'm scrambling out of bed, grabbing my tactical gear and yanking it on as I catch her up.

Meet you at the gate in fifteen, she tells me brusquely, and I get a fleeting impression of her tapping a message out to Kion and her dad before I'm full back to my own body. This Reader stuff has a lot of potential for privacy invasion, rules I should have learned as a child that I still don't know.

I'm at the gate in twelve minutes, in full gear, and waiting for Serena to show up. The roar of an engine alerts me, and then a fully equipped desert Land Rover skids to a halt at the doors, and Serena jumps out, her hair wild and pulled back into a pony.

"Papers," she spits out at the guard coming out to see, holding her tablet out for his approval, and he nods.

"Best'f luck."

I hop in the vehicle.

Serena drives like a nuking idiot, but there's no one in the streets of the slums, and we rattle over cracked and broken roads at high speed. I spend the ride holding onto the *oh-shit* handle and with my butt off the seat, because it hurts less to sort of surf than to be thrown up and down the whole time.

Serena cushions herself with her power and cares nothing for driver's ed.

We burst out of the slums into the desert a mere forty minutes after we start driving; what would usually take around two hours. It reminds me of taking ATVs out looking for Thea and Kion. I wonder why we didn't appropriate a Land Rover that time.

"Didn't have it," Serena hollers at my unspoken question. "There's only four, and they were all out."

"Right," I yell back, the wind whipping through the open sides and roof snatching the words out of my mouth.

We have a GPS bead on Leaf, and Serena drives straight for it, slaloming up the slants of dunes when necessary, and literally holding our vehicle upright with telekinesis a few times. I keep my eyes on the screens, looking for anything in our vicinity that could be danger. We have infrared on the vehicle, so I can see clear ground a kilometer in each direction, and when three hot bodies pop onto the screen ahead, I whoop in excitement.

"There!" I thump my hand on the dash, "I see them!"

"Got 'em," Serena declares triumphantly, covering the last few hundred meters as we bear down on the figures of Leaf, easily recognizable by the fact his hotspot is overlapped with his GPS beacon, my twin, and whoever else they've got with them. I hope Andrea. Leaf didn't say in his message.

Just as we skid to a halt, more heat signs pop onto the screen. "Company," I yell, hoisting myself out of the seat and propping my Zap on the front beam over the windshield to cover them. I fire off a few warning shots into the darkness, lighting the night up in streaks of white-blue that leaves afterimages on my eyeballs. It's enough to make them drop back while Leaf, Thea, and their friend cover the last few meters.

They pile into the vehicle through the back door. Serena's leaned over to pop it, and she's revving the engine as the last person climbs in.

I swivel as Serena jerks us forward, spins us around, and backs away from the danger, headlights bobbing madly over the bumpy ground.

"Thea." I climb into the backseat, beaning Serena with my foot. There's not enough room for me to sit, with the three of them squashed onto the bench seat, and Leaf obligingly worms his way around me and hops over the front seat with a lot more grace than I did.

"Toby," she sighs, and then her dirty hand finds mine, and our connection pops back into place, shimmering back into existence. She swamps me, for a moment, like at the Institute, like the first day we met, and our eyes found each other, and we realized we were part of each other.

"Womb mates." The woman next to Thea grunts, sounding half amused, half annoyed and jerks me back from the sharing.

Thea smiles tiredly at me, tugs me onto the bench seat, although I take up a lot more room than Leaf did and end up with my legs kind of jammed in behind the seats. "Hepeh-Ganuh, this is my brother, Toby."

I wedge my arm over back of the bench seat to make room for my shoulders, and Thea takes the opportunity to lean against my side a bit. "Nice to meet you," I tell Hepeh-Ganuh, already perceiving an outline of what she's done for Thea over the past few days, and before that. The "I'd be dead without her" is very, very clear in Thea's speech alone, even without the background information I've just been privy to.

"Why?" she asks. It's not a challenge; it's a genuine question, and Serena snorts a laugh in the front seat, guiding our vehicle diagonally up a dune.

"Uh..." I don't really know what to say, but nobody rescues me from my floundering, so I settle on "'Cause you saved Thea."

"Hm." Hepeh-Ganuh twists her mouth to one side, and then bares her teeth in a grin that makes me want to recoil, even though I've seen her filed shark teeth in Thea's recollections of the past few days; emotions she's sharing while pressed against my side are shadowing, coloring my thoughts, and I have to pull away from our connection a little, although I try to do it kindly.

Thea realizes she's oversharing and helps me separate back a little, giving me an apologetic, lopsided smile.

In the front of the vehicle, Leaf digs up some water, and some trail mix, and hands them back. Hepeh-Ganuh takes them and shares the snacks out so Thea gets more than twice as much as she does, and Thea tries not to choke herself on the speed she eats at.

The journey passes mostly in silence, no one making more than a half-hearted effort to break it, and when

Serena pulls over at the gate to speak to the guards, Hepeh-Ganuh ducks her head, looks around twitchily. It must be terrifying, I realize, coming to the City. I have an impression of her background, her reasons for being here, but it's hard to imagine what it would feel like. Maybe the way it was for Thea, waking up and realizing she was surrounded by Eaters, alone.

But Hepeh-Ganuh isn't alone. While we're pulled in, I wriggle clear of my wedged-in seat, and motion Thea to shift over, next to Hepeh. She might not trust me yet, but she clearly trusts Thea, so maybe that will help her relax and stop digging her nails into her palms so hard her knuckles are white with tension.

Thea scoots across and brushes my hand in thanks, and then takes Hepeh-Ganuh's hand carefully, slowly, waiting for permission before lacing their fingers together in silent support. In the rearview mirror, I catch Leaf watching them, his face unreadable.

We bump through the gate and on toward ARC headquarters. "I guess I have to go straight to report." Thea sounds more exhausted than I've ever heard her, and I scrunch my nose.

"I think I have most of it, if you want me to. I've been updating Kion on everything that you've sent me as it goes. Maybe you can go in the morning."

"Ain't gonna fly, Toby. Sorry." Serena sounds sympathetic, but she also has her soldier voice on—the one that does what she's told to do. Kion wants Thea straight at command to go over everything. We don't have time."

"Urgh," Thea sighs, leaning back and closing her eyes.

When we pull up at the garage and hand the Land Rover off to the soldiers on duty there, Kion and David Jacobs are both waiting.

Thea stumbles out of the back seat, followed so closely by Hepeh-Ganuh it's like she has a shorter, more muscular shadow. Her hair is cut even closer to her head than Thea's, except for the braided section on top, glowing a coppery color in the harsh fluorescents lighting the garage. She keeps her mouth closed, and her head ducked submissively, until Thea links their hands again, and she stands a little straighter. I move closer to her without thinking about it, our shoulders almost touching.

"Welcome back," Kion rumbles, his eyes smiling where his face isn't.

"S'good to be back," Thea mumbles in reply. "Let's get it over with." She makes to start walking toward the main building, and David Jacobs steps forward, spreading his hands.

"Your...guest...can be taken to barracks A; they've cleared some space there," he says, with a conciliatory air, but Thea shakes her head.

"She stays with me."

"We can't allow possible informants into a military briefing, Thea." He has a "Be reasonable" tone in his voice, and Thea shrugs, starting to walk, tugging Hepeh after her like a small child.

"Then you can interview me in my dorm after I've showered." She sounds more confident and sure of herself than I think I've ever heard her, when talking to the bosses, not that she was especially shy and retiring before.

Serena smothers something that sounds suspiciously like a snort, and I shrug at the ARC bosses like "What can you do?" before following Thea. Leaf and Serena are right behind us.

We've only gone a few steps, not even out of the garage, before Kion has caught up. "We'll see you in thirty minutes in the Silver Annex, if Serena can stay with... I'm sorry, what's your name?" He addresses straight to Hepeh, very politely.

She makes him wait for a moment before replying, "Hepeh-Ganuh, or Twice-Bound," giving him a sharp incline of the head. "I will happily stay with the brother or the terrible driver."

"Serena," Serena says. "I'm not that bad."

"Pretty bad." Leaf snickers. "And I'll 'ang ou' as well; tha' way yeh don' nee' ter worreh she's gonna do a blink."

"Acceptable," Hepeh-Ganuh agrees, sniffing. "I need to eat and sleep."

"Sounds thrillin'," Leaf snorts. "Seh wha', yeh both grab a shower an' a change and we'll meet yeh a' yer room, Thea?"

"Fine." Thea gives in gracelessly, clearly exhausted beyond politeness.

Clean and dressed in soft cotton, Hepeh-Ganuh looks younger, less dangerous. When you can't see her teeth, it's easy to forget she's not just another ARC soldier, except for the way she sits, like she could pull herself up into battle stance without really moving.

She's definitely not at home in this space, though. First, she awkwardly perches on a beanbag chair on the floor, and then slides off with a faint impression of "Why does this exist?" flaring about her movements. She crosses her legs on the hard linoleum instead, while Leaf takes a seat on Thea's bed, and Serena sprawls on the small storage bench in the corner, which is definitely not made for sitting on. I lean my shoulder against the wall by the door; the room is too small for this many people.

Hepeh-Ganuh is looking at everything, her eyes flicking around the room, and her hand keeps twitching at her hip like she's reflexively checking for a weapon. There's uncomfortable silence, and I open my mouth to try to break it more than once but can never think of what to say.

Leaf is fidgeting with something, a flashing object rolling over the back of his knuckles, but I know he doesn't have telekinesis. It looks impossible, and I peer over in interest.

He slows down, holds his hand out for me to see, and walks what I can now see is a burnished disc of coppery metal that holds bumps and divots on it across his brown knuckles. Ah, a coin. Serena also leans over, but in her case, it's to snatch the coin from him and balance it on the back of her own hand, try to copy his movement, and fail miserably.

She drops the coin, and Hepeh-Ganuh lets out a little bark of laughter. The atmosphere relaxes, and Leaf produces three more of the coins and offers them around.

To my surprise, Hepeh-Ganuh can already competently manipulate the little disc across her hands. I drop my coin immediately, and it rolls toward her, and she toes it back to me without stopping her own play.

I shift closer to her to watch and try to mimic her, and she glances at me from under her eyelashes, sighs, and sets to helping me.

I continue to be terrible at it, even past where Serena has the basic first flip down and is struggling to reverse directions.

"You need a bigger coin to learn," Hepeh-Ganuh tells me, more relaxed now. I abruptly realize Leaf has managed to give us something to do, loosen the tension in the room, and distract us all at once.

I'm impressed, and also really annoyed with my clumsiness as I watch Hepeh-Ganuh dance her coin forward and backward across her hand.

Thea makes us jump when she opens the door, and she looks around at the room, sighs, and runs her hand over her short hair. "Out. You can guard the door if you like, but we've been running for four days and I need to pass out."

"I'll grab a floor mat," Serena wriggles off the bed and stands up, stretching and flipping the coin back to Leaf.

He catches it easily, then follows Serena off the bed and winks at me. "Yeh cin keep tha' fer practice." Before heading for the door, he stops and speaks to Thea in a low voice, and I make an effort not to accidentally listen in, either with my ears or our link.

She shrugs a shoulder, nods, and he slips out silently. Serena pads after him. I reckon I'll wait around until she's back with a mat for Hepeh though.

"He would be a good scout," Hepeh-Ganuh announces. "Do you sleep in this box?" She asks Thea, cocking her head to one side.

"Yeah, usually."

"Sometimes she sleeps outside," I point out helpfully.

Hepeh-Ganuh looks eager for a second and then mutes the light in her eyes, masking her expression.

"You think Kion would care?" Thea asks tiredly.

"I dunno, but if you don't ask, they can't spank you till they catch you." I can feel the unease rolling off Hepeh-Ganuh at the walls and weight of the buildings over us. "I bet Serena would come for extra guard duty, and then you'd have a qualified team of ARC military personnel." I grin, because it's still a bit hilarious that I'm a soldier, these days. And everything feels better now Thea is here, like maybe we can turn the Eaters away, after all. She has a kernel of hope in her, although I didn't get too close a look at what sowed it.

Serena leans in the doorway, holding four sleeping mats and bags in her telekinetic grip. "Way ahead of you. Let's break out! And...sleep in the yard."

Thea smiles so slowly I get to watch the whole thing happen, and it puts something light and warm in my chest. I grab two of Serena's overloaded bags and shake one in the air. "And at *this* sleepover, no one gets me drunk when I have to get beaten with sticks in the morning."

Hepeh-Ganuh is in front of me before I really see her move. She leans in, intense. "Who hits you? I will snap them for you."

I very slowly lower my sleeping bag and try for a reassuring smile. "Um, it's voluntary. Voluntary being hit with sticks."

She relaxes, and it's like watching a wire uncoil. "Ah. I understand. I don't care how you take your pleasure." She steps away, out of my immediate space. "But to hurt you would hurt Two-Sides."

Thea is a step behind her, hand on her wrist and gently tugging. "It's okay," she tells Hepeh. "There's no threat here, really."

"I bet that will feel a lot more true when we're all outside," Serena points out practically, and then gives me an evil grin. "And then, we can discuss how much your brother enjoys being beaten with sticks."

Chapter Nineteen

E17

Toby huffs indignantly, and Serena chortles at his expense, and we wind our way through the long, dark corridor. No one stops us or sends us back, and we burst out into the open gardens in the back of the building, into the moonlight.

Hepeh-Ganuh inhales deeply, lets her shoulders untense for the first time since we got in the Land Rover with Serena and Toby, and I grin at her expression when she turns her face up to the skies. "It's not good to be so...inside."

"Agreed," I tell her fervently as Serena leads us down a little winding path to a patch of grass not directly under the huge windows of the main barracks.

It's ironic that our reasons for disliking walls and ceilings are so disparate. I've had enough of walls to last me my whole life, raised inside and underground, but for Hepeh-Ganuh to be somewhere locked away from the sky is an alien thing. Either way, we're both happier out here.

"Should we set a watch?" Serena asks, unfolding her mat. "Or do you promise not to kill us all and eat our brains?" She says it with a joking tone, but there's an edge of *really* in her voice that makes me sigh. But they have every right to question Hepeh. Serena wasn't with us, she doesn't know anything.

"We're tied together," I say, before Hepeh can respond. "There was a ritual. If I die, she dies. So it's in her best interest to keep me alive, and if it wasn't, she could have let me die or killed me herself hundreds of times over the last few days."

"And you're really you and not gonna lose your mind to Cassandra again?" Serena pushes, settling her sleeping bag out. "Because I will haunt the shit out of you if you kill me."

"It's me." I say quietly, and hold out my hand for hers. I'm done keeping secrets; it's gotten me nowhere so far. I already let Kion in this evening, instead of exhaustively recounting everything I can remember. Now he knows as much as I do, but I expect they'll have questions for Hepeh in the morning, once they've had time to think.

Serena takes my hand and inhales sharply as I let her share the information I have about the bond between Hepeh and I, let her see Cassandra, quiescent in the back of my Talent, and let her understand that it's me in control right now.

She also gets a lot of information about the Eaters societal structures and raises an eyebrow at me as she lets go of my hand and sits back. "You think you're gonna fight Pollux?"

I hadn't really put it into so many words, but she says it and it's true. "Someone has to. We can't fight them all."

"*What?*" Toby sounds as scandalized as I've ever heard him; clearly he missed that part.

"If someone can kill Pollux in single combat, they might be able to strike a deal with the tribes," I tell him, and Hepeh grunts agreement.

"They won't fight first meat, won't follow first meat. You two...the bond between you marks you as acceptable.

You've dropped in and out of each other enough. You...have not," she answers Serena before she has a chance to ask. "Nor has your champion—" I don't know who she means, and then she cracks her neck before expanding "—the Builder-Breaker." It comes with an image of Kion, and I huff out air, seeing the meaning. He builds us, his soldiers, and breaks those he faces.

"How come I'm the 'terrible driver' and don't get a cool nickname?" Serena asks, breaking the sputtering tension easing out of Toby into the air.

Hepeh pulls her blankets across her legs, lying down with one hand under her head. "Your names don't have meaning for me; it's hard to remember them." There's a distinct impression of "They sound funny" that comes along with it, and the added information that Hepeh-Ganuh, Twice-Bound, used to be Hepeh-Paneh, Once-Bound, and that the Eater's names are in fact words describing them in a fairly literal fashion. Hepeh smirks at me as if she can't believe I hadn't realized that before and then continues talking to Serena. "I have only seen you drive. I will call you by your meat name. Serena. Unless you have a preference."

"I want a cool nickname," she repeats, snuggling down into her sleeping bag.

"Murderballs," Toby points out, and Serena groans.

"I hate that nickname."

"And you are neither a murderer, nor in possession of...balls." Hepeh has a smirk in the corner of her mouth.

"Well..." Serena starts, and is cut off by Toby slapping his hand over her mouth promptly while shaking his head and pleading *please, no sharing.*

She pushes him away playfully, with telekinesis bracing her arm, and Hepeh cocks her head. "Iron-Bone."

"Iron-*Bone*..." Serena sounds absolutely delighted, and Toby puts his head in his hands.

"That's worse."

I'm grateful he's distracted from the idea that I plan to fight Pollux, but there's an ache in every muscle of my body, dragging me down into sleep, whether I like it or not. I lie down, listen to Toby and Serena teasing each other, and don't move my leg away when Hepeh rolls over and presses her foot against my calf.

I wake to the mind-sound of hissed voices, the feel of agitation and anger. I peel my dry, sticky eyes open to see Serena poking Ria in the chest and pointing down the path. I stretch lazily and thread my awareness that way, wafting as light as smoke, as soft as a dream; no one notices me when I can concentrate and have time to focus.

Are you insane? Ria projects at Serena. *What the hell are you doing out here? We almost pulled a full alarm.*

I left a note, Serena replies. *Me and Toby are both here with them.*

And half of ARC is convinced you're all traitors and they've come to sell our brains off. Ria is infuriated, but not with me.

You know that's not true, Serena dismisses. *Let them talk; it's not true.*

She killed sixteen people, Ria yells. *And we're letting her walk around unhindered with a mother-nuking cannibal trailing after her like a puppy.*

It wasn't her. And the cannibal saved her ass, got her out of an enemy camp, and is happy to give us information on them. Might well save all our asses. Now would you get off my case? I'll bring Thea to morning briefing and leave Toby with Hepeh, if that passes martial law.

Kion's gonna kick your ass. Ria sounds resigned now. *See you at the briefing, and for nuke's sake, don't disappear on us again.*

Done, Serena agrees. *Now piss off before you wake them up. I'm building trust here.*

Hepeh-Ganuh snorts quietly, so I know she's heard as well. Serena and Ria weren't touching, weren't trying to stay secret and quiet, and it seems only Toby missed the party. I kick him gently, and he jerks upright, sputtering in confusion with his shields slamming into place around him in an iridescent bubble before he realizes he's not in danger.

"They will want to question me," Hepeh says quietly, shifting in her sleeping bag until she can wriggle into a sitting position. She folds her hands deliberately in her lap, like she's nervous.

"Yeah." Toby agrees, yawning and not bothering to cover his mouth.

"Will it...?" Hepeh pauses, licks her lips carefully and avoids my eyes. "How much will it hurt?" I flash back to the times she's been questioned in the past, by Senep, by others, and Toby makes a distressed noise before I realize we're sharing too.

"It won't. They won't hurt you." He says, authority in his voice I haven't heard before. "Either Thea or I will stay with you and make sure of it."

"Or me." Serena rejoins us, slinging a bag onto the ground. "We get breakfast out here in case you upset the masses." She grins at Hepeh.

Over breakfast, Toby remembers what he was arguing about before Hepeh distracted him with nicknames. "You can't fight him. I saw him. I watched the battle."

I shrug, "I might get lucky, and we don't have a lot of options." I don't really have the energy to argue with Toby right now, and it's not him who will decide, anyway.

"You have very few choices," Hepeh agrees, through a mouthful of bread with cheese spread that is apparently delicious enough she's closed her eyes and wears a blissful expression. "From what I have seen, only two or three, maybe."

"Then I'll fight him." Toby gets to his feet in a flurry of limbs, just so he can start pacing angrily. "I've been training." I roll my eyes at Serena, and she wrinkles her nose in solidarity.

"The Starman would walk through you like a wind." Hepeh licks a crumb off her fingertip daintily. "You are very, very slow."

"Hey," Toby flops down, indignantly. "I'm not that bad, I could also get lucky!"

I have less than a sliver of warning before a blast of raw telekinesis roars out of Hepeh-Ganuh, smashing into the space I would have been if I wasn't already moving into a roll. Serena yells out in surprise, and Toby crashes onto his back, Hepeh on top of him, pinning him to the ground with one hand. I dive onto my feet, ready to drive her clear of my brother before I catch the grin on her face. She's just playing—Serena's seen it too—not attacking.

"Slow, and then dead," she tells him, before letting him up. Serena is clenching and unclenching her hand like it stings, looking at Hepeh with new respect in her eyes. Hepeh grins, her eyes crinkling. "You're very fast," she tells Serena before gathering a new piece of bread from the basket, spreading cheese on it, and then holding it out to Toby as he pulls himself off the ground with a grunt.

He hesitates for a moment and then takes it.

"Fast enough?" Serena asks.

Hepeh hums thoughtfully, preparing another bread and cheese for herself. "Maybe, but it doesn't matter. You're first meat, unprimed." She shrugs. "It would take weeks to pry you out of your shell."

"Is there anyone else?" Toby sounds so sad I remember he's only being annoyingly overprotective because he's so guilty about our disparate childhoods.

Hepeh shrugs again, leans back and closes her eyes to the sun. "I could tell you if you showed me all your warriors."

"Aren't you worried?" Toby does his puppy dog eyes at her. "If she dies, you die, right?"

"Yes. But...warriors fight and warriors die. I cannot stop her. I would not stop her." There's so much behind Hepeh's statement—history and respect and the-way-things-are—it's clearly not an argument Toby's going to win. I'm more concerned about whether or not Kion will hit me over the head and hide me in a cupboard somewhere until it's over. Trouble with that is I'd probably wake up to someone smashing my head in to get at my delicious, magical brains, or it might seem more attractive.

Chapter Twenty

TOBY

The early morning light is turning everything dusty and gold, silhouetting Thea and Hepeh-Ganuh as they talk about sending my twin off for a quick old fight to the death.

"It's...it's not fair," I say, helplessly, my throat is all tight and hard, and I keep thinking that she's going to die just to buy us a day more to try to get ready, to try to figure out what Cassandra could possibly have meant by turning the Wall on, to wait for them to run over us in a flesh-eating tide. If we are going to die, we should do it together, a part of me insists. Or we should run, now, while we can. We wouldn't be the only ones. People have been trickling out of the City's north gate since the Eaters started ripping them apart on the streets.

"Nothing ever is," Hepeh says simply when it seems like no one else has a response for me.

Serena touches my knee in silent sympathy, support, shared pain. I can feel the ache from her at the idea of sending Thea to fight when she hasn't had a lifetime to prepare. The fierce burning that demands she stand in front, she fights...but she can't. According to whatever customs and Talent rules these people have, Serena can't fight. And I'm just...not good enough.

My throat closes completely, and I clamber to my feet. I don't know where I'm going, or why, but I just need to be away from them and their war plans. The sun beats down on my face as I run through the gardens. I'm still faster than any of them on foot. I remember running away from those street thugs, that first day, before I used my power for the first time. I wonder what happened to them in this new war.

I just want to go back. I wish I could go back to just being Toby—safe in my parents' house with physics homework and a Rizkball game to look forward to on the weekend. The worst thing I had to worry about was getting caught with an illicit beer at the park on game night. My foot catches on a chunk of transal not dug out of the grass and I trip, plowing toward the ground hands outstretched, power bursting, soaring out of me to catch my fall. The sparkling glitter of my Talent, still shocking every time I see it, spangles over the ground, flattens the grass, and boosts me back to my feet. I throw out tendrils to steady myself and keep sprinting.

That Toby, the Toby who didn't have anything to worry about, also didn't have this power. And with this power came a twin I never knew I had, but who feels *vital* to me now. With this power, came friends...no...family. My feet slow. I'm at the base of the low wall separating the grounds from the City. Without thinking too much, I throw my power into the ground, onto the wall, hook myself up like it's rope I can touch. I haul myself up and settle down on the wide top of the wall, bringing my power back into myself. This is new too. This is from Hepeh-Ganuh sharing with Thea. They use their power so differently to us, I think the way Serena sees and uses her power is the most similar, really, the body focus of her, the way it fits into her meat. I use the Eater word without thinking about it and shudder.

Hepeh-Ganuh says Thea and I are both out of our meat, our flesh, enough that we would be allowed to fight to lead the Eaters. That's clearly because of the link between us—a link I can feel buzzing with Thea's attempts to talk to me, which I ignore. A link that Pollux had with his twin brother, Castor. Dead and eaten, now. Icarus, who is actually body-hopping, walking around in Andrea's skin—a shiver of rage passes through me at the thought— has a more direct passing grade on that particular test. Hepeh said it would take weeks to get Serena able to get out of her own meat.

Why? I throw at Thea, not bothering with niceties, meaning why don't the Eaters let you fight unless you've separated from your body somehow.

Until you leave your meat, you have never fully shielded; there's always an opening. They would suck you dry in a moment before you even lifted your blade. The only reason you've survived so far is that you're fighting outliers, stragglers. Riddled with tumors and barely thinking at all, anymore. We are not all such beasts. It's Hepeh-Ganuh who answers, her fingers laced through Thea's in a point of warmth deeper than the sun on her skin that gives me a whole bunch of other stuff to think about when I don't have a link open. Thea catches it, though, pulls her shields up tight.

I let the link go, feel it shriveling into almost nonexistence, and pull my knees up to my chest, resting my chin on them.

It's Leaf who finds me, although I assume someone told him where I was. He climbs up the wall slowly, with great concentration, but seemingly little effort. He's sleeveless, his brown arms gleaming with a light layer of sweat. It's hot without the transal shields taking a layer of heat out, I'm sweating, too, I realize. He passes me a canteen of water and folds himself up with his legs crossed while I drink, gratefully.

"I 'eard the news," he tells me. "Thea an' Hepeh been up in fron' of the council all mornin', arguin' every which way accordin' ta Serena." He pauses, tips his head back, closes his eyes in the glare of the white light. "She's gona figh' 'im. Pollux. The mad one." He sounds tired too.

"Yeah." My voice is rough, and my thumbnail catches on the plastic of the canteen as I scratch at it. "She'll die."

"Migh' not." I can't tell if he's trying to convince himself or me. "Wha' kin' of choices do we 'ave, anyway."

"We could *leave*." Emotion strangles my words, and he opens his eyes to give me a pointed look.

"An' leave all the others 'ere ta fight? Leave this lot?" He waves a hand at the sprawling city, the unpowered population going about their day. "Ya know she wouldn' come wi' ya. Wi' me."

"You'd leave?" I'm surprised, for some reason, but I remember Serena saying he used to run away from danger.

He shrugs a shoulder, "I don' like the odds 'ere, s'gotta be sai'. Bu' I owe the big man, an'...there's somethin' wi' Thea an' me. I don' wanna wonder fer the res' of my days if I shoulda stayed."

"Is that enough?" I rub my heel angrily against the smooth surface of the wall, the sun beating on my head like an anvil, making it hard to think.

Leaf twists his mouth thoughtfully, knocks his shoulder into mine. "S'pose it 'as ta be. An' there's nuffin' ter say the Eaters won' move on after they've slake' their thirs' 'ere. Mah family's jus' over there. Coul' be next." He points at the distant horizon. "Ye shoul' come down. Yer missin' all the excitemen'."

"What about Hepeh?" I ask him. He knows what I mean; I see it in the set of his mouth.

He takes a moment to respond and then grins at me, a broad grin showing his crooked eye tooth pressing against his lower lip. "It's not a zero-sum game, Tobes. If'n there's summa' there for them, tha's for them, and maybe us teh sor' ou'. Ta be 'on's I'm no' much fer monogamy, either way. How 'bout you le' us deal wi' whatever needs ter be dealt wi', and we'll letcha know."

Oh. I take the rebuke as it was intended: kindly. "Yeah. Sorry. It's just... I just want her to be happy."

"Well firs' we wan' 'er ta not be dea'." Leaf points out, practically. "So, I'm gonna clim' down an' go 'n' help wi' the plans for tha'. Ye comin'?" He swings his legs out over the wall in a way that makes my stomach *lurch*, twisting himself around and giving me a wicked grin before starting to descend.

I move down the wall a ways before I jump off, wrapping my legs, my shinbones, in power, to absorb the impact. I wreck another small patch of garden with my landing, but compared to the rest of the lawns, it's not that bad. I do feel a bit guilty, though, and toe some of the grass back into place, enjoying the shade cast by the height of the wall as Leaf descends with spidery, confident grace.

We walk back over the grounds in silence. Tentatively, I reopen my line to Thea, prepared for her to be mad at me, but there's just a sense of understanding coming down the wire, which is almost worse.

I learn that they're in the command center—Thea and Hepeh working on a map of the Eater camp and probable route for incursion, Serena trying to figure out what does and doesn't count as technology in terms of Thea fighting, and Kion organizing operatives to come and report to command in twos and threes, so Hepeh can lift her head, sniff the air and say *no*, dismissively.

The other idea on the table is firebombing the Eaters as soon as they're in heli range but that has obvious negatives—both in the form of wiping out thousands of people who might be different from us in certain ways but who nevertheless have autonomy and identities—and in the shit show that an extermination would leave behind.

I try to ignore the part of me that says *no*, not Thea, not her, and I take a deep breath before pushing into the command center.

Leaf and I are working with Serena on going through inventory and finding armor and weapons Thea could use when Hepeh says *yes* for the first time.

Cassius is in the doorway.

He leans against the frame with his shoulder and gives the room the faintest shadow of a humorless grin. "I hear you're looking for someone to fight Pollux."

My heart jumps, skips...hope flowers inside me, and Thea and Hepeh and Serena turn in unison to give me a look that makes me snap my shields up. If Cassius can fight...if he's allowed. He's good; he could win.

"No," says Thea, finality in her voice. "You're still injured...besides, you've been in hell for six years. You live." Leaf shifts uneasily at my side.

"And you weren't?" I snap, angrily clutching at the wave of hope as it washes out of me. I feel the guilt in her, though, the pain for letting Cassandra win and how red

Cassius's blood was and how sometimes, when Icarus was in him still, how he cared for Thea.

"Fight you for it," Cassius drawls, "the way they do."

"If either of you were injured...or worse, both..." Kion points out grimly, his jaw tight.

"Who is better?" Hepeh butts in, looking at Kion. "You are their master. Who wins?"

He looks sick, for a moment, shadows in his eyes that make him look old and tired. He braces his hand on the table like he needs the support. "Thea." The apology paints his words in thick, golden stripes. Sorry to Cassius and to Thea, and to me, and to Serena. And to all of us for not being able to stand in front of us and take the brunt of this army on his own shoulders.

Thea gives me a half-hearted grin. "See. I can do it."

Cassius laughs hollowly. "What's the policy on me challenging him the day after, if you don't?" He directs it at Hepeh and Thea together.

Hepeh grins, showing wolves' teeth. "Acceptable."

Cassius nods, licks his lips, and shifts his eyes to me, then back to Thea. "Try to hurt him good, then, even if he wins. Give me something to aim for."

"Done," she says, pushing confidence into her voice.

So that's it, then. Even if we find another soldier who could, Thea thinks this is her job. I stomp to the water dispenser to give myself a second. Swallowing the icy cold liquid doesn't do much for the lump in my throat, just sets a dull ache in my belly. If Thea and Cassius die, I can be day three.

"So, what, we just send everyone we can out day by day?" Serena demands. "Nuke that. Start getting me out of my meat, then. Tell me what to do." This is flung at Hepeh in a tone as sharp as knives.

Hepeh sniffs. "You do much with...consent, that we do not. It could be faster. You share with the brother. If he allows you in maybe it will take fewer tries." Hope curls in me again. Sending Serena to fight doesn't feel...*wrong*, in the same way. It's what she's made for. What she loves. What she *chose*. Thea never had a choice.

"I have a girlfriend, fiancé." Serena tells her. "No offence, Tobias, but if I'm going to do an all secrets laid bare move, you're my second choice."

I snort. "Yeah, that's cool."

Kion taps something out on his comm. "I'll try too." He looks up at Thea. "Maybe I'll be quick enough to fight first."

"He's shocked people with his speed before." Serena winces as soon as the joke leaves her mouth, but Leaf barks a laugh, and the whole room relaxes somewhat.

"Okay, so...Thea and I will figure out gear," I start.

"And fill her with your power," Hepeh tells me. You must shut the link to fight, so she has to take everything before."

Powerless. That's what that sounds like to me, like I'll have nothing left to fight with if I need. I nod jerkily.

Hepeh gives me a surprisingly soft smile. "You are a brave boy. But you still have some time before they come. You will refill."

"Wha' abou' Cassandra?" Leaf props his hips on a curving computer station. "She coul' jump in an' get ye killed, no?"

"No," Hepeh and Thea say at the same time, and then exchange a glance and a half smile. Leaf pulls a complicated face which he wipes off fast enough they miss it.

"She's...done. Small." Thea expands. "Since Hepeh showed me how to blink, it's different."

"Your power is only yours, now. She cannot take it unless you allow it. She is weaker than you and you are not first meat." Hepeh explains in a way that does very little to actually explain anything. Google, when this is all done, we're gonna have to have her write a treatise or two. Maybe more of the Eaters will want to jump ship as well...

"Peace talks." I blurt abruptly. "We need to figure out what we can offer them to leave quietly, whether or not we win the thing. Did you see Hepeh with the food? No offense." I grin at her, suddenly buzzing. "I lived some of your past—you have the farms, but limited food, barely any. No meat, really. That's..." a series of thoughts thunder through my brain. "You have rain? Out there? Or just underground water?"

"We pull the water," Hepeh tells me, a curious expression on her face. "Well, the water shepherds do. I have no nature in me."

"Water shepherds?" Now Kion is distracted from the idea of getting his not-first-meat qualifications.

Hepeh huffs, exasperated, and holds her hand out to him. He doesn't even hesitate, steps forward and clasps her forearm, wrist to wrist. He closes his eyes while she shares with him, and I watch the expressions flashing over his face too fast to follow.

"This could... This could change everything." He breathes. "They move the water, in the ground."

I figured as much from what she said, but clearly haven't grasped the immensity of it, Kion looks like he's been hit with a poleax, until Serena touches the back of his arm and he jumps.

"Peace talks." She agrees with me. "Who should be on that? My dad? Shiloh?"

Kion shakes it off, nodding, and then stilling, his eyes distant as he clearly relays a bunch of information on to David Jacobs and whoever else will deal with that.

Chapter Twenty-One

E17

After a flurry of conversation about what water shepherds can do, and a vague and imposing idea that has Kion thinking we can farm if some of the Eaters want to stay here, Serena and Kion go with Hepeh-Ganuh to try to learn to leave their meat.

That leaves me, Toby, and Leaf alone in the room. Toby, perpetually awkward, keeps looking back and forth between us with a pained expression that makes me want to pinch him.

We're pulling together orders for a bunch of equipment that Hepeh can check to see if it will get past the Eaters stringent rules about what is and isn't allowed in the arena. From the fleeting information I've managed to gather, I'm pretty sure Serena's guess that the non-Newtonian body armor is allowable will work, and that's a load off my mind, to be honest. Pollux is quick with a knife, and I'm not used to physical shielding.

"Blades'll slice it, though," Leaf points out, tapping the screen. "Ge' some of tha' stab-proof cloth over top of it."

I nod. "Yeah, that's a good idea." Kion...well...David Jacobs at Kion's request, has given us all full clearance to appropriate whatever we need. "Arm guards, as well, if the stab-proof cloth can be attached to those."

Toby dutifully notes the items we need and adds notes to our request forms before sending them off. "What about your head? A helmet?" he suggests.

I shudder. "No, I can't. Too claustrophobic. I'll just...keep out the way."

Leaf's knee brushes mine under the counter, and I freeze, then slowly relax into the contact. In some ways, I can't believe he's still here, with us, but in others I feel like wherever I go, he'd be there, beside me. Of course, now, I have someone else who plans to be there as well. I need to talk to him about whatever is coalescing between Hepeh and myself, but how can I, when I don't know and don't have words for it anyway.

"I...uh"—Toby looks back and forth between us—"need the bathroom." He lies, not very smoothly, and almost falls over as he clambers to his feet. "I'll probably be, like, ten minutes." He gives an awkward laugh and bolts for the door.

Leaf snorts, lazily moving his foot to touch mine under the table. "Subtle as a brick, tha' one."

"It's one of his charms," I agree, suddenly overcome with my own awkwardness and wishing I was anywhere but here.

"I's ok." Leaf gently reaches out, so slowly I could fold him over the table and snap his arm, or bolt in the other direction if I wanted to, and then his fingers brush my cheek. I sigh, despite myself, my eyes fluttering closed. I think he's going to kiss me, and I want him to, more than anything. Heat rises in my stomach, but confusion and fear also swirls inside me. When nothing changes, I open my eyes again. He's just looking at me with a gentle expression. "Yes. If yeh wan'. Bu' there's neh rush. We can deal wi' this"—he motions between us—"an' wi' Hepeh. I see tha' too. I'm no' fer makin' yeh choose. But whatever yeh wan' to come of this, we can deal wi' it la'er. When this'z over."

"What if... What if I die?" It's not even really a question, and my voice is small.

His face goes soft, his eyes so intense I can barely look at him. I can't Read him—never could—but in this moment I don't need to. "Yeh won'," he tells me, so sincere I almost believe him. "I feel i'."

Something balloons and bursts in my chest, pressing my rib cage outward. I've never felt so big. I surge forward, catching his lips with mine, kissing him hard enough to bruise, his teeth catch in my lip, and he curls his hand around my neck, thumb brushing over the skin of my throat, sending a shiver down my spine to coil in my belly.

I forget we're in the command room, until a wave of consternation shocks me out of the kiss and out of Leaf's lap, as my brother drops the chocolate milk he was carrying, and it splashes all over the floor.

Leaf cracks up, bending down and hiding his face on my shoulder. "Ye'd thin'...e'd thin'..." He gasps for air. "Ye'd thin' 'e'd 'ave the smarts ter check in wi' ye before tromping back in..." And then he loses it to laughter again. After a moment, I join him, as Toby pulls a face at us and uselessly tries to clean up the mess with his shoe.

By the time we have a sufficient list of stuff for Hepeh to look at, when she has time—we're stretching her pretty thin—we're all hungry, and the canteen is serving, so we head down together. I'm so aware of Leaf next to me on the stairs my skin is humming.

I can't stop touching him. Foot to foot under the table, hand brushing hand, I tuck a lock of his black hair behind his ear when it tumbles down to tickle his cheekbone. I can't stop *looking* at him, it's like I've never really seen him before, or like if I blink he'll disappear. Maybe part of that is that I can't feel him with my power. He leans into me, knocks our knees together, tangles our fingers for a moment and then away. Lets me touch him, makes space for me against him. I lean toward him, a magnet.

Toby sort of awkwardly pretends I'm not sitting so close to Leaf our thighs are pressed together, and he keeps his shields locked up tighter than I've ever felt them.

"Thea!" Aly bolts across the room, and I have an uncomfortable moment of realization that probably everyone has heard I'm back, but I haven't gone to look for any of them. Aly wraps her arms around my shoulders, giving me a gentle squeeze, and then flops down next to Toby who instantly relaxes. I can't help but giggle at him, softening under Aly's light and playful tone as she talks about nothing in particular, clearly having picked up on the semi-uncomfortable silence that was draped over our table before she sat down.

I'm so busy thinking about how delicate and strong Leaf's hands are, the way his fingers curl around the handles of his cutlery, how he uses them to gesture to punctuate the story he's telling, that I miss Serena's arrival until she sits down next to Toby.

Darcy's just next to her, and the breath goes out of me like a punch, like a knife to the lung. Her hand is wrapped in bright-blue strapping, elbow to fingertips, each finger held independently by the rigid fabric support.

Tears jump into my eyes, and a weird wheezing sound squeezes out of my throat. A hand on my back makes me jump, and Leaf rubs a little, calming circle, and the tension in my bones relaxes enough for me to start crying properly.

"I'm sorry. I'm so sorry," I tell everyone. I'm not sure if I'm apologizing for what I...what Cassandra did, or for crying at dinner, but Darcy's eyes are soft, and she puts her tray down, scoots around the end of the table, and gathers me up in her good arm, letting me bury my face in her neck.

"Shh," she soothes me, while Toby glows with protect-calm-angry-sad-help-confused from across the table, and Serena holds him there, letting me have a moment to cry into Darcy's shoulder in big, heaving sobs that tear my guts loose. It's like the tears have been waiting in my chest for days, weeks, waiting for me to be safe somewhere and almost happy before running me over with the extremities of the emotional upheaval I've been through. I remember Cassius, smashed to the ground. I remember *crushing* Darcy's hand, the vindictive wave of power it sent through my body. Cassandra's mind, but my meat. My strength did that, hurt them. Sixteen dead, Ria said. Killed them. I'm surprised they even let me sit here in this hall.

Darcy holds onto me until I pull away, and then she lets me shift back, kisses me on the forehead. "You punch him in the face for me," she tells me, using her thumb to wipe my cheek—it's a futile gesture. I'm wet and snotty. Leaf produces a handkerchief from one of his innumerable pockets, and I gratefully hide my face in it under the pretext of cleaning myself up.

When I'm not quite as disgusting anymore, I emerge to hear Serena filling the others in on how her training with Hepeh went. "It wasn't great, but she said it wasn't terrible"—she shrugs—"apparently, 'cause Darcy and I share a lot, we have an advantage. Kion's struggling. Hepeh's still with him."

I swallow some snot and gulp down some water. I don't really know what to say, because... I don't know what I want. If Serena can pass first meat, then they'll have her fight instead of me. I won't even get a say. But I feel weirdly certain that it should be me. That this is how I earn my freedom. I'd step down for Kion, but for Serena? If she dies, it would kill Darcy...Toby. Kion thinks of her like a sister. Her dad. She has so much here.

Leaf puts his hand on my back again, comforting, and Toby grins at me with an effort at reassurance, and Darcy touches my hand gently. I have things too. I know. I don't want to die, but I will, if it protects my friends.

"Don't die, Thea," Toby tells me, his face serious again. "Win."

Leaf leaves me at my door with another kiss that shakes my knees, and Hepeh is already in the room, waiting for me. She's looking at the furniture, running her hands over it, and when she turns to look at me, her face is unreadable.

"Are you tired?" I ask her. I don't have it in me to talk right now.

She nods, and it could be hurt in her eyes, or fear, but I don't know how to tell her what I'm feeling. And then I remember I don't have to, that I can offer her more than that, and I lick my lips nervously before padding across the room to sit on the bed and offer her my hand.

For a long minute she watches me, and then stalks across the room, liquid grace and muscles that stand in high-definition under her gold-brown skin. She doesn't sit on the bed with me, squats next to it, and takes my hand.

Our fingers tangle, and I feel her fear that I'm going to send her away, that she didn't do what I wanted, what I needed. That I'll replace her when she's useless to us, once we know what she knows. I let her see my heart, stripped bare, nothing but the truth of me. My pain and fear and hope. The tug I feel toward her. She breathes pure relief at me, ducks her head onto my thigh, presses her forehead against the muscle just above the knee. I hate it. I don't like this power she thinks I have over her, so I slide down onto the floor, and we sit together, in a heap, until I'm falling asleep in jerky, broken movements, and I tug her up onto the bed with me.

We sleep with her hand tucked onto my flank, just under my shirt, like she's afraid *I'm* the one that will disappear. Guiltily, I wonder if it's her need for me that's so attractive, but she hums a sleepy laugh down the connection between us and tells me to dream well.

Morning brings the insistent beeping of messages to drag me out of slumber. We've migrated in the night, both of us sleeping in our full outfits mean we've mostly stayed on top of the blankets but Hepeh's leg is tangled through mine, and she's warm against my back. Her hand is under my shirt, splayed across my stomach muscles. I can feel the six-pack I worked so hard to build swaying against her palm as I breathe.

We need to talk...we all need to talk—Hepeh and me, Leaf and me—although he did sound as if he understood that there is something with Hepeh for me to work out. For a floating, weightless moment, I remember him saying I didn't have to choose. I held hands with Hepeh and let her see the day I spent with Leaf, and she still held me like this through the night.

Your people have very strange ideas, Hepeh tells me silently. *Why would your feelings for him affect your feelings for me? It is not a competition.*

A little laugh bubbles out of me. *I don't know. I was raised by scientists.* I point out. *No one really talked to me about any of this. About feelings.*

Then it is lucky you have two people who want to. The coloration in the words she sends back is distinctly "adorable," and she reluctantly pulls her hand off my stomach, pulls my shirt down, and pats it into place before reaching out above our heads for my datapad and dropping it unceremoniously in front of me. *Make it be quiet.*

I giggle as I turn the sound off, reading through the messages quickly. Hepeh has returned to breathing heavily onto my shoulder by the time I'm done. *Kion wants you to work with him and Serena again today, and then share with the techs so they can try to figure out your people's weather power,* I tell her, feeling in no rush to get up.

Mph. It's even a nonsensical noise in her head. *I will miss you. What will you do?*

I will miss you. The sheer, honest sincerity in her thought shakes me. She doesn't just feel tied to me; she likes it when I'm around.

Of course, I like it. You are funny and clever, and you make good faces. You are brave and strong and kind. Why would anyone not like to have you around?

She sounds genuinely confused, and I definitely don't mean to start crying again, but I do anyway. I blame it on the weird feeling of safety that sinks into my bones when she's around me.

Hepeh is distressed by my tears, so I try to explain they are happy tears, but there's a roiling sadness under them that she can feel. I don't want to lose this. Lose her. Lose Leaf, or Toby, or Darcy. Aly or Serena, Jake or Demi. Any of them. I'm scared.

You are brave, and he is scared, Hepeh tells me in a soft, crooning voice, letting me curl into her body without complaint. *He does well to be scared of you; you are a paladin,* and I can feel the translation isn't quite direct, that there's a different word they have. Like a champion. She thinks of me climbing the cliff, and how I wasn't scared, how I was so brave I kept her feet moving even when she thought she couldn't go any farther. How I helped her, when we ran, how I made jokes that kept her heart light and her will strong. I didn't know she was afraid. Didn't have time to look for it in her, didn't trust her, really.

She hums a song to me, in the lilting, flowing music of her people. I think of all the slaves among them, all the unders. We have a chance to help them, help the people like Hepeh, maybe offer them a better life than scraping marrow from one another in the desert to survive.

The bound are not allowed to choose, she reminds me, and I lean up, press my mouth to her cheek.

Then we will find a way to unbind them.

Chapter Twenty-Two

TOBY

Thea's taking my power today. Although I guess it's not really mine, not anymore. It's ours—we just have possession of opposite ends of it automatically. It's a soft tugging in my stomach, like I might be hungry or scared, but neither of those things—actually, both of those things—I'm always hungry and these days I'm always scared, but that's not what this is.

We don't need to be in the same place; she's meditating and taking power and working with Ria on some advanced combat. I'm not needed for any of it, and everyone else has a task, it seems.

There doesn't seem to be anything for me to do that someone else isn't better at, so eventually I retreat to the City Library. It's undamaged but completely different. Some enterprising soul has turned off the detectors at the entrance, and even I can see at a glance that there's a lot missing. The only three members of staff I can see—most nonessential jobs have sort of ground to a halt in the wake of the attacks—look harried and overworked.

I head to the history section, doing my best to look trustworthy, which I am. I just don't want them to worry about me. I have that kind of face, my dad always told me. People tend to think the best of me. No one pays any attention to me as I download as many of the instances of

"The Wall" from the history section as my datapad can hold and install myself in a comfortable chair.

Useless, useless, names and dates and expansions and thousands of completely irrelevant mentions in entirely boring documents that have nothing to do with anything. I wish Thea could just get Cassandra to spill what she meant, to tell us what she knows, but Thea says she can't. My eyes start going squirmy, trying to glaze over or slip away from the reams of text. My finger cramps from scrolling, there's a muscle in the back of my neck that's so tight it feels as if I've been wired in place, but I don't move. No one's messaging me, so no one needs me, and no one in charge seems to have taken Cassandra's offhand comment very seriously. Kion thinks she was trying to split our attention, and I guess if that's the case, it's worked, at least for me, but this is something I can be doing.

Only the thought that if I go home I'll drive myself crazy thinking about Thea fighting that monster keeps me focused. Searching for instances of "turn" with the Wall gives me nothing at all, but at least narrows down the list of things to look at to manageable levels. I could spend months going through the lists of results for "The Wall" alone, and I don't have that kind of time. None of us do.

I think of alternate search terms. She said "turn the Wall on" like it has power, like it's a machine. I try *start + the Wall*, then *engage + the Wall*—turns out a few people have gotten married up there, over the city gates—and find nothing useful.

"Still looking?" A friendly faced librarian I recognize from the old days leans over my desk. "I'd ask if it was a school project, but it seems like that sort of thing has stopped mattering."

"Uh, personal interest," I say awkwardly, my cheeks flaring, and he grins at me.

"Well, did you check the news archives? Sometimes they're a better bet than the history section. If it was something undesirable, the old guard would have had the history section wiped. They miss news stories, though. Not that smart." He taps the side of his head. "Plus, we tried not to be that helpful."

The news archives! New energy floods me, and I nod gratefully. "That's a good idea, thanks."

"That's what I'm here for." He tips an imaginary hat at me. "Good luck."

I feel a bit stupid as I wipe the history archives off my tech before linking back into the library system and navigating through to the news archives. They go back *hundreds* of years, getting fewer and fewer as it gets closer to the dates of the Great War. Half the world gone, they always say. Seems like people would have been writing stuff about it, but maybe they were too busy surviving.

Once again, I haul every instance of The Wall onto my own machine and start trawling. There's less to go through than the history section held, but I'm tired, and my eyes are gritty. I'm worried I'll miss something, so I dock and lock for enough time to visit the bathroom and grab a coffee from the machine before settling back to my task.

Serena interrupts me to find out where I am, so I just tell her the library and carry on. She's busy, anyway, sorting out Thea's equipment and working with Kion and Thea now. Thea's shown them Pollux's fights, and they're helping her prepare.

I duck my head back to my task and ignore the following message beeps. They'll comm me if they really need me, and it's not like I'm hiding. Thea knows where I am.

I almost miss it. It's been six hours; my brain isn't catching on things properly, and I scroll right past an article talking about turning away the desert tides with the hidden power of the Wall. I'm fully onto the next article before my sluggish mind churns that up to the top for my attention, and I desperately scroll back, looking for the mention.

It's a scrap, a byline, small enough it got missed by the scrubbers, I'd guess. It talks about an attack of people-who-aren't-people, talks about their boiled-up faces and misshapen muscles. The way they can leap in the air like they're able to walk on it, and their ability to flick in and out of existence. The article is four hundred and forty years old. The Eaters were here, and in the image with the picture, citizens crowd the streets, relief painting faces wild and manic. The Wall, looming behind them, is black *and* white. It's black as night in wide strips, from top to base. I print a copy of the image as large as it will go, spread it out, and pour over it on my desk.

There's no mistaking it, once I'm in close. The huge blocks—each as tall as I am and maybe four meters wide—are *turning*. Each block is rotated on itself to show a corner, like the old-fashioned billboard they have in the history museum. The top half, above the corner, is white. Below the corner, the facet that would usually face outward, is pitch black.

Numbstone. I realize it with a shock that makes me drop my datapad. There's a side of the Wall stones that's lined in numbstone, a literal wall of the stuff that strips the power out of anyone touching it. The Eaters would never get over, they'd drop on their way up, be forced to come in the gate if they came in at all. They'd be mowed down, all in one place, a few powered-up soldiers could keep them at bay easily.

The Wall can change.

I gather the paper up carefully, undock my datapad, and run back to ARC faster than I've ever run before.

I head right for the command room, not caring who's in there. This is it, the key to turning the tide on the Eaters, the Wall is *made* for this, somehow. Somehow it was built by people who knew the Eaters might come.

A word I don't remember reading in the article jumps out and hits me so hard I stumble to a half on the main drive of the ARC building, almost falling.

Institutionalized. The captured invaders were *Institutionalized.* My knees go watery and weak. Could that be where it started? The Institute, formed to control captured Eaters, and later expanding to become the child-abducting military organization that raised my twin. Or was it there before that, even? Was it the Institute who built the Wall and knew how to defend the City against the Eaters?

It doesn't matter; all that matters is that we find the controls for the Wall and flip the switch before the Eaters are at our gate. They'll *have* to fight if they can't get in any other way, they'll have to agree to combat. Or can we turn them away without Thea fighting? Would the Wall be enough?

I lengthen my stride and kick up a cloud of dust behind me, much to the annoyance of some walkers, sprinting for the big double doors.

Sanay and a soldier I only vaguely recognize are manning the control room, and I gasp my request for them to urgently buzz Kion and Serena.

They don't seem that impressed, but they do as I ask, and I take the opportunity to uncrumple my huge print of the Wall picture and pin it up over the maps Thea's been working on.

"What?" Kion demands, but with no anger in his voice. He looks exhausted, rings under his eyes. I remember what Serena said about Kion not doing so well, wonder how long he's been working on trying to strip himself from his meat enough that he can fight for my twin.

"The Wall..." My breathing is still ragged, but I decline the chair he points at, waving my hand at the picture. "Look. The blocks; they turn. It's numbstone, there's numbstone in the Wall, and we can stop the Eaters from coming over."

I see the exact moment he understands. Serena barges through the door behind him with Ria right behind her, and I open my mind to Thea. She's sparring with live blades, and it'll do no one any good if she takes one in the guts 'cause I've distracted her, so I throw the knowledge at Serena in answer to the question on her face—we're close enough I don't need permission to pass to her, and her mouth falls open.

Serena grabs Kion's shoulder. "Holy shit."

"That does about summarize." He wipes his hand over his face. "I don't suppose you know how it works?" he asks me.

I shake my head. "But think about it; you couldn't put the controls just anywhere. They'd have to be somewhere controllable, defendable, maybe even the gates themselves."

"Like a portcullis." He nods, typing in the air with one hand. "Or the Watch, or the Institute?"

"I don't think they existed—the Institute." I open my hand in the universal signal for "It's quicker if I flood you with everything I know about this," and he nods. I flip the information from the article to them both and then pull it up onto a screen as soon as I'm done passing thoughts. They'll wanna see it themselves.

Kion nods, his mouth thoughtful. "We'll get the techs on it, see if they can find anything else to cross with the article. Toby, go and check the gates. Take this." He flips me his ARC badge with a wing of telekinesis; the gold arch with the diamond will get me anywhere I need to go. "Serena, we need you. Take whoever's not busy," he commands me, and I nod.

Whoever's not busy turns out to be Aly, clocked off for the day, and also smarter than me. She brings me a massive, dripping sandwich when I tell her I haven't had lunch, and I fill her in around mouthfuls as we hitch a ride to the Wall.

She wipes gravy off my chin with her thumb and smirks at me when I blush but listens carefully to everything I know.

"Gates make the most sense, or somewhere else around the Wall?" She offers when I'm done, tapping fingers impatiently on her thigh as we wait in traffic to cross the main street. "There could be a panel somewhere?"

"How would we ever find it?" I ask, dismayed at the thought it could be literally anywhere on the monolith.

"They'd have to mark it somehow," she points out, trying to cheer me up. I try to let her.

"Even if they have, it'll take...a day? To walk the entire Wall." I reply.

"Well...if we assume that the layout of the City districts hasn't changed that much, we should start from the gates and go out one on either side, then skip the factory district in the west and focus on the oldest part of town, City Hall and Snobsville." She grins wickedly at me. "That's where you used to live, eh?"

It's Aly who finds the panel, a block of stone not made of the impenetrable, unmarkable white stone that builds the rest of the Wall. She sends me a picture of the stone she finds. It's grayish and has a delicate black border, so narrow it looks like a shadow winding its way around the corner.

I'm half hoping she'll have it open before I get there—but I arrive, panting after running seven blocks and hitching a ride for twenty—to find her running her hands over it, looking for anywhere to press or touch that might make it move.

I join her, pressing my palms to the smooth block, feeling my calluses catch slightly on the uneven texture. It's so unlike the block next to it I agree immediately that this must be it—the control panel for the Wall. A secret kept for five hundred years.

Mundane inspection gives me no ideas, and I sink into Thea's Reader power easily, letting the slight shift in vision that comes with it paint my hands with sparkles as I sink Talent into the block.

It's hollow—that much is immediately obvious—and inside there's a lever. A lever made of iron, set into a gear the size of my head, connected to a gear the size of my chest connected to…a sinking vat of nothing that tries to suck all my power right out of me. I yank back, shaking the effects of the numbstone off with difficulty. Thea didn't even twitch down my awareness to her, though, so I must have caught it fast.

"Lever," I tell Aly.

"Pull it or comm and ask?" She leans her shoulder against mine, blinking at me in the bright sunlight. We're all gonna need a cancer booster shot after this, months with no shields. I file away the note to make sure someone shoots Hepeh up. I don't know if they've had the medics at her yet—probably, but if not, then someone needs to remind them. Last thing we need is her keeling over from a preventable disease.

"Pull," I tell her. "We're low on time; we don't know if it's gonna work, and there's numbstone all around this block. No one else is gonna get a different read to me; there's nothing *to* read.

"All right then." She grins at me. "Kiss for luck?"

I kiss her, the sun hot on my shoulders and sweat sliding between us. I kiss her deep and slow and grateful, and she pushes me away with a giggle.

"Pull it man; you're killing me."

I plant one more light kiss on her smiling lips, place my hands back on the Wall, and sink into it.

The lever is stiff, so stiff I think it's never going to happen. *I need it,* I warn Thea, deluge of information available if she wants it, and then wrap all my Talent around the bar. Thea lets go of her tug on me, and I throw my entire metaphysical strength at the lever. Nothing happens, nothing shifts. It's too old, it's been too long, no one has touched this bar for *centuries*. The traces on it are so old I can't even tell what the person was feeling, just that they were old and strong. Stronger than me.

Take it, Thea tells me, pouring strength back down the line between us until her knees buckle.

No, I yell, snapping away. *You need it.*

Have me, brother-boy, Hepeh sings down the link between Thea and I, hand on Thea's shoulder, hand under her elbow. *I have plenty.*

She does; she has *plenty.* Plenty is an understatement. She's as full as I would be if I hadn't been drained all day, fuller even, maybe, and I take it gladly, the link between Thea and me swelling full and throbbing power in rings of black light down to shudder through me, muscles protesting at the sheer strength I'm asking them to hold. I get a faint impression of her strength being why they bound her, young as she was.

I pull the lever.

I pull the lever with everything I have, everything Hepeh has, and a little bit of what Thea has taken from me. The lever holds.

It holds, and Aly slides her hands down my arms, holds my wrists where my hands are plastered to the block.

I take the strength that was filling my lungs, squeezing my heart, and throw it at the lever.

It holds.

It holds.

My knees give out, and I bite through my lip, screaming rage at the stupid piece of metal that could mean thousands of lives saved.

It gives, and so do I, dropping to my knees, and the Wall hits me in the face, but I barely feel it because I'm already mostly unconscious.

Chapter Twenty-Three

E17

Hepeh gasps in delighted surprise at the same time as I feel my brother drop into blackness, his lack of consciousness flowing down the line strung between us so I have to cut myself from him to stop the flickering dark spots from dancing in front of my eyes.

I turn to run to where he is, even though we're in the middle of a briefing from Hepeh about how we must approach the Eaters, but I stop when I see Hepeh's face, feel the sheer joy pulsing out of her so violently my stomach flips in pleasure that isn't mine. She's staring at her hands, stretching them out in front of her eyes like she's never seen them before.

She lifts her face to look at me, wonder brimming tears in her eyes. "The pull... It's stopped."

I know what she means immediately, her voice painted with meaning. The pull of the Great Rock, yanking her power always, blocked only by the meager seals I've slapped over the scarification on her palms. The pull is gone.

"The Wall"—I breathe—"the numbstone."

"What?" Serena interrupts the moment hanging in the air between us, the knowledge that Hepeh is no longer tied to me by fear, but only by choice.

I blink, the delicate connection to Hepeh's golden eyes pulling at me, and answer distractedly, "Toby flipped the Wall blocks; there's numbstone on the outside. It's flipped and cut Hepeh's tie to the Great Rock. She's free."

Serena, ever practical, draws her Zap in a split second, hands steady as she aims. "She good?"

I carefully put my body between Hepeh and Serena's weapon. I feel her loyalty to me throbbing in every direction. I could never question that. "Yes."

Serena glances at Kion, and he nods, and she holsters her gun. "All right then."

"Toby passed out," I tell her.

Kion pulls up camera footage that moves with the pace of the soldier the device is attached to. They're outside the Wall, the camera angle tilted up. The monolith is shining black, dug into the dirt and all the way to the sky.

"Must have been angled sideways," Kion muses. "In flat slats on the top of each piece." He holds his hand out palm down to demonstrate. "And now, they're flipped out, edge to edge"—he turns his hand palm to me—"making a layer that frees the tie on our friend here."

I like his choice of the word friend, and I wonder, not for the first time, how much Kion reads in our faces, not even our minds.

"Will it stay? If I am not inside these Walls?" Hepeh asks, still staring at her hands, disbelief staining her face so clearly it makes my heart ache.

"Only one way to find out." Kion rubs his hand through his dreadlocks thoughtfully. "Thea, why don't you two go for a walk. If it lasts, you can, uh, take your seals back?" He hazards a guess, not really sure—like the rest of us—how this binding works.

I nod, gently take one of Hepeh's hands in mine, and pull it down, where she can't stop looking at them; the thick scar on her palm almost matches the one Leaf gave himself trying to shed his Blankness so he could fight Cassandra. Hepeh catches the thought and gives me a small grin, just the corner of her mouth, but lets me drop her hand. We lace fingers, though; we don't let go of each other. She's pulsing with disbelief, relief, the absence of a strain that's been on her as long as she can remember. It feels like floating, like she could lift the ground and drift away. Her fingers tighten in mine.

"Let me get you an escort," Kion says in a voice that brooks no argument, lets me know that while he trusts my trust in Hepeh, he's still a commander and has to make the right choices, always.

We wait, obediently, for the two soldiers Kion requests, and then walk down to the City Wall, reckless hope dashing through Hepeh's veins so wildly I feel like shouting and running and throwing myself into a series of athletic cartwheels and rolls that I'd probably break something attempting.

We're silent, though, sharing only feelings, drifting thoughts, as we walk. The soldiers stay ten paces behind, professionally giving us space while remaining close enough to take us down if we try to run. I guess their orders were clear, their Zaps are set to stun.

The Wall looms overhead; we walk into its shadow a half kilometer before we're at the gates. It's colder, out of the sun, but not cold enough for the shiver that runs through me as we approach. If the tie reforms when Hepeh is exposed, outside the Wall, then what does that mean? That she's trapped inside for the rest of her life? I'm trapped here, in this city full of people who watched me kill their friends? For the first time the realization that I don't want to stay here when this war is over hits me, and I'm glad Toby is unconscious.

Hepeh catches my thoughts, and nerves rise accordingly in her. If the tie, once severed, remains so, then we've found our solution to the problem of the bound, without even trying. If it reconnects, we at least have a place to start researching.

Our heartbeats rise and pound in unison as we step through the gates, escorted by Kion's soldiers on either side.

Something flutters in Hepeh's veins as we step into the air, but it's relaxation, an exhale that takes her whole body. She hates being inside the Wall with a virulent passion she tries to keep tamped down. The trapped feeling echoes out of her body at me, bringing back claustrophobic memories of my own. We stand, for a moment, hand in hand, with the sun casting our shadows back under the arch of the gate, linking us to the city we both long to leave behind.

Nothing changes.

No tug reasserts itself, no building of pressure in Hepeh's breastbone, dragging her strength out to her hands where my feeble disc of power stands guard against the constant, overwhelming call of the Great Rock.

She sits down suddenly, like her knees give out, and then she's laughing.

Buoyed on the same emotions, I flop down next to her, and laugh till my stomach hurts. For the first time, hope suffuses me, thick and glowing in my veins.

The tug doesn't return, lighting all sorts of investigations into the numbstone by the ARC techs. My brother sleeps for three days, is still sleeping when the hordes of the Eaters are visible on the horizon in front of the City, when their campfires turning the black night to glowing orange march closer each day.

They ring half the City in a huge, unbroken curve of bodies moving like ants on the white and cream of the dunes, and that is where we must go to parley. Toby sleeps through the selection of attendees, which is sure to infuriate him, but all being well, we'll be back in the City by nightfall.

Still, our group seems pitifully small as we bounce over the crusty earth-to-sand ridges, approaching the desert in a group of ATVS.

It's me, of course, Hepeh having made clear the Eaters will accept no combatant who hasn't been inspected. Hepeh, to act as translator for customs and see what we may miss with our untrained eyes. Serena, in Kion's stead, leaving our commander safe at ARC in case of treachery. Serena is unquestionably his second-in-command these days, although Ria has official superiority. Sanay—some soldiers I know by sight if not name—and rounding out the group is David Jacobs, Serena's father and the leader of all ARC.

I've barely seen him since I first arrived, a busy man who looked older than his years before all this; now his hair is fully gray and the lines around his eyes are deeper than I remember. I take care to guard the thoughts, but Hepeh catches them, our bare knees pressed together in the back of a vehicle.

Leaf stayed at the camp, with Cassius—our backup champion—Ria, who works with Kion, still in the hopes of equipping him to fight in my stead, my unconscious brother and a few other worried faces who came to see us off. Leaf was the only one who kissed me goodbye, his raised chin daring anyone to question him after he pressed his soft lips against mine. Hepeh just grinned, and no one else seemed inclined to comment either. Leaf wished us luck and waved us off, then beeped me to be careful less than an hour after we left the City in our dust.

We pass the journey in tense reminders of protocol, of expected behavior. The soldiers will set up a small encampment first, armed to the teeth, which Hepeh says won't be a problem for the Eaters, who never disarm even for peace talks. Something to do with how the telekinetics are always armed, so it's pointless to ask for a showy laying down of weapons which means nothing.

Then, my vehicle, driven by a soldier I don't know—with Serena next to her father in the back seat and Hepeh and I jammed next to the driver in the front—will approach. Hepeh will go out with two guards to ask for parley. The guards are in case the Eaters decide to ignore custom and kill her as a traitor. They have submachine Zaps capable of inflicting staggering waves of damage, and enough projection ability to hold onto them as well as share freely what they're capable of.

It takes time, and by the point that Hepeh is striding out with her long-legged, comfortable walk, having to wait for the struggling soldiers with their huge weapons and lack of experience walking in the sand, I'm thirsty and overheated.

I'm too nervous to ask for a drink, though. I should be out at Hepeh's side with her. I'm still brimming with Toby's Projection power and something of my thoughts must drift outward, because Serena turns around with a canteen and a comforting smile. "She's going to be okay; she knows their ways."

"Mm." I can't really agree, having seen firsthand the unpredictability of the Eaters, especially the ones more driven by pain or older. I've realized, somehow, thoughts rearranging themselves in the back of my head, that the more bodies an Eater has been through, the less human they seem. As if they lose something each time. Sanep was on her sixth meat, the leaders Up-Shup and Karan Bethad their fourth and fifth, respectively. Less respect for life and less humanity in their thoughts than others. Comparatively, Hepeh feels no different from me and mine.

It's agony to watch the small group of Eaters trot out of their lines to greet Hepeh as she squats comfortably in the sand. The soldiers stand to her sides, pulsing readiness into the air so thoroughly it's almost surprising not to see waves of pressure threading the air above them. Just thoughts, no telekinesis involved.

The conversation is long, and I'm grateful for the canvas sheeting topping the vehicle we ride in. The soldiers have no such comfort, baking in the oppressive heat and sweating freely.

By the time Hepeh lopes back to the vehicles, a tall, bald and pale-skinned soldier has half collapsed from heat stroke and has to be lain out in the shade beside an ATV.

"They will meet your leader and your champion," she tells us, reaching out for the water bottle still lying in my lap and opening the lid without hesitation. "In around two of your hours." She drinks loudly; it's kind of cute.

"Get the soldiers under the pavilion, set a shift of watchers on each side, where the dunes are high," Serena tells the soldier waiting for orders at the front of our ATV. "And hand the water around."

"Yes Ma'am," he says immediately, turning and jogging to the tent. Serena pulls a face. "They're supposed to call me *sir*," she complains, and her dad laughs quietly.

"Not our greatest problem, currently."

Serena huffs agreement, and we settle down to wait.

When we see the approach of a small delegation, David Jacobs and I get seated in the pavilion, under cover, while the soldiers get kicked out into the hot sun. Hepeh kneels at my feet, although I wish she wouldn't. She laughed a little when I asked her to take a seat and pointed out that we shouldn't reveal her as unbound, as my equal, if we don't have to. I tell her she was always my equal and watch the blood glow in her bronze cheeks.

It's not surprising who joins us under the awning. Up-Shup Benay, Karan Bethad, Pollux and Icarus are accompanied by a small group of warrior Eaters, their numbstone gauntlets mimicking the kind Pollux wore in the ring, and their knuckles hard with callus.

I can feel Serena prowling behind me, her hands in fists radiating violence, but the Eaters don't even glance at her, dismissing her as a threat without thought. It adds to the fury singing through her veins, and her father turns to give her a glance that dampens her rage.

Up-Shup sprawls into a chair, folding themself into the stretched canvas with animal ease and dangling one graceful hand from their knee, like a giant spider.

I concentrate on thinking small and sitting big, trying to mimic Kion's air of easy confidence, total lack of fear.

Pollux smirks at me as he sits next to Up-Shup, with Icarus standing behind him, Karan-Bethad ignores her offered chair, and the rest of the warriors make a crescent behind them.

"So, you wish to fight me," Pollux drawls, breaking the heavy, draping silence.

I open my mouth to reply, but David Jacobs breaks in, all affable congeniality wrapped in a core of iron that makes me straighten my spine just to hear it. "We do. She does."

Up-Shup sniffs in my general direction. "A broken child. You have no better champion?" It's designed to irritate, and I refuse to let it, taking strength from Hepeh's shoulder barely brushing my knee.

"We have a champion—one we believe in. Your concern is only that you should accept her." David Jacobs sounds so unbelievably unflustered, calm, that I relax the tension in my shoulders and sit more comfortably. Hepeh's smile is only in the corner of her eyes, but I see it and feel her pride in me.

Up-Shup exhales dramatically, extends their hand palm out, splayed fingers. "Come, let me see you."

The whole encampment experiences a minor shift in readiness, from "ready" to "hair trigger" as I slide from my chair and try not to trip over my own, suddenly clumsy feet. I do not kneel, although I know I am intended to. I stand in front of them and force Up-Shup to stand to touch my forehead.

Their fingers are somehow cool, damp feeling. It sends a shiver of revulsion through my stomach, but behind me I can feel Hepeh, close enough that the warmth of her skin radiates into me. I allow the invasion of foreign thought to rattle into me, to look at me. I hide my skills and passions, let them only see what they need to. I feel them back, and the lack of empathy for *anyone* is as shocking as plunging my hand into fire. Their absence of humanity tears at me, a whirling vortex of hate and greed and cruelty.

A hissing sound of air through sharpened teeth, and Up-Shup pushes me back from them hard enough that I would stumble, not balanced for the physical touch, but Hepeh catches me easily, one hand to my shoulder blade, enough I barely wobble. Up-Shup looks annoyed for a split second and then controls their face back into a mask.

"She stands?" Karan inquires, leaning her hand on the back of Up-Shup's empty chair.

"She stands; she has power she did not before," Up-Shup drawls dismissively. "But she spent her best years grubbing in a hole and will be easily put down."

Anger coils in my chest like a serpent turning over, that they can look at those years with such neutrality, but Hepeh breathes through her hand on my shoulder, less than a whisper. *Be still.* And I find some composure somewhere.

"Two moons from now, dawn where we stand. I will have my unders build a place." Up-Shup turns their back on me, stalks out of the pavilion, clearly intending to return to their lines with no further discussion.

"Well then, cousin." Pollux gets to his feet lazily and stretches. "I shall see you soon." His words are varnished thick with images of my face, bloody and battered, my unseeing eyes glazing over as he sucks my power and life from me. I batter him back with Toby's strength, pouring image after image of me breaking his spine at him. Maybe it's not the most mature way to spend some strength, but hopefully Toby will wake up in time for me to replace it, and even if he doesn't, the vicious look Pollux flings me is worth it.

Hepeh grins through our connection, *easy, Paladin.* And I pull back on the power I've been exuding. Nevertheless, Icarus looks at me with fear in his eyes for the first time as he stumbles after Pollux. Apparently, I accidentally projected to all, not only to my opponent. I smile at Karan-Bethad, but it's more of a snarl.

Up-Shup and Karan-Bethad retain their dignity as they lope back across the sand, surrounded by their warriors, and the strength leeches out of my legs until I have to sit back down or risk falling.

"You did well," David Jacobs tells me, his eyes on the horizon. "And you have two more days to prepare."

I wish the fight was now, the waiting has been melting my bones to wax, but at least I know it's coming. Finally, the chance to defend my people instead of hurt them. The chance to earn back some trust?

Serena tugs me upright with her brimming strength, turning me in the direction of the vehicles. "I already trust you, Toby's dumb but he's not that dumb." She grins at me. "Let's head back and work on that lock some more."

Chapter Twenty-Four

TOBY

Apparently, I slept right through the remaining preparations, but when I awaken, I'm rested and feel strong. My power isn't full but is far from empty, having recovered itself somewhat while I slept. Hepeh loaned me enough of hers that I didn't quite drag mine out by the roots this time. Still, I'd be happy enough to leave this new habit of totally wiping myself out behind me.

I haul myself out of bed, wash my sleep-streaked face, and attempt to make myself somewhat presentable. It's today, I gather, from thoughts whisking around the place, from the constant mixed emotions buzzing down my connection to Thea, and from the excitement and apprehension glazing every face I see.

Thea, I quest toward her, and she acknowledges me at once, straightening fast enough to knock Hepeh's hand clear of her short hair.

Toby, she sounds elated, high almost, anticipation burning in her guts enough to wake a similar excitement in me. *I fight today.*

I know. I tell her simply, aware she will feel my own confused emotions down the line that ties us together.

Will you come? she asks, suddenly unsure. The worry that I'll leave her to face them alone is enough to soften the anger burning in me at the idea that she has to face them at all.

Of course, I couldn't do anything else. I won't watch her die though. I'll burst myself through her and fight in the glowing non-body of power alone before I let that happen.

She grins at me in her head, telling Hepeh I'm awake, before replying, *I can beat him, I know. I can turn them back.*

I try with all my heart to believe her.

I find her in the training rooms, resting on the side of the mat watching Kion and Ria spar. Her head is on Hepeh's thigh, her leg slung over Leaf's own outstretched calf, so I gather they've come to some sort of agreement that suits them all. I find myself glad, suddenly, that she has people more than me to fight for, to walk out of their arena for.

It's one a.m., according to my datapad, but it may as well be full day for the number of people out and about. Soldiers limber up in twos and threes, civilians watch or awkwardly try to warm their own muscles. I flop down next to Leaf's feet. I know already that the fight begins at dawn, that we have three scant hours here before we make our way across the desert. I thank whatever is listening for waking me up in time. I can't imagine anything worse than waking up to be told it was over, to find my twin dead.

"Or victorious," Hepeh points out, her voice etched deep with confidence. For a weird, floating moment, I'm jealous of her surety.

Thea pokes me with her outflung foot, her bare toes pushing into my thigh muscle. *I need it. She bolsters me, gives me courage.*

What does Leaf give you? I'm half teasing, but she answers anyway.

Peace.

We silently watch Kion bear Ria to the floor in a hold that would have snapped her spine if he'd relaxed his thigh muscles even for an instant, and I see my twin's muscles twitch, her hand ghosting a short, aborted movement of the same. He's showing her, I realize; she's splitting her attention here with me and with him, riding his body as he marches through familiar movements, learning even while she rests.

She flashes me a sharp-edged grin when she feels me realizing. She looks freer than I've ever seen her, some shadow lifted from her eyes. It's like I never even saw it was there, as though it had always been part of her, but it's faded in this new burning of her spirit.

"Warrior," Hepeh drawls, and Leaf huffs soft agreement, as though he is equally in tune with the silent communication and conversation. I wonder if he is, if he's so good with body language and silence that the absence of telepathy doesn't make him feel set aside, excluded. I wonder how he could hope to compete with the flow of comfort and support between Hepeh and Thea, so low and ebbing I doubt they're even aware of it themselves.

"It's no' a competition," Leaf tells me, echoing a thought Hepeh shared with Thea days ago, in the privacy of their own heads, and we all turn to look at him, startled.

He laughs quietly and shakes his head, eyes on the match, not bothering to expand on what he does or doesn't feel.

Thea has to eat before we head out, far enough before the fight that it doesn't thicken in her belly or tire her body with digestion. We eat with her, whether because none of us can stand to leave her alone even for a moment, or because there's nowhere else to go. I can't tell.

Serena joins us. There's a fierce light in her eyes and red flowers on her cheeks. The song of battle is already in her ears. I try to remind her that if Thea wins there will be no fight.

"Oh, there will still be a fight," Hepeh tells us, her mouth half full of porridge, which she's been shoveling down as though someone might take it away from her any moment. "The primes won't all fall in line; it took almost a year since the bright flash"—here she looks at me with a grin—"or 'the time Toby exploded,' to get the clans to even come together in peace to talk of unifying. And then you brought all the other little shouters up aboveground and the call got stronger and stronger until no one could deny the wealth on the horizon, and Karan-Bethad and Up-Shup Benay linked themselves to lead."

"So...not everyone will follow their own laws and leave when I command it?" Thea inquires, her hands overly steady and her voice too even.

"No, but enough that you might stand against the rest. The Breaker-Builder knows this, did he not seek to tell you?" Hepeh queries, her eyebrows drawn.

"I assum' as much," Leaf seems unflustered. "Hence the kitti' up an' the war parties." He jerks his chin at the steady stream of armed people grabbing food packs from a large pile on a trestle table.

We finish eating in uneasy silence. I eat mostly red meat in the hopes it will give me the strength I might need today. We rise as one, even Leaf, the acknowledgement that it is now, that it is time, undeniable after the last set of cutlery clatters into stillness against Hepeh's third plate.

Thea nods at me, and I nod back, suddenly feeling lifted, like the moment before heading into a race, where the team would slap hands and shout. Not my emotions, I realize, as Thea tightens her grip on Hepeh's hand. Hepeh blazes like a bonfire in my Reader view now, her power no longer subject to slow leak. It has time to renew itself, and she burns with it.

She catches my scrutiny and grins, a pleased, wide grin. Her teeth aren't pointed anymore, I realize abruptly.

Hepeh prods her canine with her tongue. "They were sore, and when I went to see the tooth-worker he said they should replace them. Without the rock milk, they ache and tingle."

"Suits you," I tell her. And it does. She still doesn't look like one of us, not like a citizen or a slumdweller, if those lines still existed firmly. She's deep tan over her brown skin in a glowing, bronzed way that is the sun's mark, not just genetics. There are tattoos I hadn't seen before, wrapping around her biceps, fanciful swirls and writhing lines that remind me of snakes. She'd covered her arms, but now she bares them. She's so muscled and lean, the stocky lines of her are somehow graceful, and I feel my blood warm as she stretches unselfconsciously... *Thea,* I snap at her, hauling myself back from the heat filling my twin and echoing down the line to me. *Keep it in your pants!*

Sorry. She wrinkles her nose at me in apology but doesn't sound totally sincere. Still, she tamps down on her rather visceral response, leaving me feeling vaguely embarrassed and red in the face.

Hepeh just smirks at me like she knows exactly what just happened, and I growl and clamber over the bench seat to head out. We should be at the vehicles soon, anyway.

The secondhand arousal has worn off by the time I've reached the doors, and Thea grabs my elbow. The pull of her fingers in the crook of my arm makes me breathe in sharply. It draws into focus all the growing-playing-fighting moments we never got to have. If she dies, we'll never have a chance to even try to catch up.

It has to be, she says small and just for me, her fingertips branding the words into the soft crease of my arm. *Don't be scared. I'm not.*

Probably 'cause I'm scared enough for both of us, I tell her shortly, but I slow my pace to match her slightly slower gait and let the others catch us.

"You're with me, Thea," Serena has regret in her voice that's for me. "Gotta kit you up. Tobes and Leaf, you're in vehicle four." She's always had a mantle of authority, an air of command, but she wears it more comfortably now. I nod obedience before I remember that she's my friend, not my boss, but it's too late because everyone else has already divided at the corridor split and no one is paying attention to whatever fuss I might make.

Serena wafts me a passing impression of something like blowing a raspberry, and then says, *We'll see you in the convoy. Nothing you can do except be calm and let her do her part.* I stomp toward the armory to get my own kit, and I jump when Leaf threads his arm through mine companionably.

"'S always 'arder to watch 'em go to war than to go yoursel'," he tells me, sounding comfortingly brusque.

I nod, not feeling able to find words and not able to feel Leaf at my side other than via the physical contact. I wonder if that's why he's touching me, to support me with touch, when he can't in any other way, and then I remember that he's also being sidelined, backlined, while people he cares about stand in front of him, and I knock my shoulder into his gently in recognition.

My body armor itches; the night is a physical weight leaning on my shoulders, and it's taking far too long to get this shit show on the road. The vehicles are lined up, filling the street from City Wall to City Hall, and there's shouting and yelling and movement as everyone tries to find their place and kit and get out of everyone else's way.

Thea's in the second rover, the first packed with twenty soldiers armed and ready to set up a kill zone. Kion, David Jacobs, Hepeh, and Thea ride second. The rest of us get to park and watch from our vehicles in a zone marked out for our audience, says Hepeh. The arena will be built, she assures us. Primes and unders laboring together for two days can easily level a space and stack it with seating for the crowds. It will be another place like Thea was kept in, but with no mountains at her back. She can't decide if it's better or worse.

Finally, after far too long, the wailing alarm rattles down the line, and we take off. We drive for hours across the waving dunes, and the great, flickering light of the Eater army comes into view like dawn itself is streaking the horizon.

We're guided to a spot next to another car, curling in a line around the side of a circular arena four hundred meters over. The vehicles behind us pull in at our rear and soldiers unload, pressing forward until they block my view, and so I climb onto the bonnet of our own rover, much to my driver's annoyance.

Leaf joins me after a long moment, and we sit, shoulder to shoulder, waiting for dawn to grease the sky gray in the distance. Waiting for the figure of my twin to step from the side of the ring into the center and bring about peace or a cataclysm.

Chapter Twenty-Five

E17

A strange sense of calm settles through me as I wait, stretching my muscles out, flanked by Kion and Serena. Kion oozes calm, steadiness, oneness, while Serena practically rattles with restrained energy waiting to burst out of her. We've never touched power, really, and suddenly I wonder where she would rank on the Institute's charting for strength. Hepeh rings as strongly as my brother, a pure bell of power flooding out of her when she chooses to exude it. Now the restrictions placed on her have been lifted she holds her head higher, lets her power fuzz the air around her, like a dare. A challenge. Where she stands, talking quietly with the contingent on the other side of the arena, I see her power in the Read spectrum. It's black, deep and dark, and starred with sparkles. It looks like her memory of the Great Rock itself, the way it shimmered with power as she pressed her small, bleeding hands to it and gave up her strength.

I shiver, dragging myself away from the echo, but I feel her turn and look to me across the sand, feel the throb of reassurance she sends to me. I wish I could feel Leaf like that. I know where he is only because his warm shoulder rests against my brother's, as though he can connect himself to me that way. They're too far away, and it's too dark still, to make out anything other than the power edging my brother's restlessness.

Deliberately not looking for Pollux takes concentration, and I distract myself by ranking my friends and acquaintances by strength, balancing their Projector force with their Reader insights. I know the reason I fight well—the reason Cassius isn't undeniably better than me, with his broad shoulders and well-muscled arms—is that insight. The merest whisper of escaping thought coupled with the shift of body, the minute muscular tension in the chest, tells me what to expect, and my body reacts almost instinctively, like I'd been waiting all my life to fight. Like my muscles already had the knowledge of it, like my bones remember what it is to battle.

I'm as strong as Toby now, only by merit of our blended powers, the fusion of our Talents undeniable. I wonder if, had we grown together, we would have shared strength as easily as breathing. Womb mates, Hepeh called us. Forming side by side, irrevocably intertwined, our power woven in and out of each other even as it developed. But Toby was born a Blank. His shields recognizing me as his own, but no one else. We're both high nineties in our individual strengths, and of course, the Talent pool is finite, exhaustible until rest is available, but with it accessible to us both, I wonder if we still count as nineties, or if we would break the chart the Institute had made.

Hepeh herself must be nineties also, in the Read and Project disciplines. The Eaters power is rooted in different ways to our own, or used in different, more physical ways. Less a tool and more an extension of self. There's still so much to learn.

Around me, the low hum of excitement, anticipation, fear, aggression, and other violent emotions crescendos. I can see my own hands, clenched around the baton I'll wield, defending it with my telekinesis against efforts to disarm me. Pollux will be fighting with his numbstone blade again. I'm sure of it. There will be only avoidance of that weapon, pressure exerted against the hand that wields it. If he has brought throwing weapons made of the stuff, I'll have to block them with my baton or move fast enough to avoid being hit.

Thoughts of the fight fill me, tingle down my veins like liquor, enlivening me to the moment. My breath shortens. I can smell the sweat and musk of the Eaters surrounding the arena, hidden from sight by darkness. I can feel the grains of sand hitting my lower legs through my tight, UV-proof leggings. The crowd may as well be roaring for the waves of emotions that burst over me, swelling my chest and filling my heart to burst.

Calm, Kion tells me, and it's as much a command as a feeling of relaxing. *He'll take you if you go to battle madness. You must be calm.*

I try to obey, but the wildness throbbing from Serena tugs at me, her trembling tension. She's leaning forward, her eyes narrowed against the dark, bracing her legs like she'll sprint forward at any second. Kion gently tugs her ponytail, and she subsides, letting me step back from her frustration and alertness.

Sorry. She breathes deeply, calms her own self to match Kion's stalwart patience. *They're coming.*

She's right—the group on the other side of the gaping arena is dispersing—three steps across the sand in a group, and Hepeh lopes ahead of them, back to us.

"I can't go with you," she tells me as she scoots to a halt, her breathing barely elevated. "You tell them you do, you know, and you will." She gives me a half grin, lopsided and carefree. "And you kill him."

Kion, Serena, and I catch her intention together, and they turn aside as she steps forward again, right into my space. She smells of warm, fresh sweat and sand, and I turn my face up to her, nod once, and then her lips find mine. Leaf kisses as if he's exploring me, like he's cataloguing every millimeter of skin and every shift I make against him. Hepeh kisses like she's howling to the moon, like she's celebrating, dancing, exploding with joy. It's brief, and not overly intimate, as Kion and Serena inspect their weapons with their backs to us for a moment of perceived privacy.

I pull back reluctantly, set my hands on Hepeh's collarbones, and feel the heat of her bare skin; she grins at me again, reckless and unfettered. "Go."

Leaf says "cute," Toby tells me, with mild amused distaste in his voice for being asked to pass on a message when I've just been thoroughly kissed, and I send a grin down the line for him, taut and thrumming with completeness.

I think that, if I die, at least I'll do it well, and free. For something real, and for my own people, not for a faceless, heartless organization. It seems better to be here, breathing the desert air surrounded by friends, who not only trust me, but *need* me, than anything else has ever been before. My whole body tingles with the knowledge that it is a weapon, that *I* am a weapon.

We step out together, leaving Hepeh at the border of the circle that marks our fighting ground, as the sun peeks over the horizon and finally lightens the space around us.

In the center of the marked circle, the stands of Eaters curl around us, dunes sculpted for seating but not into steps as they cut into the rockier, tougher ground of the mountainside. Here, it's only a slope, no neat rows and orderly audience, but merely pushing and shoving for the best position. I don't know if the commanders have relaxed their rulings or that the Eaters are too uncontrollable now, with the City in sight and their bloodlust whetted.

Pollux walks a little ahead of Upshup-Benay and Karan-Bethad. My bare feet dig into the packed sand. Kion wanted me to fight in boots, worried about Pollux crushing the small bones, but I wanted to feel the ground under me. I couldn't explain why, just that it felt right. Maybe it's just the echo of Hepeh in my heart.

He looks tan and strong, taller than I remember, somehow. The shadow of the crumpled, scrabbling monster I once met in the back of an elec-car is still visible, hovering just under the new, bronzed flesh of an outdoorsman. His pale eyes still remind me of a snake, and the nubs of his old controlling headgear still spike his skull. I wonder, suddenly, if I could drive one of them deeper into his brain.

Cassius sprawls indolently at the edge of the arena, a slow, pulsing hatred tingling against my shield.

"You come to fight." Karan-Bethad breaks a loaded silence with words that sound ritualistic. Hepeh blazes reassurance, a hundred meters away and right next to me at the same time.

"I do." I find my voice. The sun is brightening, spilling pink-gold over the ground, making dips and pools of shadow on the uneven sand.

"You know the laws of our people," Karan intones the second question.

"I know," I respond without hesitation, this time.

"You will obey the rules of this sacred ground." She pushes meaning at me with the last question, unloading spools of history and scripture—never written, but passed from mind to mind like this. I accept the onslaught, learning more of their ways than I would ever need to know, and trusting that the space rimmed with numbstone will protect me from any treachery.

"I will." The line that connects me to Toby is banned by the rules of the circle, and I send a brief reassurance to him before cutting it completely, as Hepeh once showed me. I feel myself shimmer as my power settles into my skin, for me only. I have Toby's power with me, too, but it's indiscernible from mine, swirling together like water into water, impossible to separate once it is mixed. Only the vessel it was shaped in could call it back to its origin.

She scans me, and I allow it openly, and then she bows her head to me and turns to Pollux.

Karan repeats the questions to Pollux, who responds somberly, with a light of amusement dancing in his eyes that is somehow, only for me. Does he think it's funny, that I have come to stand against him? Kion shifts almost imperceptibly and the reminder that I'm not alone, never alone again, gives me the will to smirk back at him, unshaken.

Everybody dies alone. The thought wafts up from so deep inside me I scarcely notice it and force Cassandra back down with the new ease of connection to my meat.

Only you, I tell her, and then it's time.

Kion's embrace is easy, proud. He presses my forehead against his cheek and breathes calmness into my skin. Serena gives me anger, clad in iron will, implacable confidence and the strength of heart that makes her who she is. I stand back from them both stronger, more complete. I'll take their hearts with me into battle.

The wind picks up like an omen, tugging at Pollux's loose shirt. He's wearing his bracers of numbstone, of course, but I can't see his blades. We'll start with power alone, almost certainly.

My skintight outfit doesn't shift, the tight fabric sealed to the gelatinous body armor that will protect me from blunt blows.

We face each other, divided by fifteen yards of sand, fifteen years of trauma and more differences than I can fully comprehend. The waiting intensifies the strumming, whining tension coiled in my guts, and I abruptly need the bathroom. I shove the demand of my nervous body away, unheeded.

Kion, Serena, Karan-Bethad, and Up-Shup Benay reach the edge of the ring, step out of the circle, and turn to face us together. They clasp hands, in a row, I feel their power humming together, curling, winding, and then they flood it at us to signify the start of the battle.

My shields snap into place, coalescing around me with less than a thought. I'm slow to start moving though, and then I'm in the air, spinning. The force Pollux has swept at me is strong enough that my shields shatter, and only the body armor I'm wearing saves my ribs from snapping as I land flat on my back in the dust.

There's no air, there's no time, there's nothing in my lungs, and there are black spots in front of my eyes, but I can't lie here, can't. I burst with power, the force that Toby shared with me explodes out of me, and I feel it crash into Pollux, feel it dissipate as it sweeps over the numbstone border of the arena. Pollux stays on his feet, but my Talent buffets him, almost of its own accord, as I struggle onto my knees.

My palms are bleeding, skinned by impact, and every breath sends hammers of pain into my side. I think I must have cracked my right short rib after all, lightning cracking over and over again as I squirm, press bloody hands to the dusty ground and push myself to my feet.

It was moments, only. Pollux breaks through my undisciplined attack, and I read his intention before he pummels more energy out at me. I drop sideways and roll, bracing my bones with power to protect them, stay conscious more by force of will than anything else.

Pollux screams, a throat tearing, animal sound of rage, and I take a page out of Kion's book, embrace the pain as it washes over me, take the pain and turn it around, push it into knives of hardened air and fling them at Pollux with no care for how it forces me backward in its wake until I have to stop because the gaping chasm of numbstone yawns at my heels.

We both stagger as I let the Talent blows fade, and then he's racing toward me. I push for his legs, a wave, dust flying in its wake. He twists and jumps, launches a counterattack; my shield creaks and holds, sheer force of will shoring it up as Pollux batters at me with invisible fists.

After a moment, he drops his assault. Glares at me from eyes that are holes in his head. There's blood under his left nostril, so something of mine got through.

For a long, floating period, we face off, both of us with shields tightly raised, waiting for the other to commit...to make a mistake.

I'm more patient than he is. I know it. I waited fifteen years for a chance to fight all the shit that's been thrown at me, and right now Pollux is the face of it. Never mind he was raised, like me, underground with prison guards instead of parents. They broke him, but now he's trying to break everyone I know and love. Everything I care about. He looked at this nation that eats the weak and kills the strong just to take what they have, and thought it was good. So, now I must break him.

Like a rabid animal, he needs to be put down before he spreads his disease.

Clarity falls over my flesh like a silk blanket, and I understand what Kion meant about battle rage. Pollux is fighting angry, fighting stupid and cruel. He's thoughtless and reckless, and if I can make him spend his strength while keeping mine back, that's how I'll win.

I sharpen my Talent to needles, designed to pick and tear at his defenses, small and deadly. If one gets past his shielding it might even break his skin. I throw them, like knives, a dozen miniscule and efficient weapons he has to catch individually.

He uses his bracers, deflects, twists his shield to strength in front of his face and neck, letting some of my mind-knives pock his legs, leaving smears of brown-red seeping through his pants. The efficiency of a shield that could stand against such small projectiles is too much for him, his control isn't fine enough. I breathe in deeply, readying a second barrage, but Pollux screams rage and needles back at me.

He learned fast, taking what I did and copying, sending shredding blades to burst on my shields dragging energy to each spot and leeching my strength.

I fling myself sideways, absorbing the shock of the movement, rolling and splitting my attention finely enough that I blast him with another round of small projectiles while I'm moving.

It distracts him from his own attack, and I follow up with a vast blow, letting Talent slam into him in the hopes he's made his shield too flexible to withstand it.

Now it's Pollux's turn to be thrown off his feet, but he rolls like a cat and catches himself on one hand, glowering at me from a crouched position. Dust swirls up, dragged from the ground by his power, forced into an unnatural tornado. I'm wrapped in it, breathless; it's impossible to see, the air swirling and thick with beige dust.

It's like trying to inhale a sandstorm. I clap a hand over my mouth trying to sieve the air, sprint sideways to escape the tormenting fingers of sand wind tugging at me. He sends it after me easily, a child spinning a top. He has me, and he knows it. He's taunting me, playing with me, showing how helpless I am against him.

But I am not helpless.

A wedge of power, the hardest I've ever made. I throw it at my sense of him, but not at *him,* where his shield will protect him. No, I hurl it at his feet. The ground splits, he loses his footing with a sharp cry, and the storm around me drops, puffing out as though it had never spun and lifted.

Coughing sends bolts of sharp white through my side and I think I'd pass out if it wouldn't mean my death. I can feel Toby hovering at the edge of my closed-down self, feel his horror and his fear. He wants to step through me, step into me and put my body on like a suit of armor, but he's holding himself back.

Serena throbs next to him in shades of brilliant blue laced with silver, the agony of uselessness darkening her to an edgeless idea. Leaf is an absence I recognize but is also a warm knee against Toby's thigh, a bastion of silent support.

My people. *Mine.* I take strength from them although not literally, this time, and force myself to stop coughing. My stomach muscles spasm in protest, threatening to reject my breakfast, but I inhale slowly past the war of my body and calm myself.

Pollux is hauling himself out of the pit I created with ropes of power thrown out like vines, sinking into the ground and hauling him up and then withering away. I remember how Hepeh cut my power from Toby, and I lash out, a whip, a blade. I slice through his harness and almost laugh as he crashes back to the bottom of the pit.

I trudge to the edge of it, worn and shuddering, my shields tight and secure. He hurls hate at me in knives, and I twist them away from myself with a swirl of power, a vortex Serena taught me in the halls of ARC. I'm not quick enough to use it as a defense automatically, but like this, in control, it's an efficient and effective move. He screams, violent frustration, sunk to his knees in dust and chunks of dry earth. He knows if he pushes himself up again, I'll snap his power once more.

Yield, I demand, barely recognizing my inner voice, twisted by effort and exhaustion that hums in my bones.

I am IMMORTAL, he screams at me silently, screams at the whole arena. I feel them pulse for him, urging him with every fiber of their hearts to get out, to kill me. I'm so busy being victorious I almost miss the movement of his blade, but my Reader senses catch the whisper impression of violence, and I turn my body just far enough to catch the numbstone blade across the top of my hip instead of in my lower belly, to sever my intestines and ensure a drawn out, painful death.

The blade punches through my high-tech stab-proof cloth like it's little more than plastic, a lash of fire snapping over the bone and into the muscle. It's deep; blood wells out between my fingers as I clap my hand to the injury. It snaps inside me, a weakened line in the blade dislodging a chunk of blackness inside me. I feel the leech of power as the skin that touches the numbstone; the blood it spilled flows full of Talent.

Toby is anguish inside me, and Cassandra is feeble, distant triumph. My power is swirling away like it was never there, slipping through my fingers as the scarlet blood oozes sticky and lurid over my fingers to drip into the pit.

Pollux arches his neck, opens his mouth like he'd drink the lifeforce from me, and I know I have only seconds before I'm empty and done. He'll climb out and kill me and kill us all. The solution is obvious.

I take two steps backward before he realizes what I intend, and his outraged scream is muffled by the ton of earth framing the pit that I destabilize with four arcing, weak prongs of power. It wouldn't be enough if I hadn't picked up a decent respect for physics and gravity through being exposed to Toby's mind.

The pit collapses, burying Pollux alive, and I drop to my knees, spent.

Chapter Twenty-Six

TOBY

The fight is over, so I feel completely justified in the twanging sensation that thuds through me as I stop trying to hold myself back from the ever-present bond to Thea. She's weak, draining. The injury is bad; there's a lot of blood, and she felt the blade hit her bone. It'll take time to heal, but we should have time now, thanks to her.

Elation soars through me as I slide down from the front of the car, which provided a vantage point for watching the fight. Surely I can go in now, any second Kion will wave me forward, and the medics will be right on my heels, and we'll take Thea out of there. She'll be back in the City before the talks are done. They'll project her over on camera to talk to the Eaters, or something, surely?

No one is waving, and my toes are digging into the dry chunks of dirt thrown clear by Thea's dramatic explosion. They half obscure the numbstone, gleaming black and oily through the overcoat of dust. When can I *go?*

I daren't contact Kion; he's speaking to Karan-Bethad, and if I didn't know him well through Thea, I'd have thought he was completely relaxed. But his body holds the shadow of tension, the hint of danger.

Thea's swaying, on her knees. I can see her blood in the sand. I'm about to go to her, regardless of what their rules and regulations might say, when I feel her eyes widen as she senses a whisper of something, and then suddenly I can't see her at all.

It takes me a moment to make any kind of sense of what I'm seeing. Not one, but two people have blinked into existence between her and me, and there's a knife scraping her cheekbone; she can feel it grating, hot blood welling up to drip down her face like a tear. If she moves, it'll slip into her eye.

It's her mind that tells me what I'm seeing. I'm in two places, straddling worlds, seeing double.

The knife against her-my face is numbstone; it's taken the last of the power that remained to her, except for the draining thread that links to me. My strength is seeping from me down that line, the numbstone latching onto the connection between us.

Icarus holds the knife; he thrust for my twin's unprotected face, determined to kill her invisibly, but his blade didn't hit what he expected.

The knife runs through Cassius. Cassius's hand is sticky with my twin's blood where he's pressed it against the angry wound in her hip. Cassius hangs from the blade, between Icarus, who's so surprised he hasn't reacted yet, hasn't thrust the blade deeper, yanked it up and split his artery before dragging it out to plunge into Thea's eye.

I try to get up. I try, but my legs are water, my spine is syrup. Why isn't anyone helping her, helping Cassius? But I know; I know it's too late for him, everything he is is falling out of the red mouth clutching black stone through his heart.

I have a present for you, Thea. His voice echoes down the swallowing rope tugging my heart out through my chest, and I clutch my throat with clawed fingers.

Serena's slapping me, Leaf is screaming for help, pressing his hands to my temples like he can stop it. There's a rock digging into my left shoulder blade, and it hurts. I want to move it. The sky is so bright white I can't see anything except the sun.

I have a present for you, Toby. Cassius tells me, and I don't know how long he's been telling me, but then I feel it.

He pulls.

He pulls.

A thousand prickling threads separate from the shape of me, a thousand thousand—an eternity passes while he pulls something away from me.

Icarus isn't moving, isn't killing my twin, because Cassius has his hand on Icarus's lip and his lip is bleeding into a slice on Cassius's palm, a slice made just for this. A slice that pulls Icarus screaming and wailing from Andrea's flesh.

Andrea lets go of the knife, falls backward. Cassius collapses into Thea, but he's pulling the blade out of his own chest, and she's okay—she's okay—she's better than okay because every tiny sucking wound Cassandra has set into her Talent, every subtle, insidious little link is being pulled away by Cassius.

He hauls her out of us both. I recognize a million bloody little mouths marking both of us, making us ready, making us hers. I feel raw, skinned. I'm Thea, and I'm Toby, and I'm both of us, and finally, I'm not Cassandra at all because she's drained into Cassius through the open wound on my twin's hip, and we are alone.

I breathe.

I breathe for the first time in a decade, and Serena's mouth is violent on mine as she forces air into my resisting lungs, my body teeters on the precipice, on the pit Thea drowned Pollux in.

Later, I'll tell her she thumped my chest too hard, and I think she's broken my rib. I can feel it stabbing into my side, but why did she hit my short rib? Not me, not me. I realize. It's Thea, hauling me to her, joining me to her, but I don't want to die.

I don't want to die here, with Leaf dripping tears on my face, his pink mouth working soundlessly, screaming at me, shaking me. I wish he'd stop shaking me. I'm so tired. I'm so tired.

Chapter Twenty-Seven

THEA

Cassandra screams, clings, digs fibers into Toby, and hauls his power through me to bolster my failing strength, to tell my body it belongs to her. I'm screaming, somewhere far away, somewhere dark and empty where there's nothing except blackness I have to swallow until it chokes me.

It's so dark, it should be the morning, but we must have fought all day because I can see the stars popping out in my eyes. I don't know why no one has come for me. Did I let them down? Did Pollux climb out somehow? Cassius is a warm weight on my lap, and I don't know what blood is his and what is mine, but we're covered in it, a sticky red blanket that's dragging me out to bury in the sand.

But Cassandra is flailing, losing. Cassius has his teeth in her; Cassius has his *everything* in her; Cassius has seven years of hell burrowed into Cassandra, bolting them together. He drags her with him. He dies, and he dies, and he dies for days, and all the while he's dying, he holds Cassandra and Icarus tight to his Talent in bloody little fingers.

Cassius dies and he's using his death to free me.

I'm crying blood—no—I'm bleeding—no he's bleeding.

Why is Toby screaming?

There's no echo, nothing except my own thoughts rattling into emptiness. There's something heavy on my chest, something violent in my side. The pain is distant but annoyingly demanding. *Thea,* it says. *Thea.* My meat is far behind me, lying in a thick puddle of life seeping down into the sands, just like it's meant to.

The sky is vast and clear, the biggest thing I've ever seen. *Wait until you see the water,* someone whispers. They're crying, and I wish they wouldn't; their tears hit my face in broken diamonds, memories dropping into my skin, pulling me back to my broken body.

I thought it was night, blackness, but now I see that was only blood in my eyes, or shadows on my soul, or something dramatic like that. The sky is blue, the bluest, clearest blue I've ever seen. The sky is the color of Serena's eyes, the sky *is* Serena's eyes. She's leaning over my brother and screaming his name into his face. Did I bring Toby with me again? I find him, shredding into the wind around me. He has no boundaries, no sense of ending. I'm so tired, but he's disappearing, blurring into me and into the sky and into nothing.

I grope after his unravelling pieces and haul him back together, far above where hands pound our bodies and scream and scream and scream into our deaf ears.

Are we dead? Toby asks me, woven in and out of me, so close we may as well be one.

I don't know. I tell him. There's threads pulling at both of us, and I seize the end of the yank in what might be my belly and pull, trying to free myself. Below, far below, my meat jerks.

Hepeh is black and gold sparks, and she roars like a fire, she burns up the thread that ties me to my body and curls herself around me and Toby both. She doesn't have a face, but if she did, it would be blurring, shredding. We aren't supposed to be here until we are ready to disappear.

Please. She shudders with it, pressing her meat down on my meat. Next to her, Cassius stares at the sky. He's smiling. *Please,* she begs, running threads of power around us. We're sinking with the weight of her, and Kion grabs my meat-arm. He's gold, a sun inside a man. His hand is so big he can wrap my whole bicep in his fingers.

I'll miss you. He doesn't beg or plead. He releases me of duty, frees me from all the pain and exhaustion and fear and doubt. He gives me permission to go, and my heart aches for the pain I feel in his gold heart.

I don't want to go, Toby sounds young and small, but determined. He throws out power down the line to his flesh-self, but we're almost empty; there's almost nothing left of us. It hurts, a burning pain in my hip like someone's spilled acid down my side.

I don't want to die. It's stronger; he's stronger. Leaf's hands are the only thing blocking the smallest trace of him inside his body. Serena's lungs and palms force life into his meat. Hepeh is holding me against her chest, holding us inside her power, disintegrating with us just to keep us whole for one more moment.

Toby drifts away from me, hauling himself down the link to his meat and stepping willingly back into the pain, the pain, the pain. It's too much, and I let go, ready to be gone, ready to disappear.

Below, so far below I see it only with my heart, Toby jerks and shudders his way back into reality. *Help me,* he tells them, and Serena lifts his weak body up over her shoulder. It would be funny, watching someone so small carry someone so large, if only I could remember what it is that's funny about anything.

Hepeh has a spark of me in her hands, but all else is drifting out over the sky, tattering away into nothing. I am bright sparks falling as rain over the people gathered below. I understand, suddenly. My death will bring Talent to the people it touches, will water the power inside them. It is good, it is a circle. All things will continue, and I will sleep.

Serena drops Toby on my body. It's like having an elephant stamp on my broken rib, a sudden and violent reminder that I am *not* nothing. I am not everyone. I am Thea and Thea is me, and that damaged meat on the desert ground is *mine*. His hand finds mine and clutches it convulsively.

Serena takes his other hand, Kion takes hers, Hepeh takes his, and Leaf skids to a halt next to them, desperate for something to do. Hepeh gropes blindly across the sand and finds my fingers, curls them in hers protectively. This is the circle.

"The cut." My mouth moves as Toby, Serena, Kion, and Hepeh tell Leaf what to do, how to bring me back, and his fingers dive into me.

It's sticky and slippery and it *hurts* more than anything I've ever felt, an icy burning that fries against his fingers as they tug and move inside the open wound over my side.

He pulls it out. A piece of sharp black poison. Fresh blood surges in its wake, and he claps his hand flat over the mouth of the wound. His hand is a call I can't refuse, and I trickle back into myself under his palm, spreading out inside my own skin until I'm seeing through my own eyes, and Toby is laughing sheer happiness at me even while he's crying.

I try to tell him I'm back, I'm here, it's okay, but all that comes out is "Nuke, that hurts."

Chapter Twenty-Eight

TOBY

"You're getting a reputation as a layabout. You slept right through the two-day-long battle, and now you haven't even come to help set up the dance floor and tables." Serena snickers from the doorway to my new bedroom. Sometime during the reorganization of the last month, it had been decided that I rate a private room now, and so I no longer have to wake up with Jake's stinky feet in my face. My new digs are small, but mine. Or, well, glancing around makes it clear that Aly regards the space as at least partially hers.

I put my nose in the air, dropping a bookmark on the fantasy novel I've been reading and then throw a pillow at Serena with my free hand. "Excuse me, Hepeh and I single-handedly leveled and cleared three-hundred square kilometers of slum."

"Single-handedly...with your four hands." Serena flops onto the end of my bed and puts her dirty, booted feet on the blankets. She's an animal. Sometimes I wonder what she was like before Darcy had a calming influence on her.

"I am down a finger." I grin, kicking out at her foot. "How's the reno going?" I can see stuff happening on the cams but it's hard to make sense of it.

"Pretty good." She huffs in irritation and puts her feet on the floor in order to wiggle her boots off and curls back up on my bed like it belongs to her. I deliberately don't point out the dirty sock that's resting only a few inches from her hand. "The land grants should be marked out by the end of the week. Still a lot of citizens up in arms about the property seizing, but the tube will be fixed soon, and they can take their complaining elsewhere."

"It's rained three times this week." I grin just thinking about it, watching the water stream down the transal. Seeing it sink into the earth before I had to move a boulder the size of a house and exhausted myself.

"Thanks to the now unbound water-shepherds. But it's sunny today, and I'm getting married in—" She checks her datapad. "—six hours."

"You nervous?" I wriggle into a sitting position. She doesn't look or feel nervous, but she's pretty good at keeping stuff low-key if she's concentrating.

She beams at me, half laughing, "Nuke, no. I've been ready to marry her for years." The confidence in her voice is nice to hear. "She's shitting her pants though. Thea's been doing a good job calming her down, but I can feel her panicking at least once an hour."

I snicker. I can't help it. Serena thumps me, which I suppose is fair.

"It's mostly the public speaking"—she shrugs a shoulder—"you know how private she is."

"Aren't there only like ten people coming to the ceremony?" I point out with a broad grin.

"Six, and that's six too many." Serena grins. "But you have to at least have the officiant, and it's not as if Demi would agree not to see her only sister getting hitched."

"And Darcy's best person is bringing two dates." My grin is definitely leaning toward "shit-eating."

Serena rolls her eyes. "Who are meeting us *after*, for the food."

"Mm-mm food. I can't believe you've managed to secure a pig." I'm so excited about the approaching hogroast my stomach rumbles in anticipation and Serena snorts.

"You literally haven't changed at all since I first met you." She laughs at me.

I clutch my chest, mock-wounded. "I think you'll find I'm about an inch taller, have *several* more hairs on my chest, and a much worse sense of style."

"Military-chic!" I join her in laughter, and then we slump together in companionable silence for a bit until she straightens up. "Right. Out of bed with you. We have to go and set up chairs and shit."

The sun streams down from above, but the blue sky is punctuated by scudding white clouds. A canvas awning has been set up for shade down by the statue garden, but the gazebo is shelter enough for the small party gathered around to hear Serena and Darcy's vows.

Kion is officiating, standing at the back of the gazebo as we walk up the four steps to join the waiting group. He grins as we approach, pride in his eyes. His hair is tied back neatly, and he's clad in a fantastic red suit emphasizing his broad shoulders. His ARC pin is at his curving lapel, the tips of his shirt are shining gold to match it.

Thea and I are in matching blue-black with crisp white shirts, rather than the monstrosity Serena promised

I was going to be wearing, right up until it was time to get dressed. We looked quite fine when it was just the two of us, standing together for a photo, but next to Serena and Darcy we look almost drab.

Serena is wearing... I don't know how to describe it other than as a black and gold combat suit. She looks like an ancient Valkyrie about to ride to war, or a person you'd see on the back of a dragon. The main base is black, a deep, soft-looking leather, with metallic gold detailing curling around the shapes of reinforced plates. It's equal parts ridiculous and amazing. Her hair is brushed back from her face into sleek braids, woven through with gold thread.

Darcy is wearing a floaty, pale pink dress that's so light it's almost a pearlescent white. It sets off her deep mahogany skin perfectly. The floral lace that traces across her chest is attached by what must be Talent only, as I can see no other way that it could be held against her skin. I slip my eyes into Reader vision and see the tracery of pink-tinged Talent. The effect is magical.

They walk together in perfect step, and halt in front of us with matching enormous smiles, although Darcy looks a little wild-eyed, and I can see their hands are clasped tightly together.

Behind them, David Jacobs, Shiloh, and Demi make their way up to the gazebo floor and complete the circle. Demi is wearing a dress version of Serena's armoresque outfit, and it's completely adorable. She looks thrilled to be here, standing up for her sister.

Kion greets them in a calm, low voice. There are flower petals on the floor and a light breeze blowing through the iron latticework posts. Darcy makes it through her vows without choking or tripping at all, and

Serena cries her way through her promises in a way that makes my eyes sting, just a little, at the strength of her emotion.

When the vows are finished, I grab the bottle of fizzy wine that Serena and I secreted away earlier in the day, and we raise glasses to Serena and Darcy's future.

After we've finished the bottle, which doesn't take long between eight adults and one overexcited twelve-year-old who gets a half glass, we get our nicest boots messy in the freshly rained-on grounds of the city park as we stroll down to join the party.

It's an open event, ARC personnel mixing freely with city folk who have turned out with wary interest, and even a few of the more outgoing and less feral Eaters who chose to stay—exchanging labor and skills for land and unbinding—roaming through the trees and splashing through the newly running waterpark area.

I find Aly by the drinks and laugh as she drags me out onto an impromptu dance floor made of rubber matting decorated with bright paint—Darcy's handiwork if I'm not mistaken. Her hand is free of her cast now, and while she'll never regain the fine motor control she once had, she's moved onto larger, spray paint projects with enthusiasm. A pink lion chased by turquoise birds gets trampled with mud stains from my heavy boots as I try to keep up with Aly, spinning her around under my arm. Serena and Darcy are dancing slowly to an upbeat pop tune. They're in the middle of the floor staring into each other's eyes like they can't see anyone else, while next to them, Kion is teaching Demi a complicated-looking bit of footwork.

Thea has somehow contrived to dance with Leaf and Hepeh at once, and with a lot of silliness at that. They spin and whirl one another around, moving confidently together.

I sweat through my shirt, dance with everyone I know, and plenty of people I don't, and watch the sunset spill shades of carmine and apricot across the lightly rippling ankle deep "pond" with Aly curled into my side.

Epilogue

Thea... Hepeh's sending is no more than a murmur, but I straighten immediately. My wristpad lights up with a green dot that shines through my pale shirt. Leaf has them in sight; he's trailing them.

The four Institute agents of Second City, Leaf's hometown, round the corner. The faintest trace of my Reader power draped over them in gossamer threads lets me know they're still calm, relaxed. Returning to their current base with no clue that I'm already inside. I blink out of reality into invisibility, pulling Toby's power through me as easily as breathing. He grumbles a small complaint in the distance as he adjusts.

I pull back from the window as Hepeh glides like a shadow across the street. She'll enter with the flashcard Leaf arranged as soon as she feels me call.

Smash lifts her wrist to the scanner, and the apartment door obediently clicks open. Angel, Rhino, and Helo follow her in. I feel them coming up the stairs, feel Hepeh buzzing herself in in their wake.

Leaf guards our exit on the streets. I can't feel him, of course, but I'm peripherally aware of the empty space his mind stands in, the nothingness and quiet of him.

Smash is through the door first, of course; she doesn't see me, invisible as I am, pressed against the wall next to the entrance. Angel senses me as something out of place even past my nonexistence, and he's pulling his weapon as he turns.

With the ease of long practice, Smash, Rhino and Helo try to fall into fighting formation, but Hepeh is through the door behind them, and I am moving already.

Angel is an easy takedown, his shield pathetically weak in comparison to my double-reinforced Serena Slam to his temple. He drops like he's been axed, and I use his falling body as a propulsion point, flipping in the air with ropes of telekinesis to guide me and swing myself around onto Smash's back.

She puts up a fight, but I'm invisible and twice as powered as she is. Hepeh takes Helo and Rhino down with slightly more difficulty and much more grace.

It's over in a matter of seconds, Angel unconscious, Helo and Rhino the same. Smash struggles in my grip, on the verge of panic.

Peace. I tell her, imbuing it with the truth of the sentiment, and she relaxes slowly, panting. I let myself blink back into sight, and she gasps, seeing my face.

Do it, Hepeh tells me, with the knowledge that Rhino hit an alarm, and help will be with them in minutes.

I'm sorry, I tell Smash, placing telekinetic bonds around her body and pressing my hands to her temples. Her eyes widen as she anticipates the snapping of her own vertebrae, but what I give her is worse.

My flood of memories swamps her, drives out the false imprints left by the Institute as they reordered her experiences to suit them best. She remembers and remembers and remembers.

Her brown eyes flash with the violations and the deprivation and the hardships, until she coughs and chokes and pushes me away from her with trembling hands. I let her. She has the shape of it now, the purpose that brings me and mine to Second City. I didn't steal from her, didn't take the knowledge of the bases and protocols that she holds. Three people aren't enough to bring down an organization like the Institute, no matter how good a thief Leaf is, no matter how well Hepeh fights.

We'll need an army, and I intend to make it from their soldiers.

How do we start? Smash wipes her mouth, and I regret the shadows I've put in her laughing eyes. But the lies she's been told were never freedom.

She'll have to take that for herself.

Like I did.

Acknowledgements

This has been a ride and a half, and I can't believe it's finally over. Although I have started making notes on a possible universe continuation, mwahah. I'm so grateful for all of the love and support I've received in the writing of these books, from the most unexpected of places. Thank you to everyone who has asked how it was going, who's picked up a copy, who's spent some time with these characters in this world I dreamed up, and who has cared about their journeys.

If you could do me one more favor and leave a review, or tell your friends to pick up a copy, I'd be eternally grateful.

Thank you to my editor, BJ, my copy editors, and the family at NineStar Press who have shepherded these stories to their conclusion. You've been a wonderful home, and I appreciate each and every one of you.

Thank you to my wife, Marie (we got married!) who has been the foundation of my adventures in literary creation since she first dared me to write what later became We Are the Catalyst.

Thank you to my family, blood and chosen.

And finally, thank you to everyone who's been part of my growing and changing circles over time. I am a richer person for having known and loved you.

About the Author

Tash is a Welsh-Canadian author, teacher, speaker, and educator. Their debut novel series, *The Psionics*, has been well received and they've published multiple short stories in anthologies.

Tash teaches Comp Sci and English at the high school level on unceded territory in Vancouver, BC. They've worked with youth for almost two decades in varying capacities, including as a writing mentor, toyshop product demonstrator, queer competency trainer, and martial arts instructor. They've lived on four continents but made their permanent home in Canada.

They write fast-paced, plot-centric action adventure with diverse casts. They write the books that they wanted to read as a queer kid and young adult (and still do!)

Email: tash.mcadam@gmail.com

Facebook: www.facebook.com/tashmcadam

Twitter: @tashmcadam

Website: www.tashmcadam.com

Other books by this author

I Am the Storm
We Are the Catalyst
They Are the Tide

Also Available from NineStar Press

Connect with NineStar Press

www.ninestarpress.com

www.facebook.com/ninestarpress

www.facebook.com/groups/NineStarNiche

www.twitter.com/ninestarpress

www.tumblr.com/blog/ninestarpress